Spyfall

(The King's Rogues Book 2)

by Elizabeth Ellen Carter

Copyright © 2019 by Elizabeth Ellen Carter
Print Edition

Published by Dragonblade Publishing, an imprint of Kathryn Le Veque Novels, Inc

All rights reserved. No part of this book may be used or reproduced in any manner whatsoever without written permission, except in the case of brief quotations embodied in critical articles or reviews.

Additional Dragonblade books by Author, Elizabeth Ellen Carter

Heart of the Corsairs Series
Captive of the Corsairs
Revenge of the Corsairs
Shadow of the Corsairs

King's Rogues Series
Live and Let Spy
Spyfall
Father's Day (A Novella)

Also from Elizabeth Ellen Carter
Dark Heart

★★★ Please visit Dragonblade's website for a full list of books and authors. Sign up for Dragonblade's blog for sneak peeks, interviews, and more: ★★★
www.dragonbladepublishing.com

Dedication

A huge thank you to the Dragonblade team: Kathryn, Scott, Kris and Shawn. Your support and encouragement keep me going. And thank you to my darling husband, Duncan. I couldn't do this without you. I love you.

*Never give up, for that is just the place
and time that the tide will turn.*

– Harriet Beecher Stowe

Prologue

May 1803
Denge Marshes

"GET BACK HERE!"

She ignored his command and ran for her life. Her jaw ached from where he'd struck her. Her arms sported bruises from where she'd been grabbed and shaken.

She watched the sandy path through the marshes carefully, the ebbing twilight making it more difficult to see her way at a run. She prayed she knew the treacherous landscape better than he, but still the man gained.

And she dare not stop.

The town of Lydd was two-and-a-half miles away by road, but only half the distance directly through the marsh. Only by going forward would she find safety. Going back would bring her death.

She knew *that* with a certainty deep within her bones.

"Bitch! I'll cut your throat before I let you speak against me!"

The woman choked back a sob, knowing that to give voice to her terror would rob her of the air her lungs cried out for. Her running footsteps splashed up water, so she corrected her course, lest she stray too far and be dragged into the silty bog to drown.

All too soon, her pursuer was in reach. He grabbed her, tearing the sleeve from her gown. She screamed and pulled away, stumbling as she went, but it was enough for him to yank her arm and throw her to the ground.

"I'll have you then cut your heart out, slut," he spat.

He reeked of booze, as he so often did. Too often in their seven years of marriage, she'd borne his assaults soundlessly, saving her tears until he left or fell into alcohol-fueled unconsciousness.

The sky had changed from a lilac hue to a deepening lavender. His face was in shadow but she did not need to see it to know his murderous intent was real this time.

He had threatened to kill her before, but the color of his rage was different tonight. All the maidservants in the house fled to the kitchen. The manservants, who were little more than lads, stood by impotently, powerless to act against their brutal master.

As mistress of the house, it had been up to her to try to calm him down.

To no avail.

And now they were here.

Made clumsy by the knife in one hand, he had only just slipped the second button of his breeches when she sprang to her feet and ran again.

The square, castellated tower of All Saint's Church stood out as a beacon against the darkening sky. The water that lay between the grasses turned silver as the remaining landscape around it became grey.

And yet she ran through it, resigned to the fact this night would be her last.

If she were to die, it would be better to drown while fleeing this brute she called husband, rather than have him kill her. It would be just one thing in her control, at least.

With little light and few features in the landscape to guide her way, she hurried as fast as she could, letting instinct and fear drive her forward. She zigged and zagged, somehow finding a path through the wetlands.

She chanced a glance back. He was slower, lumbering, hindered by his loose breeches – *she should have let him get more buttons undone!* – but he eroded the distance between them. She zagged left, running as hard as she could at an angle that should take her to the road and one of the cottages where she might find protection.

He swore an ever-increasing string of vile and terrible curses from behind, and cut at an angle also, intending to head her off. She heard the splashing caused by his heavy footfalls.

A sudden yelp of surprise was followed by bigger splashes.

Then his yells became screams.

She slowed, gasping for breath, the stitch in her side now agonizing. She ventured a few feet back to where she could now see her pursuer in chest-deep water.

Absently, she pushed the ruined sleeve of her gown up onto her shoulder but it fell down her arm again.

"Help me!" he yelled. "Don't just stand there like an imbecile. Help me, you stupid bitch. Pull me out!"

She started forward, her arm extended, then halted.

"What are you waiting for, you idiot?"

If she waded in, she might drown.

If she waded in, he might kill them both.

She took a step back.

If she waded in, he *would* kill her.

Seeing she would draw no closer, he growled and surged forward.

Suddenly, he disappeared below the surface.

She held back a scream as the water covered the top of his head.

A moment later, his face emerged and she imagined she saw through the darkness that his rage had turned to fear. There began a furious thrashing and grunting that seemed to last an eternity. She clutched her arms about herself tightly and watched, unable to move even if she had wanted to.

The grunts became screams and the screams became higher in

pitch. Then they became gurgles.

The last of the light faded, luring the moon from its place low on the horizon.

The thrashing in the water slowed to a weak, listless struggling that barely made a sound.

Then it stopped, leaving only the soft cries of the water rails and the low croaks of the marsh frogs.

Chapter One

October 1804
St. Sennen
Cornwall

SUSANNAH MOORCROFT BROUGHT the wagon to a halt in front of the three-story square building and chanced a glance at the passenger beside her, waiting for the woman's reaction to the structure.

She knew what *she* saw when she looked at it – an overgrown, neglected, isolated inn. No wonder it had been for sale so cheap. Had she been too hasty in signing the contracts on the dilapidated estate?

"What do you think?" she asked.

The housekeeper, older than her mistress by ten years or so, held on to her straw hat and looked up.

Susannah watched Peggy's sharply angled features in profile with some trepidation as her gaze seemed to fix on the metal straps shaped like the letter "x" over the grey stone. There were two of those cross shapes between the second and third stories. And she knew what they were for.

They were anchors for the iron rods which ran right through the building to keep it square. Lines of rust stains running down the wall offered mute testament to how long the repair had been there.

Suddenly, she couldn't bear the silence any longer. "This will be your home, as well as mine. I'd rather have your honest opinion than not."

Her companion offered her a game smile. "Perhaps it won't be too bad inside."

Susannah inwardly breathed a sigh of relief. She had come to rely on Peggy's uncommon good sense following the dark days of her marriage – and its aftermath.

"Well, go take a look inside," Susannah offered. "Then you can give me your final verdict."

Peggy held her hand out for the key, trying – and failing – to keep a skeptical expression from her face as she clambered down from the wagon. Susannah also climbed down and took hold of the horse's bridle to bring it closer the hitching post.

She didn't join Peggy inside the inn.

Better to let her explore the place on her own without having to worry about saying nice things she did not believe just to please her mistress.

When Susannah came here to look at the inn three months ago, the deceased estate seemed an answer to a prayer. It was quiet, a quarter of mile away from the main road that led into the nearest habitation, the village of St. Sennen.

The inn came with a liquor license, three acres of land, a small stable block, and even a small boathouse out the back beside one of the tributaries off the River Pengellan that ran into the sea just a half a mile to the west.

St. Sennen itself was only a mile and a half away in total. It was a pretty little fishing village set on the mouth of the Pengellan, the estuary protected from the Irish Sea by two large rocky headlands.

It was peaceful here, silent but for the rustling of the leaves in the wind and the squeak of the inn's naively painted sign swaying on a high whitewashed post by the corner of the building. The sign depicted a woman in Tudor dress carrying her head under her arm. The block lettering gave the inn's name.

The Queen's Head.

Named for Anne Boleyn, executed for betraying her husband, Susannah recalled. That *she* should now be the owner of a place so named struck her as macabre but apt.

She stepped inside the dusty, neglected building and listened to Peggy upstairs, opening and closing doors, no doubt giving the inn's six letting rooms a thorough going over.

Susannah decided to remain on the ground floor and let Peggy explore in peace.

Opposite the front door was the bar. On the floor behind the bar was a hatch that led down to the cellar.

Around the bar to the right, past the staircase, was the dining room. It could seat thirty guests at a squeeze. The bar and dining room each had an entrance into the kitchen.

To the left of the front door was a short wall with another door which led to two more rooms. The first served as a private parlor. Leading from that room was a bedroom.

Peggy returned downstairs. Susannah listened to the squeaks and groans of the worn risers and treads while she ran an idle hand over the bar's countertop, polished smooth by many hands over the years.

"I haven't made a ghastly mistake have I, Peg?"

"Don't be worrying yourself, Duchess," the woman said with genuine affection. "You know, with a bit of work this place'll come up all right."

Susannah allowed herself an audible sigh of relief.

Peggy picked up on her mistress' expression. Grey eyes sparkled. "And, if it's all the same to you, Duch, I'll claim the big attic room for myself. With a clean-up and a lick of whitewash, I'll have a cozy little nest of my own with a bird's eye view down to the sea."

"Of course! It's yours, anything you wish." She couldn't keep the gratitude from her voice.

Peggy walked to the bar to join her.

"Well, go on, show me the kitchen. That ought to be the first thing we set up, eh?"

The two women shared a smile. One of reassurance, the other of thankfulness.

"It's just through here." Susannah pushed the dining room door open and they peered into the musty room together.

"I'll go see to old Sid and start unloading the cart."

Peggy's face dropped. "You shouldn't be doing that."

"Come now, I thought we agreed. I'm no longer the lady of the house and you're no longer a servant. We're equals, companions. Friends, I hope… and, as of today, business partners."

Susannah caught the open-mouthed look of surprise for a scant second before Peggy threw herself into Susannah's arms.

"Oh, Madam! Thank you!"

Susannah returned the embrace and wished her declaration was made from kind-heartedness and friendship alone. But it wasn't.

If she were to pay wages to Peggy as her housekeeper, she would be out of funds within three months and Peggy would be out of a job. But if they worked together and split the income, Susannah was sure they might manage.

She squeezed Peggy once more and pulled away. "You go and set the fire. I found a trolley around the back. I think it's for moving kegs of beer and such. I can use it to bring in the barrels and tea chests."

"Yes, Ma'am."

Susannah's mock stern look saw Peggy return one of her own.

"Well, I can't call you by your Christian name. That just wouldn't be right," she retorted. "And I can hardly be calling you Duchess, it wouldn't be respectful."

Susannah sighed. "Well, never call me Mrs. Moorcroft, not under *any* circumstances."

Peggy balled her fists and placed them on her hips.

"It's been over a year now!"

One year or twenty, it wouldn't make a difference. She would never feel safe as long as she carried that name. The sound of it said aloud still had the power to frighten her.

"I can't take any chances, you know that," she answered softly.

Peggy regarded her with great sympathy.

"If we're going to make a new life here, I've got to call you *something*," she said. "I mean, people are going to want to know your name, like. What about your maiden name?"

Susannah shook her head immediately. "That's on the church records. It wouldn't take too much effort for an associate of Jack's to work out what name I went by. No, it has to be something different."

She cocked her head and thought a moment. When was the last time she felt safe?

Back home with her late father at the vicarage, in a sweet little cottage called Linwood House in Buckinghamshire.

Yes, *that* would do. Especially since the marriage registry listed her place of birth as Essex...

"I'll use the name Linwood, originally from Buckinghamshire."

"Susannah *Linwood*." Peggy's brows furrowed, processing the name, sounding it silently, then sounding it aloud once more. She nodded her head in approval. "I think that suits you right well. Will you be a Miss or a Mrs.?"

"We'll stick close to the truth. It's easier if our story is more-or-less true. I am a widow who has bought The Queen's Head and I live here with my friend and companion, Peggy Smith."

"Linwood..." Peggy pretended to mull it over a moment before offering an exaggerated shrug. "If I forget, I'll just call you Duchess like I usually do."

Susannah laughed, leaving Peggy to attend the hearth.

Duchess...

Susannah shook her head. She hadn't even known the servants had given her a nickname until after her husband was dead.

She worried when she first heard it, fearing the servants thought she put on airs and graces rather than the truth, that she was just naturally reserved.

However, Peggy had reassured her the name came from a place of true affection.

How naïve she had been when she married Jack. He was thirty-five. She had only just turned eighteen. She knew little about being a wife or even running a sizable household. Even now, the truth of the matter was she needed Peggy's practical skills.

She regarded their old horse and cart. Sid was only burdened with items of necessity – linens, crockery, kitchenware – everything contained in four barrels, three tea chests and two large trunks. They brought few bits of furniture and finally, their personal belongings.

The Queen's Head had been sold lock, stock, and barrel so Susannah had been able to sell furniture that she no longer needed. She was grateful for the extra coin.

She led the horse across the courtyard to the separate stable building which, in turn, opened out onto a fenced paddock bounded to the north by the watercourse. Attached to the stable was an open-sided lean-to. She urged Sid along until the wagon was under its shelter.

She unbuckled the grey gelding from his harness.

He didn't seem in a hurry to leave the shaft. Susannah slapped his rump to encourage him to take in his new surroundings while she did the same.

The stables and paddock were large enough to agist another four horses. Across the way from the stable was enough room for a chicken coop. Then there were the boathouse and the little jetty. It was as dilapidated as the rest of the place, but not in serious disrepair. She had yet to consider how the boathouse might provide further income.

There were so many possibilities here. All she had to do was hang on until the money started coming in.

Now *there* was a dilemma.

How could she have miscalculated so badly? Her solicitor told her that taking on the liquor license from the late owner would cost no more than fifty pounds per year – which was a princely enough sum.

Yet when Susannah applied to the local justice of the peace, a landholder by the name of Martin Doyle, he told her that, because she was new to the community and there was no one to stand surety for her, she would have to pay *one hundred and seventy-five pounds* as recognizance.

A hundred and seventy-five pounds!

The amount was almost all of her reserves. It left nothing to make repairs to the inn, let alone the improvements she wanted.

Susannah knew as well as Mr. Doyle did that the true value of The Queen's Head was in its license to serve alcohol. Who in their right mind would stay at an inn without at least beer or cider served with meals?

Being allowed to run The Queen's Head only as a boarding house would cut its income potential by three-quarters.

So, she had paid. There was nothing for it but to work harder still.

She climbed up on the back of the wagon. She tilted, turned, and rocked one of the heavy barrels until it sat on the back edge of the tray.

She clambered down and tugged at it, imagining to lift it down. Instead, it fell in a more or less controlled drop onto the ground. Crockery cushioned by straw inside the barrel rattled. She listened as she rolled it onto the trolley and felt confident nothing had broken.

The damned thing was heavy!

She leaned all of her weight on the trolley handles until it tilted, then shoved and willed the heavy cast iron wheels into motion. She was sweating by the time she had navigated her way along the half-overgrown path to the back door of the kitchen.

"Well at least there are brushes, brooms, buckets and mops here," said Peggy. Her back was to the door, her attention on setting a fire. "Not that you'd suspect they'd ever been used."

"One barrel down, three to go," Susannah puffed.

Peggy turned and gave her a look. "I wish you'd let me fetch one of the boys from the village to do the heavy lifting."

"No. I must learn to do these things for myself."

"Well don't blame me if you're abed all day tomorrow because you're too sore to move," said Peggy. "You're a lady. You weren't brought up to do a day's work like I was."

Susannah heaved the barrel off the trolley and rolled it edge-on to just inside the kitchen.

"If I didn't work, then I'd truly earn the name Duchess, wouldn't I? No, this is the new life for me – 'in the sweat of thy face shalt thou eat bread, till thou return unto the ground; for out of it wast thou taken: for dust thou art, and unto dust shalt thou return'."

Peggy did not look impressed. "Well, I still say you'll ruin your hands. You're still a young woman. You could marry a nice gentleman if you had a mind to."

"No, thank you. I thought I'd married a nice *gentleman* the first time."

The edge to her voice blunted any comeback Peggy might have offered.

Susannah dragged the trolley out and returned to the stable.

She wasn't afraid of physical work, but Peggy was right – it was hardly the life she had been used to. As the daughter of a rector, she had been raised to manage a little household with a servant or two. When she wed Jack Moorcroft, she thought she was marrying a successful merchant with a big household.

Oh, the many, many lies that man told... to her, to her father. To everyone.

Susannah wrestled another barrel down and onto the trolley, then stopped to catch her breath. She looked across the quiet road that cut through the valley, the tree-studded Arthyn Hill on one side and the wind-shaped grassy Trethowan on the other, like arms embracing her, drawing her closer to the sea that she loved.

There was no threat here, she told herself, not even from the officious Mr. Doyle. Perhaps Peggy was right. Perhaps almost a year and a half was long enough to stop looking over her shoulder.

She had moved across to the other side of the country for a new life, far away from the reminders of the seven years of hell she endured during her marriage to Jack. Anything she did that was different was good. It made her less frightened. It made her forget about her past.

By the time Susannah brought the last of the chests inside, there was something smelling absolutely delicious bubbling away on the stove. Peggy had lit the lamps in the kitchen, making it feel like home already.

She lowered herself wearily into a chair at the old and scarred kitchen table just as Peggy returned through the dining room doors.

"Most of the kitchen is unpacked," she pronounced. "And fresh linens are on your bed. That's the thing to help a body feel at home."

Without missing a beat, Peggy picked up a bottle of cider from one of the work benches and brought it to the table, along with two glasses and two spoons.

Susannah opened the bottle and poured two glasses before taking a long draught of her own. She set down the glass with a satisfied sigh then pronounced, "You're a miracle worker!"

Peggy ladled two bowls of vegetable and barley broth into bowls and joined her at the table.

When the worst of her hunger was assuaged, Susannah outlined her plans.

"We should go into St. Sennen tomorrow after we've taken inventory of anything we need for the inn. I think it would be useful to get to know the shopkeepers of the village. There's no quicker way to be accepted than being a regular customer. And I want to pay a call on the vicar of St. Catherine's Church, too."

Peggy lowered her spoon and gave her a considered look.

"The sea air here really must agree with you. You never did that back in Lydd."

Susannah wrinkled her nose and took another sip of cider. "Ha! Ever since I took off my widow's weeds, you've been at me to go out in public instead of locking myself away, and now I do it, you tease me!"

"Well, by all means, have tea with the vicar, Duch. But I draw the line at helping you with the church bazaar." Peggy's voice became proud. "*I* have an inn to run."

Susannah raised her glass.

"To The Queen's Head."

Peggy raised hers also.

"And to women who don't lose theirs!"

Chapter Two

May 1805
Ascorn, Brittany

HE STARTED AWAKE from a dreamless sleep and was on his feet silently before the creeping figure got closer than three feet away.

Nate Payne gripped a short piece of timber in his hand, its end sharpened to a point. He'd managed to keep his weapon hidden for weeks in this squalid French prison and, by God, he'd use it.

Blackness was near total in this place. The only light was from a line of narrow slits high up on the walls – fifteen feet away Nate estimated, but tonight was moonless.

The man before him looked like a specter, his features covered by the cowl of a cloak.

"You're awake then, English pig," the man whispered. *"Bon, then it's time to release you from your sty."*

Would he be simply hung, or would they use the guillotine? He searched the blackness for the rest of the guards to take him to the scaffold.

There was no one save the man before him.

"Follow me, *silently*. Your life depends on it," he instructed.

The man used a key to open the cell door. Once open, he pulled out a wire from his voluminous cloak and dug scratches around the lock before dropping the wire just inside the cell and closing the door.

"Better the guards believe you picked the lock than know someone simply let you out, eh?"

The question didn't require an answer, so Nate didn't give him one. In fact, it had been so long since he had uttered a word, it was debatable whether he still had a voice. Instead, he attuned his ears to the slumbering prison.

Silence.

Nate suspected the hour was well after midnight, although hours away from dawn. Not only was it silent, but it was also cold. At least that's what he told himself as gooseflesh crept up his legs and across his arms. He could not give in to fear.

The rescuer moved swiftly through the lower chambers of the Fort St. Pierre and climbed the stone steps up to the ground level. Nate kept pace, only too aware of the many aches caused by lumps and bruises from various beatings.

Here, there were dozens of men, perhaps a hundred or more.

Some slept on cots, others on pallets on the floor with hardly enough room to walk among them.

This was where Nate had spent eight months, here among the English prisoners – mostly sailors from captured ships, but one or two, like himself, were smugglers, swept up in the raids against black marketeers.

He had thought it was hell on earth. But that was before he was sent to the donjon below for knocking out a guard who had struck another prisoner.

The fort commandant told Nate he was lucky not to be executed on the spot. But after six weeks interred in something no bigger than an oubliette, Nate begged to disagree.

His rescuer did not linger. Behind a column lay a door Nate hadn't known existed. It was narrow and smelled of dank dustiness that suggested it was rarely used.

Perhaps he should find his voice and ask where he was being led.

The man stopped before a closed door on the landing.

"Stay there," he instructed before he opened and slipped around the door.

Nate had no trouble complying. Six weeks alone in that small cell seemed to have sapped him of his stamina. He breathed deep to stop his shallow panting.

He scrubbed his thick black beard impatiently and dreamed of being freshly shaved, of a steaming hot bath and his back scrubbed by the very charming and very accommodating Yvette from *Le Pomme d'Eve*.

Nate opened his eyes and started. A French solider stood before him.

He inwardly cursed. He hadn't heard the door open or close. How had he fallen asleep so quickly? That was careless. Exhaustion could be no excuse. Distraction was deadly.

It took him a moment to realize the solider was the same man who liberated him. "Here, put this on."

His benefactor threw a hooded cloak at him. Nate donned it, grateful for its warmth as well as its disguise. He pulled the cowl as far forward as he could.

"Keep your head down," the man instructed in a low voice. "And when I tell you to run, *goddamn, tu cours comme l'enfer*."

Nate nodded once.

Run like hell.

He didn't need to be told twice.

They slipped through another side door close to the barracks room and into the cold night air. Staying close to the shadows, they approached a small outbuilding. Light blazed from its windows, smoke from its chimney also brought with it the aroma of freshly baking bread.

Right now, Nate would sell his own grandmother twice over for a slice.

His nameless escort walked right up to the door and rapped sharply three times. The door opened. A heavyset man with a white rag tied about his head peered out then glanced at him.

The two men spoke rapidly. Nate struggled to keep up with the conversation, but it didn't appear to be a happy one. The baker grunted, lumbered toward the closed postern gate and waved him over.

The moon emerged from behind a cloud. From the direction of the barracks, the breeches and cross belts of an approaching patrol glowed white. Nate didn't wait for an invitation. He moved toward the gate with alacrity. As he passed his *friend*, Nate heard a distinctive sound.

It wasn't good.

He turned. The man who had brought him up from the cells held a musket. It was cocked. And it was pointed at him.

"You have friends, Nathaniel Payne," he said. "You also have to the count of five."

"*Allez, allez, allez!*" the baker called hoarsely.

"*Un...*" Nate shucked off the cloak and sprinted toward the open gate. "*Deux...*"

Before him were twelve feet of tunnel between the battlements. He prayed the gate on the other side was unlocked.

The count continued in his head.

Troi... quatre... cinq...

The musket fired just as he made it past the door the baker had unlocked. The ball chipped the wall, a splinter of masonry cut his face.

Nate shoved open the second gate and didn't slow. He headed for the cliffs some twenty yards ahead.

The rocky coastline, a perfect location for a defensive fortification, now served his escape.

Nate scrambled over boulders, working his way down through the crevices that hid him from his pursuers.

Despite the cold, he sweated with exertion now.

The sky lightened, going from inky black to a steel grey. He could see a little further ahead so he concentrated on making the descent, ignoring the sound of the pounding waves below and the yells of the search party on the cliff above.

Ahead, about three hundred yards away, pinpricks of light from the township beckoned him. One hundred yards down and across would bring him to the rocks at the shore.

You have friends, Nathaniel Payne.

Who was his mysterious savior? The only man he could think of was Michel Piaget, the owner of *Le Pomme d'Eve*. He must be desperate to get his goods to England if he had gone to all *this* trouble.

On the other hand, the reason why he'd spent the past eight months in prison could be laid at Piaget's feet as well.

Nate's legs felt like rubber, hardly able to take his weight. How he was able to remain upright was a mystery to solve another day. The morning sky tinted the world around it a rose hue.

The first glimmer of sun started to peek over the hills by the time he'd reached the kitchen door of the tavern.

He stumbled through it and collapsed just as the cockerels marked the dawn.

IF THIS WAS a dream, it was a very pleasant one.

Nate was on the softest bed he could ever recall laying on. The vision through half-open eyes was that of a woman, her curvaceous silhouette revealed beneath her thin chemise backlit by the daylight which now streamed through the window.

The woman raised one leg and rolled a stocking over a slender ankle, a perfectly formed calf, over the knee, before smoothing it across her thigh.

He couldn't help himself, he let out a sigh.

The woman turned, her curly blonde hair shone like a halo. An angel, although Nate wasn't sure heavenly hosts were supposed to look like *that*.

"I was wondering when you would awake, *mon cher*," a husky voice greeted him.

Nate felt his body start to respond, to a degree, until his more awake brain reminded him there was another need that had to be satisfied before he could contemplate anything else.

He forced himself to ignore his full bladder for the moment, not to mention his nakedness, and struggled up to a half-seated position, resting his elbows on the mattress.

"How long have I been here, Yvette?"

Yvette pulled the shift over her head, now nude but for her stockinged feet, and strolled to the wash bowl and ewer, heedless of the man in her bed.

"You have slept for a full day."

The sound of water trickling back into the bowl was too much. He forced protesting muscles to pull him upright and made his way to the chamber pot behind a painted Chinoiserie screen.

Nate tried to remember whether he'd undressed himself or whether Yvette had done it for him.

"And the soldiers?" he called.

"They did not look hard and did not stay long," she said. "There was a fire at the fort, the entire barracks building is gone."

Nate thought of his mysterious benefactor.

"Arson?"

"They say not," Yvette answered. "Apparently a workman repairing the leading on the roof knocked over a brazier. There's talk of the garrison being relocated to a chateau ten miles from here but who's to say?"

Blessed relief at last!

Having finished his business, Nate emerged from behind the screen.

Yvette now wore a fresh shift and was brushing her hair. She eyed his naked form appreciatively. Ordinarily, he would have allowed her to persuade him into her bed. Instead, he wanted a wash and food more than he wanted a woman.

He kissed her on the cheek in passing. Yvette wrinkled her nose.

"I do not like the beard. Use Michel's razor, it's on the *coiffeuse*."

Nate spotted it and a pair of scissors next to the soap.

"I will bring you some coffee when I am dressed."

He picked up Yvette's sponge and plunged it into the bowl from which she had washed.

"And food," he added.

"Ah, there you ask too much, *mon cher*. We never eat before noon, you know that."

He turned to see the twinkle of a tease in her eyes as she slipped a dress over her head and worked the stays at the front.

"I'll need clothes, too."

"Such a pity."

"I'm sure your husband doesn't share your view."

"He's not standing where I am."

Nate angled the mirror on the dressing table so he could see *her* and the bedroom door, and watched both while he trimmed the dark black beard and shaved it away.

Even with a straight razor in his hand, he was vulnerable in more ways than one.

"Where is Michel? I presume it is to him I owe my escape?"

"I don't know anything about that," Yvette shrugged, "just as I know nothing at *all* about his business. He told me to make sure you were fit enough to sail out on the high tide this evening."

Bloody hell, that was so typical of Michel – all business, all the time. No wonder Yvette sought consolation elsewhere.

"What's the cargo?"

"I do not know. I suspect not even Michel will know the inventory before tonight."

"Do you at least know the destination?"

"St. Sennen. In Cornwall."

Home!

Or at least as close to a home that he had. The only person he could think of who would command such a large order from Michel was Martin Doyle. He certainly had the resources to arrange his release from prison.

And the power to put him there in the first place...

The thought came to Nate unbidden as he scraped the sharp razor down his chin.

Grey eyes stared back at him.

That would be so like Doyle – not man enough to call Nate out for his affair with his wife. He'd rather throw around his influence than his weight.

And what better way to teach him a lesson than have him molder away in a goddamned French prison for eight months.

Bastard.

Lillian Doyle probably thought it was amusing, too.

Nate set the razor down and rinsed his face. God, he was a fool for ever taking up with *her*. That was a lesson learned the hard way.

He threw the bowl filled with soap and bristles out an open window before returning to the washstand. He poured fresh water into it and washed using Yvette's lavender soap – a reminder that he was dallying with yet another woman who could be equally dangerous.

No. The next woman he pursued would be sweet, uncomplicated, and unattached. She'd come with no baggage from her past. They would do things the old-fashioned way, with courtship. Hell, he'd even entertain marriage if he ever found such a paragon.

Nate's reflection responded with a wry, self-deprecating grin.

He was a fool and he knew it – he may as well wish for the moon.

Downstairs, he heard the sound of pots and pans banging in the kitchen, then a tentative knock at the door.

That was not Yvette. She never did anything tentatively. Nate found a cloth and wound it around his waist.

"Entrez-vous."

There was a rattle of tray things, and the door opened. A young maid entered and started at seeing him unclothed. She blushed, keeping her eyes to the floor, and set down a tray on the bed. The welcome aroma of black coffee made its way to him. The girl returned a moment later with clothes which she put on the back of a chair, then bobbed a curtsy and left. Not once did she look directly at him.

Nate made his way to the tray and lifted the cover over a plate.

Bread, butter, and a small dish of preserves...

An English cooked breakfast with ham and eggs *had* been too much to hope for, he supposed.

He poured a coffee from the small pot and took one sip from the cup. The brew was bitter and soured his already diminished stomach. Nate dropped six lumps of sugar in the cup and turned to look at the clothes.

They were freshly laundered and *his*. Sitting by the door was his own satchel with a new pair of boots he'd ordered from the bootmakers before he was captured.

Nate's mood lightened immediately. He lathered butter and strawberry preserves onto a thick slice of bread, folded it in half and shoved as much into his mouth as he could, then chewed. Then he swigged down as much of the cooling, sweetened coffee as he could manage.

He wanted to go down to the dock as soon as possible and check the *Sprite* for seaworthiness.

The more Nate thought about Martin Doyle, the more he was certain the magistrate had something to do with his imprisonment – not that he'd ever be able to prove it...

He'd been used.

Forty-two Channel crossings he'd done over the past seven years and *never* had there been a problem at the French end. He cursed the man – and his wife, too, for good measure.

Nate made himself another vow.

No more. No longer would he be at any man's beck and call. If he were to risk his life and risk his boat, he would do so for his own profit, and for no one else's.

Chapter Three

May 1805

"HEY HO! AND a fine mornin' to you, Mrs. Linwood!"

In the reflection of a newly cleaned window, Susannah could see a stocky, middle-aged man jauntily approach The Queen's Head.

She set down her cleaning cloth and turned to greet Clem Pascoe.

Clem was aged in his mid-forties and owned the ironmonger's in St. Sennen.

Susannah liked him – and not just because he was a regular customer at the inn. He was the type of chap to restore one's faith in mankind. Nothing was ever too much trouble – advice, an extra pair of helping hands, even extending a little credit to them when they needed additional tins of whitewash for the walls. And if he could not help directly, he always knew someone who could.

More than that, Clem was rather sweet on Peggy. Despite the woman's protestations and frequent rebuffs, Susannah suspected her friend was more than fond of him, too.

"Good morning, Mr. Pascoe. If you're looking for Peggy, you'll find her 'round the back tending the garden," she said.

"Oh, after the way she treated me last night," he began theatrically, "I think it's the end for us, Mrs. Linwood, truly I do."

Susannah laughed before lowering her voice conspiratorially. "If it's any consolation, she spoke of no one else but you this morning."

"Did she now?" Clem's gap-toothed grin grew brighter.

"Hey ho! That's somethin' to cheer up a cove! But is there any chance of a pint? A man's got to wet his whistle before he woos a pretty woman."

"The bar isn't allowed to serve until noon."

For any other patron, Susannah would stand firm on her opening hours. She had no wish to draw herself to the attention of Magistrate Doyle. She had no wish to attract the attention of anyone.

Clem touched a finger to the side of his nose and gave her a wink.

With mock exasperation, she dropped her cleaning rag into the bucket of water and went inside. Clem chuckled, then followed her.

PRINCE, SUSANNAH'S NEWLY-ACQUIRED dog, raised his head from his place inside the door and beat a tattoo with his tail in recognition. Clem gave the half-breed pointer a pat in passing before slapping a couple of coins on the counter. He whistled a sea shanty while Susannah made her way to the service side of the bar and poured a tankard of ale.

Prince went back to sleep.

As Clem savored his first mouthful of beer, Susannah caught a glimpse of Peggy coming around the front of the inn bearing a basket of vegetables from their garden.

"We've got a lovely crop of cucumbers and asparagus," Peggy began as she entered the bar. Her face brightened at seeing Clem.

On hearing her voice, the merchant set down his mug with an emphatic bang on the counter.

"How's the prettiest girl in five counties?" he said, turning around to greet her.

Susannah hid a smile as Peggy set a dismissive look on her face.

"Last night you said six."

"Ah, it's because I haven't had enough of your smiles – and a big slab of your hevva cake."

"Oooh, the cheek of it!" exclaimed Peggy. She turned to Susannah. "Have you ever heard the like?"

"I'm certain you took a cake out of the oven just this morning, didn't you?" Susannah replied, innocently. She reached forward to take the produce basket from Peggy.

"You're both in it together!" said Peggy. She opened the hinged countertop. Clem picked up his tankard and bowed to indicate the ladies should precede him into the kitchen beyond.

Susannah set the basket at the end of the table and started sorting the vegetables. Some would be used for meals at the inn for the next couple of nights. Others would be pickled and preserved. If the autumn harvest fared well, they would be able to make it through the winter on their stores.

Clem settled himself at the kitchen table, eyeing off the fruit-filled cake which had been set to cool. Peggy carved out a few slices. He reached out to take one when she slapped his wrist.

"None of that until you've washed your hands," announced Peggy.

Clem meandered outside to the pump, rinsed his hands and returned.

"The paper there at your elbow is a list of things we'll be needing to enlarge the chicken coop," Peggy continued, "and to fence off the area for the fruit trees before we buy the goats."

Clem slipped the paper into his pocket without even looking at it. "I'll get my lad on it when I get back to the shop."

He picked up the thickest slice of cake and took an enormous bite.

"No plate and no fork! I despair of you, Clem Pascoe!" Peggy exclaimed.

"Enough of that, Lady Muck," he responded around a mouthful of food.

"Go on, you uncouth fool! Just finish that and I'll show you the idea I've had for shelving in the cellars for our preserves."

Susannah let them carry on like an old married couple. Her attention was caught through the window by a large flash of white between the trees. Was that a sail?

Indeed, it was. Before now, she'd only ever seen the occasional angler in a rowboat venturing this far upstream to wet a line or set a lobster pot, but this boat had a sail. Had its skipper chosen the wrong tributary? The harbor at St. Sennen was near the mouth of the Pengellan – a much larger waterway than this.

Yet, it did not sail past. In fact, inch-by-inch, the sail dropped below the willow trees that lined the bank.

Susannah glanced behind her. Clem and Peggy were gone. The sound of Peggy's voice was muted, coming from the cellar below.

Susannah looked back toward the creek.

"Prince! Come!" She opened the door and, with the pointer at her heels, headed past the pump and the kitchen gardens, then into the paddock which lay between the inn and the river.

This was the first stranger she had seen around here for months. Perhaps this would be their first lodger. The boat was anchored by the boathouse.

She heard the sound of the skipper's voice before she saw him, singing a Cornish folk song she recognized.

My sweetheart, come along!
Don't you hear the fond song,
The sweet notes of the nightingale flow?
Don't you hear the fond tale
Of the sweet nightingale,
As she sings in those valleys below?
So be not afraid
To walk in the shade,
Nor yet in those valleys below.

She walked a wide berth until she could safely see the boathouse, the boat, and The Queen's Head all in one.

A ten-foot long plank bridged the river between the boat and the small jetty. The jetty was *not* in a good state of repair, but had been low on her list of priorities to fix.

The stranger had overcome the structure's failings by adding a plank to span three broken timbers.

Both boathouse doors were flung wide open. A padlock dangled open on the chain which had kept both doors shut. More shocking was the fact that the lock still had a key in it, *exactly* like the one on the keyring she saw not a minute before hanging on a peg on the kitchen wall.

Susannah glanced back to the inn. She ought to run back now and fetch Clem. The song became louder as the singer approached.

Pretty lady, don't fail,
For I'll carry your pail,
Safe home to your cot as we go;
You shall hear the fond tale...

The second verse trailed away as the stranger emerged from the shed.

He was taller than her by several good inches. Dark hair fluttered in the breeze. His clothes were already sweat-stained, evidence of hours of work already although it was not yet noon.

"Good morning, Miss," he greeted her with the confidence of a man who was sure of his right to be there. "I've not seen you around here before. Are you one of the maids from old Gilliam's inn over there?"

Anger was her first reaction. It was not an unexpected emotion, but one so long repressed it made it difficult to find her tongue. And then, if this man did not like what she had to say, she would see the stranger off with a command to Prince.

"Cat got your tongue?" the man inquired in a mildly mocking tone. But he didn't seem interested in an answer. He turned to cross the damaged jetty. "I'll be done here shortly. Let the old man know that Nate's back, will you?"

The sailor pressed a heel down onto one of the damaged jetty treads. It squeaked, then splintered.

Prince stood and gave an emphatic *"woof"* in protest at the sound. Susannah laid a hand on the dog's head. The pointer sat but was still watchful.

"He'll have to do something about the landing here. The boards are pretty rotten. I nearly fell through this one."

"Mr. Gilliam is in no position to do anything."

The stranger gave her an absent glance. "Ah, the quiet woman speaks after all."

She ignored the barb and worked to put a lid on the simmering pot of her temper.

"What's wrong with the old man, anyway?" the stranger inquired.

"He's dead," Susannah answered.

NATE WAS TOO late to hide his expression from the woman on the river bank.

He was stunned. Gilliam had been as ancient as Methuselah, but he was hale and hearty. The man often joked that he would outlive them all.

The woman now regarded him with more sympathy and slightly less suspicion.

She wasn't as young as he initially supposed. A faded grey work dress hinted at a pleasant figure beneath. Her not-unattractive face was rather appealing. The morning sun highlighted strands of gold in her light brown hair which had escaped from a threadbare scarf.

"When did that happen?" he asked soberly.

"About nine months ago," she answered and not unkindly. "I was told he fell down the stairs overnight and wasn't found until some of the locals were concerned the inn hadn't opened. I take it Mr. Gilliam was a friend of yours? I… I'm sorry for your loss."

"We were, um… business partners."

The woman's expression closed and the suspicion returned.

Pity. He could grow to rather like the "nice" woman.

"Who owns the place now?"

"I do, *Mr. Nate.*"

The flint returned to her voice.

Damn, he had miscalculated all 'round. The female before him was a gentlewoman, despite her faded working clothes. She was well-spoken with an accent which marked her from being from a county further to the east.

He needed her cooperation in order to quietly store Doyle's contraband, and she was not likely to give it now.

Something which looked like triumph spread across her face.

"Cat got your tongue?" she asked sweetly.

If he couldn't order her about, perhaps he could win her over with some charm.

Nate gave an obvious slump to his shoulders and heaved a theatrical sigh.

Did he detect there the hint of a smile?

"Nathaniel… Nate Payne, at your service… *Miss?*"

"Mrs."

Nate quelled his disappointment.

"Mrs. Linwood."

"Does Mrs. Linwood have a first name?" he inquired.

He watched her consider the question while she patted the dog, a pointer whose intimidating size seemed to be more for show. But he'd rather not get close enough to discover whether its bite was worse than its bark.

"Susannah."

He breathed out, feeling he'd won a victory of sorts. A little flattery would go a long way, he suspected, so Nate offered his most winning smile.

"Then, Mrs. Susannah Linwood, please accept my profound apologies for calling unannounced. Gilliam would allow me to rent out his boathouse as a store. I hope you would allow me to continue the custom – with financial consideration, of course."

For the first time since he first saw her, she moved. With a mistrustful, but faintly amused expression fixed, she approached the boatshed.

He met her at the door and watched as she took in the four barrels of brandy and two crates of tea.

What she did not know was that still on board the *Sprite*, were another half-dozen barrels, bolts of silks, lengths of lace, and several small chests of spices.

He observed the woman in profile. She had an aristocratic face – finely proportioned features, pale skin that suggested she did not habitually work outdoors. He glanced down to her gloveless hands folded in front of her. Long and slender fingers with nails cut short. Hers were the hands of a lady newly introduced to labor.

Who was she? How did someone who ought to be gracing the drawing rooms of fine houses end up owning a smugglers' inn?

He would not dream of insulting her intelligence by pretending the goods before her were anything other than contraband. He waited for Susannah Linwood to name her price. She couldn't be any more avaricious than Gilliam.

The silence stretched on a moment before she seemed to return to herself, embarrassed to have two sets of eyes looking at her, for the dog gazed up at her, too, his tail sweeping the ground. She dropped a hand on its head.

Her eyes, a deep blue, met Nate's for a moment.

"I want these gone by the end of the day," she said quietly, almost apologetically, before turning away.

"You what?" he yelled.

Susannah Linwood took a few steps back, the look of fear written clearly on her face. Even her canine companion barked his disapproval.

If Nate wasn't already bone weary from his midnight voyage across the Channel, every joint still aching from his long imprisonment, he might have controlled his temper better. He certainly regretted the outburst now. The woman's fearful reaction to his raised voice dismayed him and he sought to quickly make amends.

"Forgive my imposition, Mrs. Linwood," he said softly with bitter resignation. "I won't bother you again."

To make good on his promise, he shouldered a barrel of brandy. The edge of it rested on a deep bruise. He winced away the pain and moved past the woman, making sure to give that dog of hers a wide berth.

He squinted against the glare of the sun on the water which instantly set off a headache. His stomach reminded him it had been more than twelve hours since he'd last eaten and longer still since he had slept.

All he wanted since leaving France was a place to dump Doyle's illicit goods, find a middling meal, and a bed without bugs in it where he could sleep for a week without drawing attention to himself.

He *had* hoped to find it at The Queen's Head.

Bugger and bollocks!

If he showed up directly at St. Sennen, he'd get no peace and quiet. No doubt he'd also receive a visit from Lillian Doyle, and she was the last creature he wanted to set eyes on.

Perhaps he should set out to sea again. He could be in Ireland by nightfall and sell off Doyle's goods as his own – that would teach the *prig* for keeping him moldering in prison for nigh on eight months.

"Hey ho! That's the *Sprite!*"

Nate recognized the voice. He dropped the barrel on the deck of his ketch and shaded his eyes to look for a familiar face.

"Clem Pascoe, you old bastard!"

He found a last reserve of energy and hurriedly left the boat to where his friend waited. For an ugly, old midget of a man, Clem was the finest sight he had seen yet.

"And it's the devil himself!" his friend replied. "After so long away, I thought Neptune had claimed you for one of his own!"

Nate clasped Clem's shoulders with true affection.

"A sight for sore eyes you are, too!"

It was strange – Nate could feel himself smile and respond but the pounding headache grew worse. A cramp cut across his gut. Clem's face turned from overjoyed to shock, just before Nate doubled over.

"Get him out of the sun," ordered a female voice, but it did not belong to Mrs. Linwood. "I'll get this pirate a bed."

He managed to raise his head to see a shorter woman hurry away with the dog at her heels. He felt his weight supported by Clem on one side; to his other, the mysterious Mrs. Susannah Linwood.

He stumbled over the uneven paddock ground and Clem held him more firmly around the chest. The man bit back a curse. If Nate wasn't in so much pain, he would have chuckled at his friend's effort to mind his manners in front of the woman.

"What did those Frenchies do to you, man? I can feel your ribs!"

"Long story," Nate gasped.

Chapter Four

PEGGY BUSTLED ABOUT the kitchen with an efficiency and intensity that left Susannah feeling useless. She returned to the bar with the plan to stay out of the way and stay there until she had washed, dried, and polished every last glass and goblet to within an inch of its life.

She watched the light change through the windows as the day advanced. Now, the setting sun cast the landscape in a warm peach hue. The ticking wall clock told her the first of the regular evening diners would be here in about an hour.

"Well, I'll say this about our guest," Peggy called to her amid the banging of pots and pans, "he's certainly quiet."

Indeed, Nathaniel Payne had accepted convalescence with little argument – which worried Susannah just a little bit. No man who could stand on his own two feet wanted to be coddled. But then, he could barely stand, could he? She offered to call for the doctor, but he refused it, although he did eat the beef broth Peggy had prepared before collapsing into bed.

That was over a day ago now and he had slept since.

"Where's he come from, I ask?" Peggy continued. "I'd have pried it all out of Clem, but Old Boots disappeared as quick as you please once you got the pirate upstairs."

Susannah heard a creak from the floorboards above and glanced up to the ceiling. "Clem mentioned something about France," she replied, lowering her voice a little.

"Oooh, he must be a *smuggler*! But that doesn't explain why he's been away for so long."

No. No, it didn't.

Against her better judgement, she had allowed Clem to talk her into storing Nate Payne's smuggled goods in the boatshed temporarily until the man recovered.

"Don't you worry none, Missus," he told her. "Two days from now, you can forget you ever saw Nate and the *Sprite*."

But the truth was she *did* worry.

Even after two years in the grave, Jack Moorcroft gave her cause to worry even now – and her fear took the form of a ledger she kept under her mattress. Not even Peggy knew about it. She had only discovered it herself by accident after she had sold up the house at Lydd.

It had been in a secret drawer in her husband's large, oak desk.

The small, leather-backed volume listed names, addresses, and sums. Large figures they were, too – amounts of two hundred, three hundred, five hundred pounds. And beside the amounts were the description of goods. Jewelry mostly – diamonds, emeralds, and rubies, but also silverware such as candles and platters. It was a veritable treasure trove.

None of it had been familiar. Certainly nothing so fine had ever passed through her doors that she had seen in seven years of marriage. The bitter truth was that not only was her husband a brute, but he was also a criminal, a *fence,* receiving goods stolen from the great houses in London.

She knew only one of Jack's associates, a man by the name of Robert Lawnton. He had looked respectable enough, but there was an air of menace about him that frightened her as much as Jack had done.

Lawnton had shown up the morning of Jack's *disappearance*. He did not take kindly to the news his partner was missing. The look he gave her when she told him was full of unspoken threats that she knew he was capable of carrying out. He insisted on joining the search party.

She had not seen him since Jack's inquest, but she knew in her bones that while he lived, there would be unfinished business between them.

She shuddered. Two years and four hundred miles hardly seemed any distance at all.

There were simply too many things she wanted to forget. But no matter how hard she tried, there they were, lurking at the edge of her consciousness, just out of sight. The idea that they would one day return to destroy her would not be quelled.

"Can I help with those?" said an unexpectedly close voice.

She fumbled the glass in her hands, which were soon enveloped by two much larger ones.

The captain of the *Sprite* now stood before her.

"Easy there!" said Nate. "I don't know how much bad luck it is to break a glass, but I know it's seven years bad luck to break a mirror."

For such large hands, they were gentle. They cradled hers rather than gripped. When she finally pulled herself together enough to look into his grey eyes, she found them kind rather than mocking.

"Only bad luck for anyone stepping on it," she answered.

Having seen she was now composed, Nate took away his hands. She put the glass gently on the bar.

"I didn't mean to frighten you," he said.

She picked up a cloth to continue polishing. "You didn't... I didn't expect you to be up, that's all."

The expression Nate returned suggested he didn't quite believe the answer, but was content not to press further.

"Is there one for me? A polishing cloth? Since Clem isn't here, I may as well do something useful."

"But you're a guest."

"Until I can get paid for my goods, you'll just have to consider me a hired hand, instead."

Susannah handed him the rag she was using and reached under the bar for another.

"You're a smuggler." Her tone was as flat as her mood.

"I take it you don't approve?"

She shook her head. How could she condone such a thing considering the "enterprise" her late husband engaged in?

"Laws are to be obeyed," she said softly.

"Including bad laws? Taxes set so exorbitantly high that the cost of goods is higher than decent men can afford?" Nate set down one glass and picked up another to continue polishing. "A man is a better custodian of the fruits of his own honest living than some man in Parliament, is he not?"

"I might agree, except smuggling is not honest."

He shrugged. "Those selling the goods get paid a price they're happy with and those buying pay a price they're happy with. It's only the big wigs at Westminster who are upset. Smuggling will disappear as soon as the tariffs reduce. Perhaps the representatives should learn to manage their money better, like the rest of us do."

"And you get a cut from both the seller and the buyer."

"Enough to make it worth the risk."

"Is that why you do it? The excitement of staying one step ahead of the revenuers?"

"Perhaps that was true in my younger days, but eight months in a French prison is enough to change a man."

The conversation trailed off as they worked on polishing the remaining glasses.

Susannah supposed she could be persuaded that there was a difference between smuggling and the outright theft and receipt of stolen goods. If Jack had been caught, would it have changed him? Somehow, she thought not.

And what of his ledger? Should she hand it in to the authorities?

The goods had been destined for foreign shores – France, Flanders, Holland, Spain. There would be no hope of recovery. It would only be of value to one man – Robert Lawnton – and the threat of its exposure was the only weapon she had against him.

Soon, delicious savory aromas were emerging from the kitchen and the work of polishing the glasses was done.

She looked up again and found herself caught by Nate Payne's eyes, silvery in the late afternoon sunlight. He said nothing, but he waited until he had her full attention.

She ought to be frightened by such an intense gaze but, for some reason, she was not. Strange how *aware* of his masculinity she was, and yet it was different to the force of power shown by Jack Moorcroft.

When he finally spoke, his voice was soft, little more than an undertone.

"I'm sorry to have put you in an uncomfortable position, Mrs. Linwood. For what it's worth, my word is good – for a smuggler. Those goods will be out of your boatshed by this time tomorrow."

She drew breath to steady her rapidly beating heart. "I... I feel I owe you a further explanation, Mr. Payne. Peggy and I are still new in St. Sennen and..."

Nate shook his head. Once more, she felt his gentle but firm hand over hers. She managed to pull her gaze away from his eyes and was drawn to where their hands touched, his deeply tanned skin in contrast to her pale hand.

"Then say no more. Let's leave it at that, shall we?"

Susannah jumped at the sound of the kitchen door being flung open.

"Duchess, do you think the pirate will want his tea upstairs?"

Nate pulled his hand away.

Peggy gave Susannah a puzzled frown, before looking past her to see Nate on the other side of the bar.

"Oh," she gasped before flushing crimson.

Nate offered Susannah's companion a lazy smile – one of those confident smiles designed to charm unwary women. Susannah took it as a sure sign he'd heard his nickname. "I'd be delighted to dine with you ladies tonight," he said.

Peggy was having none of it. She matched *the pirate's* look with a very direct look of her own, one that said she had his measure and was more than a match for him.

"You try that charm of yours on someone else, *Pirate*. Mrs. Linwood and I are much too busy to dally with the likes of you."

NATE ATTACKED THE roast beef on his plate with gusto but got no further than the third forkful when his stomach announced its fill.

For more nights than he cared to remember, stuck in that detestable French prison, he'd dreamed of eating hot roast beef with potatoes, gravy and Yorkshire pudding. Tonight's meal was better than any memories he could conjure up.

Sitting across from him, Clem continued to shovel in the food but slowed as Nat set down his knife and fork with regret.

"A froggie prison did this to you?" he asked.

Nate straightened in his seat, hoping the knot in his gut would ease of his own accord.

"For the last six weeks, I was in the donjon. I was lucky to receive one meal every couple of days. It's going to take a while to get used to proper English cooking, I'm afraid."

"Well, you're not goin' to find better than the cookin' here. The landlord at The Rose and Crown has had to lift his game since Peggy Smith and Mrs. Linwood came here."

Nate took a tentative sip of beer. That might help his stomach some.

It didn't work. The knot grew bigger. Perhaps distraction would help.

He nodded across the dining room to where Peggy and Susannah worked.

"What's *their* story?" he asked. Clem's eyes trailed Peggy as she made her way around the room with plates piled with food. It smelled delicious but Nate's stomach complained once more.

He hadn't appreciated how old and haphazard Gilliam had become until he saw the dinner service tonight.

The last time he was in The Queen's Head, there had been just him and two other drinkers all night. Come to think of it, the place had been as tired and run down as the old man himself. Gilliam's percentage from storing smuggled goods was probably his main source of income by then.

Now, with the walls freshly limewashed and the floors actually *clean*, the dining room looked bigger and more welcoming.

Tonight, the place was half-full – and not just full of drinkers propping up the bar, either – most of the men and women here tonight had actually come in to *dine*.

"Dunno where they're from exactly," answered Clem.

Nate forced his wandering mind back to his friend.

"Kent is all Peggy'll tell me. They got here six months ago and have done a right good job bringin' the place up to snuff." Clem leaned forward and dropped his voice. "Peggy's a girl after my own heart. I could see myself settlin' down again with *her*. She's good to Sam as well, treats him like a young man, not a boy."

Clem's announcement surprised Nate. The man had been a widower for nigh on a decade. Nate believed the status was a permanent one, especially now that his son was sixteen and had no need of a mother to raise him.

"Does Peggy know your intentions?" Nate asked.

"Nah," Clem answered with a grin. "But she *will*. A man's got to be patient. It's a bit like fishin', you see. She hasn't taken my bait, but she's nibblin' about. Sure, she'll swim away a bit, so I'll reel out a little more line…"

Nate focused his attention on Peggy as she made her way back to the kitchen. She was long past the first bloom of youth. He wouldn't describe her as beautiful, not even conventionally pretty with her sharply angled features and mousy brown hair, and yet he had to acknowledge there was a liveliness to her step and her manner which gave her a presence that was hard to ignore.

"Well, I haven't spoken with her before today," said Nate, "but I'm pretty sure Peggy wouldn't take too kindly to being described as a fish."

"Not a fish," his friend grinned. "Nope, Peggy is my own real life mermaid."

Nate liked Peggy already and was secretly tickled by the *pirate* nickname she'd given him. In fact, he felt well enough now to try another mouthful of his dinner. He cut a piece smaller than usual and chewed the morsel slowly.

A burst of laughter came from the direction of the bar. He glanced up. A group of three men chatted animatedly among themselves. Serving them behind the bar was Susannah. Her expression was relaxed, less guarded. She said something to the three and they laughed once more, drawing her into their conversation, although from what he could see, she mostly listened.

"Peggy's very protective of Mrs. Linwood," said Clem.

Nate heard the warning.

"And what's *her* story?"

"Peggy warned me right at the first that Mrs. Linwood had been through rough times and I shouldn't make a nuisance of myself."

"And what of *Mr.* Linwood?"

"She's widowed, but she never talks of him. Peggy's more effective than that hound of theirs at keepin' men away. And there were a few sniffin' about at first, but after Mrs. Linwood showed no interest and

Peggy bared her teeth, they've given her no trouble."

"So, who do *you* think Mrs. Linwood is?"

Nate waited for Clem to polish off his meal for an answer while he attempted another bite of his own dinner. He caught a whiff of spiced apple and saw a redheaded woman at the table opposite break open the pastry with a fork. Nate's mouth watered and he cursed his lack of appetite.

"I heard Peggy slip and call her 'Duchess' once," Clem admitted.

"I heard her say that, too, this afternoon," said Nate, idly picking at the dismembered remains of the Yorkshire pudding.

"I'm not sayin' she isn't a pleasant woman – *she is* – but Mrs. Linwood is the type who keeps herself to herself. It took months before she addressed me as anythin' other than Mr. Pascoe. *Mister!* Blimey, I don't think I've ever been called that in my life!"

Clem plastered a winning smile on his face as Peggy approached to collect their plates. She looked dolefully at Nate's.

"I'm sorry I couldn't do it justice, Peggy."

"If you'd had the stew, like I said, you'd have finished it all," she gently chided. Nate inclined his head in silent agreement.

"Any chance of gettin' an apple spiced pie and another pint, my bird?" said Clem, swatting her on the bottom to get her attention. The woman didn't react.

"Perhaps," she answered, turning away from both men, *"when* you've learned some manners."

They watched her leave. Clem turned back to Nate and grinned.

"She likes me, you know."

Then the man's face sobered and Nate found himself under his friend's scrutiny.

"When you didn't return after a couple of months, we'd wondered whether a storm had taken you, or whether you'd had enough of Lillian Doyle and moved on."

Lillian Doyle.

Nate pulled a face. Clem laughed.

"There's not much to tell," said Nate. "I got picked up in a raid. When they learned I was English, I was taken to a fort where they were holding prisoners of war."

He really *didn't* want to talk about it. There was too much unsettled in his mind – his arrest, his release – little of it made much sense. He needed time to think it through.

Clem looked ready to insist on hearing about it now when Nate had good fortune in the arrival of Clem's son, Sam, a gangly youth who was as tall as his father was short. Only the nose and the grin gave his parentage away.

Sam insisted his old man join him and his friends in a game of darts.

Nate waved them along and pointed to his unfinished beer as explanation for not joining them.

A flash of memory hit him. He was once more in the middle of the overcrowded prison. His hand shook as he reached for the tankard and another mouthful of beer.

Those poor souls, those haunted men... they'd only see home again when the war was over – and only God knew how long that would be.

This afternoon as he napped, he dreamed of one of them who had been in the oubliette along with him. The man had been there for a long time. The fullness of a beard hid a gaunt, pale face. His voice was rusty from disuse. He coughed frequently.

The man insisted that Nate write to his family. He actually dictated a letter but it was nonsensical, filled with references to mythological creatures. Each day, the wretched man would recite the same letter over and over and insisted Nate learn it word perfect.

To occupy his time, as days became weeks in that hellish hole, he did memorize it and recited it back to the man who, despite his weakened condition, could rouse enough energy to yell if he got the text wrong or embellished it.

Then one morning, Nate woke and found he was the only one alive.

That had given him nightmares this afternoon – and he counted himself fortunate he'd not awakened screaming.

Even now, the phlegmatic words of his companion came back to him.

Dear Aunt Runella,

Your nephew has been remiss in writing, but the Gorgons have been insistent on having their way...

Rubbish! The ravings of a man gone mad and yet the man had given him a perfectly sensible address.

Charteris House

Truro, Cornwall.

Perhaps a few words to let the poor bastard's family know of his end would help assuage his guilt that he survived when so many other men did not...

Chapter Five

S USANNAH SOUNDED THE small brass gong which sat on the counter behind the bar.

"Time gentlemen, please! Last drinks!" she called.

And like cows ready to be milked, the men made an orderly line, more or less, eager for one last pint before the clock struck eleven.

As she and Peggy served, Susannah glanced around looking for Nate Payne. He wasn't here, nor was Clem. Perhaps he had taken her insistence of removing the smuggled goods to heart and decided to do that tonight, instead of on the morrow.

He didn't need to do that, especially since he was obviously recovering from his ordeal.

During the course of the evening, she'd glanced his way from time to time. He seemed to struggle to eat the meal set before him and nursed the same pint for hours.

Eight months in a French prison is enough to change a man...

Enough to change his appetite at least.

Just before the eleventh hour chimed, Nate returned alone. He ran a hand through his wind-ruffled hair. A day-old beard darkened his cheeks. His concession to the evening was a navy blue coat that somehow altogether made him look every inch a dashing pirate.

"I'm afraid the bar has closed," said Peggy, "but since you're a staying guest, I suppose we can bend the rules."

He shook his head and flashed Susannah a smile before addressing

Peggy.

"I wouldn't want to get the landlady in trouble," he said. "But I'd kill for a cup of tea."

"I'll do that, Peggy," Susannah insisted. "We've all earned one tonight."

She slipped into the kitchen without waiting for an acknowledgement. The truth of the matter was she found Nate Payne interesting and, yes, if she was being honest, she was starting to find him physically attractive, too.

And that simply wouldn't do.

She set the water to boil and finished drying and stacking away the plates, then put away the cutlery from the meal service.

Prince lay asleep in his usual spot in a corner near the fire, his large body curled up on a faded mat made of fabric rags.

Susannah liked the life she had made in St. Sennen. The villagers welcomed her and didn't pry into her past. The one or two men who'd expressed their interest in her were firmly but politely rebuffed and did not persist. After a while, she could even feel at ease in any company – just as long she kept her distance.

Out by the bar, she heard the sound of laughter as Peggy and Nate apparently shared a joke.

Oh my, yes. She should most certainly keep her distance from *him*.

Surely that would be easy to do. It was one of the attractions of buying an inn, after all. No one stayed for long – a night or two that's all. They could pass in and out of her life just like the flow of the river that ran alongside The Queen's Head.

Nate, too, would move on, and everything would be back to normal.

She heard the conversation between Peggy and Nate grow louder, then they both came into the kitchen together.

"I was going to bring the tea into the dining room," she said, mindful her words carried a hint of admonishment in them.

Peggy's face dropped and Susannah knew why. She hadn't used *that* tone of voice ever since they arrived in St. Sennen. She knew it to be standoffish, prissy, *cold*. Very much like the lady of the manor.

But didn't Peggy see? The kitchen was *their* domain – hers and Peggy's and, more recently, Clem who had been welcomed into their group. It was too soon to invite this stranger.

She braved a glance at him. He, too, looked reserved, although she wasn't sure whether it was a reaction to her own coolness.

"I'll take my cup upstairs," he said, not once taking his eyes off her.

She shook her head to clear it. "No, there's no need to do that. I'm sorry. You're welcome here, Mr. Payne."

"If you're not going to call me Nate, then I insist you call me *Pirate* like Peggy here does."

Susannah felt heat rise up her face. Peggy spoke before she could think of a reply herself.

"Oooh, you're not going to let me forget you overheard that, are you?" said Peggy, lightly tapping him on the arm. She addressed Susannah. "Nate's offered to build that chicken shed and those shelves in the cellar, starting tomorrow. Isn't that wonderful, Duch?"

"I spoke to Clem tonight," Nate added. "If I can borrow your horse and trap first up tomorrow morning, I can have certain *goods* away from here and be back by mid-morning with the timber."

She tried a tentative smile as her apology. "That's most generous of you, *Nate*."

The simple act of using of his name seemed to bring genuine joy to his features – not lasciviousness or mockery. Susannah didn't know what to make of it, so she turned her attention to the kettle on the stove but Peggy had beaten her to it.

When she looked back, Nate stood by their kitchen room table.

"Generosity has nothing to do with it," he said. "As I told you this afternoon, I'm throwing myself on your charity until my buyer pays for his goods."

Susannah dropped her chin to hide a smile. Nate Payne was a man who looked less in need of charity than any person she'd ever known and, yet, were his circumstances so much different to hers? After all, both of them needed a fresh start.

Here, Susannah felt on firmer ground.

"Let's not call it charity then," she said. "Let's call it a trade."

Nate waited a beat, then gave an emphatic nod.

"That seems eminently fair, Mrs. Linwood."

He held out his hand, not as a man would to aid a lady, but rather to shake hands as one would do for a man. An equal. A *partner*.

Once more, Susannah searched his face for hints of the mockery or malice she'd learned to detect in people's faces – chiefly those of her husband and his cronies. There was none, only an expression of equal caution. The only difference was that in his actions, *he* was prepared to risk rejection.

Wasn't it about time she learned to do the same?

She breathed in deep. She took his hand and shook it firmly.

The three of them didn't linger over tea. Nate had asked them questions about the work he was to start on in the morning and, with those answered, he announced his retirement.

After he had left, Peggy looked at her over the rim of her teacup and it was a *particular* look.

"So, what do you think of our pirate, then?"

"We've known him for two days. Is there a particular opinion I should have of him?" Susannah parried.

"Well, for my mind, I like him," Peggy announced, "and I'm a good judge of people. Now, I'm not saying he doesn't have his faults. He's a bit too cocksure of himself, I'll wager, but all men are."

"But more importantly, Clem vouched for him, did he?"

Peggy's eyes dropped in silent confirmation and Susannah tamped down a small feeling of triumph. See, Peggy was not the only one who could read people.

"Aye, he did."

"What did your *beau* have to say?"

Susannah let out a small laugh to see Peggy bristle at the term. Oh yes, it *was* love – as long as her friend wasn't too stubborn to see it.

Peggy told Susannah little more than she had already gleaned for herself. Nate had been in a French prison.

"Nate was never really expected to come back, even if his smuggling run had been successful. He'd sold up everything to buy the *Sprite*, but some kind of business venture went sour. Clem wouldn't say more, but I'd say there was a woman involved because there usually is with his sort."

"But other than being a smuggler with dubious business associates and a woman in every port, the pirate is a good man?" Susannah inquired mildly.

Peggy picked up on her tease and grinned. "Something like that, Duch."

To whom it may concern,

My name is Nathaniel Payne. I write with news which may be of interest to your family.

My fear is the tale I tell is so nonsensical and so out of sorts that it causes unnecessary distress to your family.

This story concerns a man I only knew by the name of Felix. His surname, I regret I did not learn before his death. I met him while a prisoner held at Fort St. Pierre in Brittany. I do not know how long he had been held there, but judging by his state, it had been some time.

He insisted if I should find my way back to England that I was to convey a message to you. In fact, he was so insistent, he had me memorize it and recite it back to him.

I would have dismissed his request as the sad delusion of someone so far gone, but he gave the address to which I write you.

Below is his message, transcribed faithfully.

If it means something, I hope it brings you and your family comfort.

If it does not, then I regret the distress this letter from a stranger brings you.

Yours faithfully,
Nathaniel Payne.

Nate looked up from the dining table and out of the window with its view into the garden and the paddock beyond. It reminded him of where he was. He was no longer in that dark, dank prison he'd been so recently released from – the one he still saw in his dreams.

Susannah asked no questions when he asked to borrow pen and paper to write a letter. He suspected he'd given something away in his face that the missive he needed to write was not a happy one and had to be written in private. She had offered him a commiserating look and disappeared through the dining room doors, leaving him alone.

In the small hours of the morning, he gave up sleep and wrote and rewrote the covering letter in his mind. Over the past hour, he had warred with himself over whether to write the letter at all.

But that was done and now to commit to paper the words Felix had asked him to commit to memory.

He stared at the blank second sheet and heard the voice of the man with the death-rattle cough who shared the cell with him.

Dear Aunt Runella,

Your nephew has been remiss in writing, but the Gorgons have been insistent on having their way.

Iris reports Aristeaus has three hundred and Phorcys brings another hundred to his aid.

Ares has taken to the skies. Eurus brings his usual bad luck, Apheliotes might be prepared to cooperate.

Adrastus should be aware of betrayal. Pyeois wanders closer.

Deipneus still plies his trade.

Thanatos draws closer, too, so this letter will be my last.

Your faithful nephew,
Delas

If Nate didn't know better, he'd think it was a code of some kind, perhaps a game, instead of the ravings of a man near death.

He stared at another piece of paper and considered whether Felix's kin would want to know more of his final days. What could he tell them? Hell, he couldn't even know where his body was.

Before he could wallow in the poor man's misfortune any longer, Nate took the sheet, fashioned an envelope, and addressed it to Charteris House in Truro before sealing it. The wax dripped blood red on the paper.

There. It would be posted tomorrow and he would have discharged his duty to Felix, God rest his unfortunate soul.

WORKING OUTSIDE WAS a godsend. The spring sun of late May on his bare back was invigorating. The breeze making its way from the sea up the valley cooled him as he worked and made his chore a pleasant one.

Nate continued the task he'd started at the beginning of the week. The uprights had been set into holes filled with mortar and packed with dirt and then cross-braced to keep the length of log perpendicular. He used lengths of twine to get his levels before fitting the horizontal connecting girts that would keep the structure rigid.

It felt good to be doing something with his hands. Perhaps he could build his own cottage not too far away from the river.

While he worked, Nate indulged in the fantasy of rebuilding his life. He would take on another hand to help him manage the *Sprite* and establish a legitimate trade around the coast of Cornwall. Every night he would return, knowing he had somewhere to come back to.

He lifted the girt into place and shoved until the timbers bit. He pulled a mallet from his belt and tapped along the length of the beam, feeling it further mate with the uprights. When he was done, this structure would stand sturdy against the wildest of storms to blow in off the coast.

He stopped at a sound and mopped his brow. Susannah had shut the front door. She had a basket in hand and was making her way across the paddock to the meadow across the road from the inn. Her hair was pulled back to her nape in a loose chignon, but it was a losing battle against the breeze.

She put down the basket and removed her straw hat. Light brown hair fell out of it to hang halfway down her back. It glinted gold in the light. She faced into the prevailing breeze to better deal with her hair. The skirts of her dark green gown fluttered around her ankles.

Nate admired her form as the gown stretched tight across her bust and trim waist while she reached both hands behind her to deal with the wayward pins in her hair.

She hadn't noticed him. He suspected she would be less carefree if she did, so he picked up another length of timber he'd earmarked for the lintel over the door and started hammering it into place, so if she *did* happen to glance his way, she would find him at work.

Although she was no more than forty yards away from him, Susannah seemed to be in a world of her own. Walking on again, she stepped lightly though the grasses, more like a girl than the cautious woman he'd come to know over the past week.

A look of delight came over her face as she spotted something in the field ahead. She headed for it with a spring in her step.

She bobbed down. She'd plucked something red, most likely ripe fruit from a wild strawberry plant.

The simple honest pleasure of her actions touched something within him. How long had it been since he stopped and looked at the world around him and acknowledged its beauty?

Nate knew, willing or not, he had been privy to something special.

The woman in the field before him was the true Susannah, the one who lay within the quiet, reserved proprietress of The Queen's Head.

He wanted to know her better, and wondered what he might have to do to bring another expression of joy to her face.

He cast his eye across the landscape – the valley in which they stood, shaped over eons by the flow of the river between the two hills. He used to wander through the woods of Arthyn Hill. They could find mushrooms there – perhaps even sheltered parts where sorrel and mallow might grow. There were the paths that crisscrossed Trethowan where blackberries were found.

Would she enjoy the outing? Would she give him the smile she now reserved for the wild strawberries?

He'd like to find out.

Chapter Six

SUSANNAH CROSSED THE road to the field opposite The Queen's Head and looked back.

What a difference six months had made. She and Peggy had worked hard and the fruits of it were beginning to show.

Windows frosted with unwashed years of grime now gleamed in the sun. The timber sills were painted and tubs of red geraniums and the spikes of rosemary in flower were welcoming and inviting.

Arthyn Hill, dark green against the bright blue sky, provided the most spectacular backdrop to the inn. Susannah allowed herself to feel pride. *She* had done this. She had lost sight of who she was and what she could accomplish after so many years of being told she was useless; an adornment and no more.

With Peggy's help, she had done it.

She turned away and headed into the field. The breeze tugged at her hat and her pins loosened. She dropped her basket and removed her hat to secure the pins.

There was much to do, but the thought of it brought anticipation, not dread.

One floor of The Queen's Head had been refurbished and was now letting, although they'd only had one or two paying guests so far. But soon, when news spread during the market days, overnight trade would pick up.

Until then, she was not so concerned about reopening the other floor until the other was regularly occupied. It would happen in its time.

What pleased her the most were the growing number of regulars who came out to dine and have a drink. And not just because she enjoyed their custom. She was beginning to enjoy their company, too.

How good it was to learn to trust again. It was like seeing the sun emerge from behind storm clouds and seeing the rainbow filled with promise.

Were those ripe strawberries in a patch ahead? She grinned. *They were!*

She approached and sat cross-legged in the middle of the patch. There was an abundance of them! Tomorrow, she would make preserves.

From the money left over from the day-to-day expenses, she had saved enough to pay for the renewal of the liquor license and, bit by bit, was saving enough to pay for more improvements.

Like the materials for the chicken shed. As she picked strawberries, she listened to the sound of the coop taking shape.

Across the way, Nate was at work hammering things into place. What a bit of luck his arrival was after all – and his willingness to work for his room and board. With the money she would have had to pay someone else to build it, she could now consider hiring a girl from St. Sennen to help Peggy in the kitchen.

She was beginning to like Nate Payne as well.

More than that, she was getting used to having him around. He volunteered to do the heavy chores even when they cost him – like two days ago when the new barrels of ale arrived.

She saw the set of his jaw when he volunteered to go down into the cellar to remove the old kegs and store the new. It was always cool down there but when he emerged, he was sweating, and she was convinced not all of it was due to his labor but to his still weakened state from his imprisonment.

She leaned forward, searching for more ripe red fruit. From beneath her hat, she looked back toward the inn where she could see the man at work.

He was stripped to the waist.

She ought to blush at that and look away. The only bare-chested man she had seen was her husband, whose body had been pale and soft. Yet even so, he had been so much stronger than she.

There was nothing pale and soft about Nathaniel Payne. Certainly, his ribs showed and his arms were thin from starvation; his back was discolored with bruises from beatings. But his bruises would fade and a return to regular meals would fill him out. And still, in spite of his mistreatment, he was strong and muscled.

Yet he had shown himself gentle; a *gentleman* despite his plain speech and no-nonsense manner. He was also virile and male. The few times their hands had touched, she felt... *aware.*

Surely it couldn't be desire beyond the basest sort. Besides, how wicked was she for letting her imagination go in such a direction? By the same token, how much loyalty did she owe Jack in death when he showed her none in life?

She shook her head and rose to her feet. Further in the meadow, she thought she spied the light purple heads of mallow in flower. She went to investigate.

It was not time to be distracted by handsome men. Besides, Nate and the *Sprite* would be moving on soon. She already knew a couple of the regulars had approached him about work. He would have his own place and own life to lead.

Better she should concentrate on what she could control – her business – rather than the mysterious workings of human nature.

Her rambling took her further up the rise to Trethowan where she could see the road that led to the headland and to Trethowan House, home to Martin Doyle and his wife, Lillian. She had seen the couple only twice since moving to St. Sennen – the last was at the Christmas dance held in the church hall.

Doyle had remembered Susannah and introduced her to his wife. She appeared to be a few years younger than her husband. If Susannah had to hazard an age, she would have thought Lillian Doyle was closer to forty, than thirty.

The woman was an aristocrat, born and bred; everything from her lustrous black hair dressed with pearl-topped gold pins, her fine features and clothes, exuded wealth and power.

Susannah owned little of her own that was fine, apart from a pair of pale amethyst earrings surrounded by seed pearls. They had belonged to her mother. Everything Jack had bought her was sold, either by him when he wanted fast money or by her after his death. How could she possibly keep things when she did not know whether or not they had been stolen?

She had worn her mother's earrings on the night of the Christmas dance with a pale rose silk gown trimmed only lightly with lace. It was cut befitting a young matron.

Mrs. Doyle wore a gown of deep blue which showed off her pale and unlined décolleté. When Doyle made the introductions, his wife had looked at her with mild disdain.

"The Queen's Head? I had no idea the place was still standing," she said. "Such a disreputable place. I believe you have your work cut out for you, Mrs. Linwood."

"I am well up to the task, Mrs. Doyle, although I do not underestimate it."

Susannah watched the older woman's face change to mild interest as she spoke. Susannah knew the reason why. Her speech was cultivated, educated, with none of the inflection of the local dialect.

"You're not from around here, are you?"

"Mrs. Linwood is a lady. Did I not tell you, my dear?" Doyle interjected with sly humor. "How very remiss of me."

Susannah had been left in no doubt the *oversight* had been deliberate. Lillian Doyle knew it, too, judging by the brief expression of displeasure that flittered momentarily on her face then was gone.

She ignored her husband and kept her attention on Susannah.

"We're going to London for the Season and we'll be back in spring. I look forward to better making your acquaintance, Mrs. Linwood," she said. "There is always room in our little society for people of quality."

When the quarter day in March that marked the beginning of spring came and went, then the date for tax collecting also passed without the Doyle's return, Susannah ceased to think anything more of Mrs. Doyle's invitation.

She raised her face to the sun overhead. No, there were better ways to spend her day than joining Mrs. Doyle and her friend for tea and whist – such as helping Peggy prepare for the noon diners and for the supper meals.

The sound of a coach – the crush of wheels on the gravel and the rhythmic trot of horses in harness – reached her before she saw it. Around the bend, the matched pair of black horses made their way steadily down to the crossroads. That meant it was heading toward the inn and not St. Sennen.

Susannah removed her hat and put it in the basket to protect her haul of strawberries and mallows. She picked up her pace down the hill and across the field to The Queen's Head. If she ran, she might just make it back before the coach came to a stop.

AT A DISTANCE on Trethowan Hill, Nate watched Susannah break into a run. He looked about for its cause and could see nothing amiss, but felt the urgency of it clearly. Had she been stung by something?

He dropped his mallet and set out at a jog and met her.

"Go back," she called when he was about thirty yards away. "A coach is coming. I'll let Peggy know."

Nate raised a hand to indicate he'd heard her and turned back. He glanced up the road and saw the approaching vehicle – and inwardly groaned. He didn't need to see the livery to know who it belonged to.

Well, he supposed it couldn't be put off forever. He would need to confront Martin Doyle, the man who owed him nearly two hundred pounds for the contraband goods that he and Clem had stowed in the smugglers' caves on the beach below Arthyn Hill.

The same man he suspected of arranging his arrest in France.

Only one thing could be worse than seeing that snake. And that would be if Lillian accompanied him.

He exchanged a glance with Susannah as she hurried around the back of the inn to go through the side entrance into the kitchen. Nate picked up the tools and dropped them in the trug before grabbing his shirt to follow Susannah inside. There'd be no more work on the shed until this afternoon.

He looked down at his sweat-stained breeches – hardly fitting for a business discussion. Nate started upstairs to his room when he heard the door open.

"It's an honor to see you, Mr. Doyle; Mrs. Doyle," said Peggy in a mannered tone he'd never before heard. If he hadn't known better, with those rounded vowels, she sounded like the housekeeper in a stately residence, rather than a cook at an inn. "Do take a seat. Mrs. Linwood will be out presently."

Nate hurriedly unlaced his boots and stripped out of his grey working breeches. He hung them and his shirt up to air. Then he poured water from the plain ewer into the bowl and picked up the sandalwood soap. He hurriedly washed before dressing once more in clean clothes.

The latest haul was the last. If the revenuers had caught him, he'd have swung for sure. It was no longer worth it. Even the satisfaction of cuckolding Doyle was short-lived.

He made his way quietly downstairs, deciding the best form of defense was a surprise attack. There by the bar was Martin Doyle, looking every inch the county magistrate. His roundish face made him look younger than his fifty-or-so years, his grey hair more distinguished than old.

Today, he was dressed in a navy wool suit tailored to make the most of a figure still reasonably trim. His ensemble was finished with highly polished black boots and a black silk topper.

Standing beside him was Lillian, fashionably – and no doubt expensively – attired in a gown also of dark blue, but of a lighter shade than her husband's suit.

"Good morning, Martin," he said, descending the last three steps.

The magistrate turned and stared at him as though he'd seen a ghost. The look of shock on the *tuss'* face was unmistakable.

That's interesting, Nate thought. If Doyle was surprised to see him, perhaps it wasn't him who had arranged the escape from prison…

To the man's credit, he recovered his composure quickly. Nate observed Lillian's expression had not changed a jot.

"Why, Nathaniel Payne, I thought we'd seen the last of you," said Doyle.

"Well, you know me; I keep showing up like a bad penny."

Doyle moved toward him stiffly, as though still uncertain whether he was flesh and blood or a haunting spirit.

Nate wondered if a punch on the jaw might effectively establish his corporeal status.

The magistrate wisely stayed well out of reach.

No, best to suppress his violent impulse, reflected Nate. He stayed where he was, a few paces away from the stairs, but far enough into the dining room to see Peggy edge toward the door marked private which opened to Susannah's quarters.

"How long has it been?" said Doyle. "Six months?"

"Ten. And we have business to discuss."

Doyle straightened, a smile snaked across his features, the same smug little prick he always was.

"You can make an appointment like any other constituent, but now I have business to discuss with Mrs. Linwood."

Doyle turned to Peggy.

"Will your mistress be much longer? You did tell her *I* was waiting, didn't you?"

Peggy dipped a curtsy but that was where all semblance of respect ended.

"She is aware, Your Honor."

As though on cue, the private door opened. Susannah had changed into a blue dress, and her hair was severely pinned back. Nate owned to a private disappointment. He'd enjoyed seeing Susannah's hair down. Now the reserved proprietress of The Queen's Head had returned.

"Forgive me for keeping you waiting, Mr. Doyle," she greeted. "Your visit wasn't expected and you caught me at work in the garden. I understand you wish to speak to me?"

"I do require a moment of your time, Madam, especially to go over the books for the previous quarter's taxes."

If Susannah was surprised at the request without notice, it never showed on her face. In fact, her face seemed made of marble – beautiful but expressionless and remote.

"Yes, of course," she said before opening the door a bit wider, giving Nate a glimpse into a room – he spotted a tapestry-covered settee with matching armchair and a hint of a desk – a *private* room that was off-limits to everyone but Susannah and Peggy – and now Martin Doyle.

For some strange reason, it felt like a kick in the guts.

THE WAVE OF tension in the room had hit Susannah the moment she opened her parlor door onto the bar. Her eyes had fallen straight to Nate. He looked angry, no, more than that... ready for a fight. Mr. Doyle's back was to her but, even so, she could see a line of tension across his shoulders.

Surprisingly, the Magistrate's wife maintained an expression of cool composure at odds with the air of hostility surrounding the two men.

A glance sideways told her that Peggy, too, felt the tense atmosphere.

Susannah was aware of a tingling in her toes and fingers, and her rapidly beating heart. Jack had made her feel like this whenever he came home. She never knew whether she would get affable Jack or savage Jack.

Thank heavens for the mask of plain, neutral indifference she could conjure up at will.

"Peggy, will you bring tea into the parlor and see to Mrs. Doyle's comfort?" she asked.

The magistrate did not even acknowledge her presence. He just pivoted on his heels, stalked right past her and into her quarters.

PEGGY, UNCHARACTERISTICALLY, SAID nothing, but bobbed a curtsy instead as Susannah followed Doyle into the room and shut the door.

This was damned odd, and a touch alarming thought Nate. Peggy was acting like a servant while Susannah behaved like an automaton.

"I'll give you a hand, Peggy," he called out, but the woman gave him a blank stare rather than a customary saucy retort.

As he moved past Lillian, Nate felt the woman grab his arm. "So many months away and not a word for me?" she asked.

Once upon a time, that seductively low and husky voice would have him standing to attention, but no longer.

"How about 'let go of my arm'?"

"You're angry," Lillian pouted.

Nate snatched his arm away. "Angry doesn't begin to describe it, Lillian. I spent months in a stinking French prison, and I *know* your husband had something to do with landing me there."

She looked him up and down provocatively. "It doesn't seem to have done you much harm."

He clenched his fists, forcing them to his sides. The most vile of curses danced at the end of his tongue. Nate was afraid that if he uttered them, he'd do so at a volume to bring everyone running, and if he raised his hand, it would be to strike – and he'd *never* hit a woman before in his life.

He turned his back to her and chewed on his rage, pulling whatever control he had back under his mastery.

"Goodbye, Lillian," he ground out in a voice that didn't much sound like his. "And this time, I mean it for good."

Lillian may have said something else, but Nate was too consumed with his rage to hear it. He shoved his way through the dining room door that led to the kitchen.

SUSANNAH CLOSED THE door behind her as though a few slabs of wood could bar the hostility from entering her quarters.

Now she could see Mr. Doyle's face. There was a firm set to his jaw that revealed the man had not recovered from the shock of seeing Nate.

He made his way to her settee and sat down unbidden. She didn't like that. Only half of her parlor was for business – the part with the desk. The settee and chairs by the fire were *her* private sanctuary.

She'd had a sense right from the beginning of their acquaintance that he'd like something more than financial consideration in their relationship. She had made it clear that the only business there would be between them would be purely professional. She had no desire at all to encourage any familiarity with the magistrate.

"I suggest you will be more comfortable at the desk, Mr. Doyle," she said. "I encourage you to take a look at the ledgers. I've laid it out for you—"

"How long has that man been here?" Doyle asked, his voice a mix of low annoyance and anger.

"Mr. Payne has been boarding with us for the past couple of weeks," she answered.

"*That* man is a known smuggler who ought to be rotting away in prison. I would be very careful of the company you keep here, Mrs. Linwood."

Susannah placed a shaking hand on the high back of a wingback chair between herself and the magistrate. The tingling in her toes was making its way up her legs to her knees which wobbled, threatening not to hold her weight.

She forced all her courage into her voice. "I run a very respectable establishment. I tolerate nothing dishonest at The Queen's Head."

Doyle looked at her levelly as he rose to his feet. Susannah didn't have any trouble keeping eye contact with him. Every word of what she said was true.

"Nathaniel Payne has a hide showing his face around here again," Doyle muttered as he made his way around her desk, sitting at *her* chair and turning the books around so he could view them. He pulled a small pince-nez from his inside coat pocket.

He looked at her over the rim.

"I trust these books are a true and accurate account of the transactions here? Nothing... under the table?"

Susannah felt a flush of anger and used it to dispel her fear. She lifted her head haughtily.

"They're true down to the last farthing. I'll get you your tax money, Mr. Doyle."

She turned on her heel and stalked into her adjoining bedroom. She let the door close loudly to give voice to her resentment. Susannah retrieved her locked cashbox from beneath the floorboards, between two joists and pulled out a small cloth bag.

In it was everything Doyle was entitled to. And no more.

PEGGY BUSTLED AROUND the kitchen at speed. Nate staked a position by the wall and kept out of her way.

"What's going on, Peggy? Martin Doyle has never collected taxes personally in his life. What's his interest in Susannah?"

Nate winced when Peggy set down a teapot so heavily he was surprised it didn't break.

"It's not *Susannah*. It's The Queen's Head," she said. "Doyle refused her a liquor license at first and without it, we couldn't have made this a going concern. So he offered her his surety."

"In exchange for *what,* exactly?"

Bile burned its way up his throat. The thought of Susannah forced to *consort* with that man…

For the first time since the Doyles' arrival, the hint of the old Peggy returned with quirk of her lips.

"Settle down, lover boy. The man's here for his five percent cut of the takings – the price of the bond to make sure the Duchess is running a *respectable* establishment."

"And *that's* what she's told you?"

For a while, Peggy didn't answer. She set out the teacups and cut a couple of slices of hevva cake. Nate wondered if he was being comprehensively ignored.

But when she had finished dressing the tea tray with neatly pressed napkins, she pinned him with a gimlet stare.

"Know this, Mr. Pirate. There's no other woman I know who has the decency of Susannah M..., *the Duchess*. Even during the worst of times, she was *always* an honorable woman. If she says that's what the arrangement is, then that's what the arrangement *is*."

He held his hands up to surrender and lowered his head momentarily in contrition.

"Forgive me. The last thing I want is to offend you or impugn Mrs. Linwood."

A drawn-out sigh and a softening of Peggy's features was a promising sign.

"I know you don't," she admitted. "I can see you're a decent man Nathaniel Payne. But don't go thinking you're some knight on a white horse. This is the first time in that girl's life she's been able to make some of her own choices, so let her make them."

Nate approached Peggy and lowered his voice. It wouldn't surprise him if Lillian had an ear to the door.

"I saw her face, Peg. Susannah was terrified. And as much as I'm loath to defend him, I know what kind of man Doyle is – a rutting reprobate – but he wouldn't force himself on a woman."

Susannah's companion fiddled with the hem of her apron.

"So what kind of man was Linwood that would leave his widow so afraid even years after his death?"

"His name wasn't..." Peggy shut her mouth with a snap. The little enough she said was obviously too much.

She simply picked up the tray and left the kitchen.

The roiling emotion Nate thought he had under control threatened to bubble over. He pushed through the door into the mud room, snatched up his tools and went back outside, clean clothes or not.

Pounding timber would have to suffice for physically pounding Martin Doyle and this mysterious husband of Susannah Linwood's.

Chapter Seven

June 1805

TODAY WAS A local holiday for the church fete to mark the end of spring. Held on the common opposite the little square Norman church, the fete attracted merchants from as far away as Wales and Dorset, selling spices, trinkets, laces, and iron goods.

It was early. The sky had been a soft shade of peach, highlighting the mist which clung to the ankles of those setting up their stalls. As the sun rose, the pink gave way to a golden apricot-hue, heralding a clear fine day.

The largest of the structures, on the far side of the common past the rows of stalls featuring games and amusements, was the beer tent erected by Simon Sitwell, proprietor of The Rose and Crown.

For Susannah, as the owner of The Queen's Head, the lucrative opportunity was something she had had equal claim to. However, during one of the planning committee meetings, she herself raised the motion that, to demonstrate a spirit of goodwill and cooperation as newcomers to St. Sennen, The Rose and Crown should be given the concession.

Her offer endeared her to Reverend Johnston and his wife who had been wondering how to broach the delicate subject of competing commercial interests. Even Simon Sitwell himself had come over to The Queen's Head to thank her.

She smiled at the memory. This was what she wanted – a place that felt like home, to be welcomed in, to be part of a community where one's individual differences mattered less than everyone cooperating together for the mutual good.

It was what she had hoped to do when Jack moved her into the house outside of Lydd. But he had kept her isolated at home. Only the servants were to go to the village. If Susannah wanted to go anywhere, she would first have to consult her husband – more often than not, he refused.

At first, she did not voice any dissent – after all, as a new bride, she took her vows of "honor and obey" seriously. And, after a while, isolation became habit – then a relief. How could she face another soul after bearing the brunt of that man's violence?

Only since his death and the discovery of his ledger had she realized there was another reason why Jack shunned company.

Now, two years later, Susannah felt she could breathe again.

"The pirate likes you."

Susannah smiled to herself as she pulled the jams and preserves out of a crate and placed them on the trestle table while Peggy pinned fabric bunting to the canvas awning on their stall.

"Does he?" she responded innocently. She managed to catch a glimpse of Peggy out of the corner of her eye. The expression was priceless – slight exasperation mixed with the knowledge that she was being teased.

Now that Peggy was secure in her own romance with Clem, she was turning a matchmaker's gaze in *her* direction.

Susannah picked up another crate and started unpacking it. Even with her back to the woman, she could still feel Peggy's attention directed her way.

"I like him, too," she said softly so only Peggy would hear.

And it was true. She *did* like Nate. How could she not?

Despite the fact she had known him for only about a month, she felt as though she had known him a lifetime.

Never once had he complained about helping with chores around the inn. Every morning, he went out and tirelessly labored. Moreover, his temper was even and his sense of humor was unforced when he bantered with Peggy and Clem.

You could tell a lot about a man by the way he took teasing at his own expense.

And as days went by, Susannah felt herself lose more of her reserve to him.

Last week, they received the first eggs from the half-dozen chickens now living in the shed and run Nate had built for them. Now a portion of the paddock had been fenced off by him. In a few weeks' time, they would plant apple trees and she would also try her hand at growing Kea plums which she had ordered from a farm in Falmouth.

She thought how, before dawn this morning, as she and Peggy hitched Sid to the loaded trap, Nate had set off on the *Sprite* to take a cargo of salted eels down to Newlyn. He'd probably be there for at least a night, if not two.

She would miss him when he eventually left for good. She tried not to think about it too much.

"Do think you think it's time to tell him about Moorcroft?"

Susannah's smile vanished. She fought off a shudder.

"Why would you ask *that*? There's no need for *anyone* to know."

Yes, she thought about Jack Moorcroft often. But she was careful to keep those thoughts to herself. Not since that first day they moved into The Queen's Head had Peggy spoke his name. Susannah set down the jar in her hand and waited to catch Peggy's eye. She did. The woman looked down from her step stool.

"You haven't told Clem about my past have you?"

Peggy looked appalled. "No! I wouldn't do that without your say so."

Susannah nodded, accepting it as the truth.

"My past is behind me; behind the both of us. There is no reason on earth why anyone other than we two ought to know any of it."

"Hey ho!"

Never before had Clem's call of greeting been so welcome. Susannah smiled as he approached.

"A smile from two of the prettiest women in St. Sennen can only make this day brighter!" said the ironmonger.

Peggy climbed down from her step stool, accepting Clem's hand as she did so. "You silver-tongued devil! It's going to get you into trouble one of these days."

"You'll just have to stick by my side, old girl, and make sure I stay out of strife then."

Peggy turned a becoming shade of pink.

It was really quite sweet. And since Peggy seemed keen on playing matchmaker, then perhaps Susannah should return the favor.

"Why don't you two explore the markets this morning? I can manage here on my own for a few hours."

The look of delight on Clem's face was worth making the offer. Peggy's frown added to her amusement.

"How are you going to do that while also keeping an eye on thieving little tinkers?"

"*I* shall manage. Besides, I suspect most of our sales will be at noon when the beer tent becomes too crowded," said Susannah. "If it makes you feel better, consider it a mission. I hear Mrs. Doyle's cook is excellent and expects to win a medal in the baking competition. I want to make sure we at least take home a ribbon.

"So shoo! Off you go," she added, waving her hands. "Enjoy the fete for a couple of hours."

She watched the pair walk off hand-in-hand and her heart lightened. She was certain that in the not too distant future there would be an offer of marriage. And, if that was the case, she wanted Peggy to be free to follow her heart and not refuse it out of some obligation to her.

The best way she could do that was to demonstrate she was capable of managing on her own.

By the time the sun itself peeked over the hills, the reedy drone of a hurdy-gurdy could be heard sounding over the common, calling people down to the fete.

The morning passed quickly. And profitably. Susannah was down to her last dozen jars of lemon curd. The pickled asparagus was selling very well.

After a while, she got to know the types of visitors – the idle browsers, the locals who simply wanted a chat, the fellow stallholders who would casually buy a bottle or two to evaluate the quality of the competition, as well as the genuine enthusiastic purchasers.

One of those early idle browsers returned and browsed through the goods again. The stranger was as tall as Nate and about the same age from what she could see of his face beneath the tricorn hat. But the thing that stood out was the crossed anchors tattoo on his web of his hand between the thumb and forefinger.

A sailor, without question. But the nearest naval port had to be fifty miles from St. Sennen. Was he a local man who had returned home? Without knowing why she should suspect so, Susannah believed there was more to the man's business than merely enjoying the day.

The aroma of roasting meat filled the air as preparations for the noon meal approached.

Peggy and Clem would be back again soon and she wouldn't mind taking a walk around to stretch her legs after several hours on her feet.

Then the mystery man returned a second time and picked up a bottle of rosehip cordial, examining its deep pink color.

A ghost of fear whispered in her ear.

Who is he? An associate of Jack's? Of Robert Lawnton?

Run!

She swallowed, forcing the panic back down. Truly, it was ridiculous to let her imagination run away from her. Who could possibly harm her here in the middle of St. Sennen? One scream would have neighbors running to her aid.

She should talk to him.

"If you're thinking of taking the rosehip cordial, I suggest you don't wait. The ones you see here on the table are the last I have left."

The man set down the bottle and looked at her directly for the first time.

"You're wondering why I've been lurking around your stall, aren't you?" The man sounded a little sheepish, as though embarrassed to have been caught.

She inclined her head in acknowledgement.

"How about I take four of each of your remaining stock?" he said.

"I won't refuse a sale, but I would put it to you that you're not a man who usually buys preserves."

The man grinned. "I'm truly that obvious?"

"I'm afraid you are," Susannah answered, trying to sound casual as she retrieved a crate in which to place his purchase.

"Usually my wife does all the buying of this sort."

"And she's not with you today?" Susannah knew full well that she was not. Whenever she had seen him, he was alone.

"No, she's at home in Truro."

"I see."

There was just enough censure in those two words to catch the man's attention and to broaden his grin.

"I'm in St. Sennen on business for a few days. Trading; international exports, that kind of thing. I'm looking for someone I thought might be here today. Nathaniel Payne? He's given The Queen's Head inn as his address and whenever I've asked about him, it's led me back to you."

Susannah shucked off her wariness. This man was not an agent of her late husband's after all.

"Mr. Payne has been staying with us, but I'm afraid he won't be back for a couple of days," she said. "If you're looking for a place to stay then you can't do better than The Queen's Head."

"You've sold me, *Miss*—?"

"Mrs... Mrs. Linwood, and I didn't catch *your* name. Mr...."

The man gave an informal bow.

"The name's Hardacre. Adam Hardacre."

THE TRADING RUN down the coast was as smooth and fine as this late spring day. As a result, Nate completed unloading the cargo of salted silver eels well before lunch. And if the winds favored him this afternoon, he could be back at St. Sennen just on nightfall.

The lingering twilight made navigation easier than sailing at night.

Everything seemed to go his way today. He took it as a good omen.

His pockets were full and his hold was clear. Exactly as it should be.

And, yet, he wasn't returning home empty-handed. Inside the cabin was a lady's fan for Susannah. It was a purchase made on impulse as he'd waited for the warehousemen to unload the cargo and wandered around the harbor markets.

It wasn't expensive, but the folding fabric was prettily painted with multicolored roses and the nicely crafted pierced-work on the sticks made it stand out from the ordinary.

Nate imagined Susannah dressed in her finest gown, her light brown hair swept up and set with ribbons in the shade of deep pink. When in all the time he'd known her had she enjoyed herself without a care in the world, knowing she didn't have to prepare for the next day's trade or cajole a drunkard out of having one more pint?

Nate wasn't a wealthy man by any means, but he'd give a lot to see Susannah as the grand lady he suspected she was. Even after spending every day for almost a month in her company, he was still no closer to knowing any more about her past, from her at least.

Did she not trust him? Or was the truth of the matter that she trusted no one but Peggy? What was it about her past marriage? Apart from a wedding band, she wore no rings and there were no remembrances to the departed Mr. Linwood that he had seen at The Queen's Head. But then, he'd never been invited into Susannah's private quarters either.

He set those thoughts aside and put his full attention to sailing. All that really mattered was making good time back to St. Sennen so he could enjoy at least one dance with the proprietress of The Queen's Head before the night was over.

HE YAWNED AND scratched at the day's whiskers. If Susannah was Cinderella, did that make him a prince? Good Lord, he hoped not. His tolerance for mannered fools was limited at the best of times. It would be just like him to insult a sodding earl.

The sound of the band could be heard in the Pengellan estuary.

Nate furled the sails and dropped anchor. He wouldn't risk docking the *Sprite* at St. Sennen in the dark and without assistance. He would row the rest of the way in and tie up the rowboat at the jetty.

Any vestiges of exhaustion fled with the sound of music, laughter and merriment in the center of the fete. After sating his hunger at one of the food tents, he went in search of Susannah.

The stall had been taken down and, presumably, packed into the cart. Hopefully, Susannah was enjoying herself among the dancers and had not made some excuse to leave early. As he got closer to the tent with the dancers, a couple hand-in-hand passed him grinning, the girl fanning her face with a folded piece of paper.

Nate thought of his gift which he'd left on the boat to give Susannah on the morrow. Was he being forward? Perhaps that had been a mistake. He circled around back to the big tent scanning the heart of it where dozens of dancers enjoyed a lively country dance.

"Hey ho! You're back!"

Nate felt a thump on his back. He turned and was greeted by Clem.

"We didn't expect to see you back before tomorrow! Come and join Sam and me here."

Clem indicated a bench. Four men on it duly slid along to accommodate one more. Nate hesitated a moment. If he sat, he couldn't see the dance floor properly and he suspected that was where he'd find Susannah.

"Why aren't you out there with Peggy?" Nate asked, nodding to the knot of dancers.

Clem rubbed the back of his head and looked sheepish.

"It's like this. After the third time I stepped on her foot, she called me a lumberin' oaf and threatened to cut off certain unmentionables. And since I'm fond of my certain unmentionables, and I like the fact that Peg's been thinkin' of my certain unmentionables, then the least I can do is sit out the dancin'."

Clem and Peggy. Nate laughed until his eyes nearly watered. He couldn't think of two people so well suited.

"And Susannah?"

Nate hoped the question didn't come across as too obvious. Clem's expression told him he hadn't been successful.

"She's still here – and dancing every so often… including with the new lodger."

"What new lodger?"

"Someone who introduced himself to Susannah today."

Hell, he was *not* going to be a jealous man, Nate told himself, even as he rose to his feet to view the crowd.

The music came to an end. Dancers applauded as they left the floor. He spotted Susannah immediately. Her face shone and not just from exertion. There was a brightness to it he'd never seen before. Then that beautiful face broke into a genuine smile as the man she was with said something evidently amusing. She looked up to answer.

Susannah looked his way. The surprise and added delight on her face as she left her companion to come to him made Nate feel triumphant. That extra smile was for *him.*

"You're back!" she said, touching his arm. Nate doubted Susannah would be aware she had done it. "Clem was certain you'd stay at Newlyn overnight. Nate, this is Adam Hardacre, he'll be lodging with us for a couple of weeks."

Hardacre. The name was *familiar.*

The man held out his hand. Nate shook it.

"Mrs. Linwood, thank you for the dance," said Hardacre, "but if you'll both excuse me, I'll sit the next one out."

Nate mentally saluted the man for his impeccable sense of timing. He picked up Susannah's hand and bowed over it.

"I was going to stay at Newlyn, but I wanted to be back in time to dance with *you.*"

Chapter Eight

NATE WONDERED WHETHER the color in Susannah's cheeks was merely from the recently finished dance or whether he was the cause of it.

He liked the way her bright blue eyes regarded him around the circle of dancers, as though there was no one else around but him. A landlady did *not* look like that at a tenant.

He made sure Susannah was left with no uncertainty about his interest. A lingering touch at her waist, a quick-step turn that forced her up close to him. He found himself growing aroused. He liked it, this slow burning desire – especially when he could see an expression of it mirrored in the eyes of the woman in his arms.

Susannah agreed to another dance, and then a third before declaring herself well and truly done in.

She accepted his arm once more and they went in search of Peggy and Clem. The new lodger was nowhere to be seen.

Hardacre...

Nate shook his head and forced himself to concentrate on Clem's humorous tale about almost coming a cropper when fishing off the rocks.

"A body was soaked right through! I cursed my luck and scrambled my way up to the rock, only to find the fish had stayed put and *I'd* gone into the sea! 'Hey ho,' I said. 'If you're up here on land and I'm the one in the sea, then who caught who?'!"

Here, Nate could watch the light from the lamps fall on Susannah's face, highlighting high cheek bones. She listened attentively to Clem's tale and then told one of her own about how she and Peggy found themselves flapping about like birds to get rid of the family of seagulls that had made themselves at home in one of the rooms due to a broken window pane.

Once during the evening, Nate saw Lillian Doyle moving around and about, dispensing a word to one of the villagers and doling out the occasional coin to a child. How very *good* of her to condescend to grace St. Sennen with her presence as though she was some sort of Lady-bloody-Bountiful...

Her charity and piety was only for show, unlike Susannah whose generosity showed itself in many different ways – and Nate was cognizant of the fact that he was one of the recipients of her kindness.

Here within this inner circle, she was no longer on guard. And he was struck by the sense that he ought to consider himself lucky that Susannah deemed him worthy to be included in her trust.

Mid-evening was heralded by a shift in the breeze. The smell of brine from the sea also brought with it the sound of waves pounding against the protective embrace of the rocks and cliffs which guarded the estuary.

Nate, Clem, Susannah, and Peggy made their way unhurriedly back to where Sid peacefully grazed. When the ghost-grey horse saw them, he raised his head and approached. It looked as though he, too, was eager to be home.

Soon, Hardacre and Clem's son, Sam, emerged from the thinning crowd.

"Well, this looks like a full house," Peggy observed gravely as Nate and Clem harnessed the horse between the shafts of the cart. "We're not all going to fit on the trap, not with all the timber and canvas from the stall."

The new lodger went to move his satchel. "I'm afraid *I'm* the imposition – I don't mind trailing along behind. Besides, it will give me a chance to talk to Mr. Payne. I have a feeling w—"

Peggy was swift to interrupt. "Now, we can't be having that! You're a paying guest. Nate, why don't you escort Mrs. Linwood home? You can meet us there, and we'll have a nice cup of tea and get Mr. Hardacre settled in."

Nate exchanged a look with Susannah. She looked mildly amused. Clem, by contrast, was utterly bewildered.

No one said a thing for a moment until the silence was broken by Hardacre who shrugged, then vaulted up onto the back of the trap.

"Well that suits me," he said. "I've been on my feet all day."

He was soon joined up there by Sam.

Clem looked Nate's way as though he expected an objection either from him or from Susannah.

"But wh—"

"Well?" Peggy called down to Clem. "What are you waiting for, Old Boots?"

"You go on ahead," Susannah touched Clem's arm. "It's a lovely evening for a walk."

Peggy flashed them both a triumphant look as Clem clambered aboard. With a smart snap of the reins, Sid began the mile-and-half journey back to The Queen's Head.

As blindingly obvious as Peggy had been, Nate wasn't going to knock back a chance to spend time alone with Susannah. And the fact she hadn't overruled her friend was all the encouragement he needed.

Susannah waved them off into the darkness before bringing the shawl more closely over her shoulders. She looked at him almost shyly, not quite reserved, although he knew *that* part of her waited in the wings.

"Have you ever been sailing?" Nate asked.

She shook her head. "I've never been on a boat, even though I've lived by the sea a lot of my life. Perhaps you'll take me one day."

"How about now?"

"What? Tonight? In the dark?"

The surprise on her face was an image he wanted to hold forever.

"Sure, why not? The *Sprite's* here, the tide's running in, and there's a breeze we can pick up."

Susannah worried her lip. Nate watched hesitation play out over her face. It seemed she warred with herself. Would she retreat back into herself?

She nodded as though concluding a silent discussion to which only she was privy before looking back at him.

"I can't believe I'm going to let a pirate take me sailing."

Nate fought the urge to sweep her into his arms at that moment. He was going to do this courtship thing right. Susannah was a lady and ought to be treated like one.

Instead, he took her hand in his and watched her face carefully as he drew her closer to tuck her arm through his. Did he presume too much? His experience with other women had been much, much different. They wore their desire as plainly as he did and were not shy in expressing what they wanted and how they wanted it.

Susannah wore a veiled expression as they walked through the moonlit streets with some of the other villagers until they reached the dock.

Nate boarded the small dinghy first, holding it steady with one hand while offering her the other. She placed her hand in his and squeezed as she stepped into the little boat and allowed him to guide her to sit down on the stern thwart.

"I should warn you," she said. "I can't swim."

"With me here, you don't need to."

"I'm safe with you, am I?"

It was the smallest of teases, a tentative attempt, as though it was something she had never before tried.

He gave her a smile in return.

"For the most part," he said, turning to untie the rope at the mooring. "Let me put it this way, I've not lost anyone yet."

That elicited a laugh.

He settled himself a-thwart, then used an oar to push the boat away before settling them both in the oarlocks and beginning to row. It didn't take too long to reach the *Sprite* and they didn't speak during the journey. Between glancing over his shoulder occasionally to check their progress, he looked at her and she at him in enigmatic silence.

Finally, he helped Susannah aboard the *Sprite* before pulling the dinghy aboard and lashing it to the deck.

He started his preparations to set sail while Susannah remained at the railing, her attention fixed across the water on St. Sennen, deep in thought.

SUSANNAH THOUGHT IT best to remain where she was, out of the way, while Nate moved around the *Sprite* with brisk efficiency.

It was an odd feeling being out here on the water, looking at moonlit landscapes that were familiar, yet different from this perspective as the vessel bobbed gently. It was like seeing the whole world anew.

After a moment, Susannah felt the boat move decisively; little more than a tug at first. She looked up to see the white sail flap and then fill out. The decking beneath her feet shifted some more. Susannah stepped back to maintain her balance.

"It might take you a moment or two to get your sea legs," said Nate, making his way back to the rear of the boat – the stern – that much she did know. "Keep your knees slightly bent and walk smoothly, you'll soon get the hang of it."

After a couple of unsteady steps, she made her way to the wheel where Nate was, positioning herself a few paces behind him against the stern rail. She breathed in. She could smell the salt and that certain indefinable quality distinct to the sea.

She didn't want to distract the man at his task, but she did want to stay close enough that if anything did happen…

She looked at him. Firm legs stood braced apart, accenting a trim waist. Strong arms held the wheel…

Peggy was right to dub him the pirate – especially now that the long day had covered his face in stubble. The only thing he was missing was a gold earring.

And a parrot… a big red parrot.

She giggled at the thought.

"You're not laughing at me behind my back are you?" he asked.

"No!" she lied.

He shot back a glance and his grin gave her the confidence to speak truthfully.

"Well, perhaps a little bit," she said. "If you want the truth, I was thinking of the nickname Peggy gave you. Watching you at the helm, well, it seemed rather apt."

"The pirate…"

"You're not offended?"

"I overheard her the day I arrived. I rather like the idea of being a dashing pirate."

"Not a villainous pirate?"

"Nope."

"Not a murderous pirate?"

"God, no – not unless you're talking about murdering one of those fruitcakes you make."

"Then that would make you a ravenous pirate."

"Oh, I'm definitely a *ravenous* pirate."

His tone dropped, and his words were laden with meaning. But more shocking was her own reaction. Susannah felt it in her chest, a feeling of tenderness toward the man before her; even desire.

Nate took another glance ahead and again up at the sails, trimmed just enough to take the breeze.

"Come and join me."

Susannah frowned. Perhaps there was something of the pirate in him after all.

"No, thank you," she said. "I'm comfortable where I am."

"You may not be shortly. We'll be crossing the bar between the two tributaries and the ocean. The change in tide will make it rough."

And, as though he'd ordained it, Susannah felt the deck beneath her feet and the vessel begin to rock gently from side to side.

Without looking back, he reached out a hand toward her. "I might be a ravenous pirate, but I don't bite."

She took a deep breath and pushed herself away from the stern rail. She took the four unsteady paces forward.

The *Sprite* pitched a moment.

She clutched his shoulder. He placed a hand on the center of her back and urged her closer to him, closer to the helm.

"Here, step in, put your hands on the wheel," he said. "Set your feet apart just a little until you feel well-braced."

She followed his instructions and gripped the exposed spindles where he did while he settled himself behind her.

She felt a shove broadside. The *Sprite* bucked fore and aft like an untamed horse but, encircled in Nate's arms, Susannah was steady.

She was safe with him.

She closed her eyes at the thought.

The last time she had felt truly protected was when her father was alive. In the years since his passing, and during her marriage to Jack, she had *never* felt at ease.

One error on her part would have Jack scream at her – call her stupid. Worthless. A waste. She became too afraid to do anything for the fear of his raining blows. She swallowed against a lump in her throat, relieved Nate could not see her.

She felt his warmth at her back. If she stepped back just an inch, she would be against his chest. If his arms closed around hers more fully, she would be in his embrace.

"Steady yourself," he said softly in her ear, sending delicious shivers down her arms that had nothing to do with the cold. "It will be rough for a bit until we get further up the mouth of the Pengellan."

The *Sprite* was picked up by a wave rolling through the estuary mouth. Her stomach plummeted at the unexpected motion. She let out a small gasp.

Nate pulled the wheel down hard to pull the boat back from the crest of the wave. Susannah's hands gripped tightly, but she had no choice but to follow where he led.

"Don't fight her," he said. "The *Sprite* knows what she's doing. Just relax and go with it. Work with her."

After a moment concentrating on how the boat reacted to the change of the current and the push of the wind, she started to understand. If she was aware, there were subtle cues that told her what the boat was going to do next and she adjusted her stance in anticipation of it. Her unease became exhilaration as the *Sprite* and her able captain crossed the bar and headed for the calmer waters of their creek.

She couldn't help a grin. Had she ever felt this alive before? Possibly never. She breathed in deep and stood up on her toes, so she could see the rise and fall of the bow.

The *Sprite* followed the river course around the protection of Arthyn Hill until, up ahead, she saw the lights in the ground floor windows of The Queen's Head. In the moonlight ahead was the boatshed.

Nate let go of the wheel and worked the complicated web of ropes overhead that gave him control of the mainsail.

"Keep the wheel where she is," he instructed. "Just line up the bow to the jetty and the *Sprite* will do the rest."

Nate stepped away. Susannah adjusted her grip on the wheel, feeling the true resistance of the water through the wheel for the first time.

"How do you sail her on your own?" she called back.

"See the two eyebolts on the deck, either side of where you're standing?" Nate called. "I lash the wheel."

"And you're always on your own?"

"No, I used to have two other men sail with me; Clem has joined me from time to time."

She was about to ask what happened to them, but thought better of it. He'd never spoken about his imprisonment in France. Moreover, he had asked her nothing about *her* past. It seemed only right she did not ask him about *his*.

They drew near to the jetty, now just a few yards away. Nate released the mainsail which dropped down the mast, allowing them to slow their progress to a drift. He sprinted forward and tossed a rope around one of the uprights and drew the *Sprite* into dock, then did the same with a second rope toward the stern before dropping the anchor from the bow of the boat and making his way back to her.

She felt the weight of his hands on her shoulders where he gave them a squeeze. "You make a fine first mate!"

She hoped the moonlight hid the heat rising in her cheeks.

"You make a very fine teacher," she replied.

His right hand left her shoulder and touched her cheek gently. The breath she took was unsteady. He wanted to kiss her. She could see it in his eyes. But she was confident he would not; not until he was certain of *her*.

Jack was the last man to touch her, and she had vowed to never let another. A foolish promise. Especially when all she wanted now was to step forward into Nate's arms and have him hold her with all the tenderness she saw in his face.

And what harm would a kiss do? She was no man's wife. She could kiss anyone of her choosing or no one.

Would she dare?

She ignored her whispers of doubt and took half a step forward. He met her the rest of the way, taking her into his embrace.

She breathed in deep. The smell of him was unique. He smelled of the sea, of cedar and lemon – like no one else.

"Will you let me kiss you, Susannah?" he whispered against her ear.

She raised her face to his, closing her eyes as his lips descended. The kiss was warm, soft, and all-too-brief.

She opened her eyes. She wanted another, but the words wouldn't come out. His embrace firmed a moment then their lips met again in a slow exploration that lit a spark of long-dormant desire which turned into a slow burning heat.

In the end, it was he who broke off the kiss.

"Oh God, Susannah..." He breathed in deeply and touched her cheek once again. "You know nothing of me, and I'm afraid that if you did, you'd run a mile."

She reached up and stroked his hair.

"And you know nothing of *me*, but I've had enough of running away. I've done it for far too long," she said, looking at him directly in the eyes. "I'm willing to take a chance on a pirate, if he's willing to take a chance on me."

This time, the kiss was a chaste one to her cheek.

"Then let's not run. Let us walk together, slowly, and see where this path leads. Agreed?"

Chapter Nine

NATE AWOKE FROM a light doze.

The floorboards creaked once more as the occupant of the room next door moved about.

This Adam Hardacre was an early riser, it would seem.

Last night, Nate's attention was all on Susannah, but he did recall this Hardacre man saying he wanted to talk business. Well, no time like the present, especially as the first order of business was to find out exactly *how* this man knew him.

He quickly washed, shaved, and dressed and went downstairs. It was still quiet in The Queen's Head.

From outside, a soft grey early morning daylight spilled through the mullion windows, across the oak tables and chairs, and onto the floor highlighting places where the varnish had worn away.

He heard a sound in the kitchen. There, he found the fair-headed stranger making himself quite at home, stoking up a fire in the range. The man looked round at him then returned to his task.

"You can make yourself useful by finding where these ladies keep their tea and preparing a pot for us," he said.

"You know, Peggy will kill you for being in her domain, and I'd do nothing to stop her."

"I consider myself suitably warned," the man laughed, but he continued on his mission. He lifted the kettle and swirled it, evidently looking to gauge whether there was enough water in it.

Nate let out a sigh of resignation loud enough to be heard, then walked to the cupboard to pull out the locked tea chest. He tried the lid; it was locked – just as he knew it would be.

"It looks like you're well out of luck, mate," he said. "The box is locked and I'm pretty sure Peggy sleeps with the key."

"Don't tell me you've never picked a lock before."

It was too damned early to be butting heads like two rutting stags. Nate shrugged and refused to hide a full open-mouthed yawn. Hardacre fumbled in his pocket and turned with a piece of shaped wire in his hand.

"What the hell do you think you're doing?" Nate kept his voice low and harsh. Susannah's bedroom was only two rooms away.

"I used to be a ship's carpenter, so I've worked a lock or two in my time, but I ended up taking advanced lessons from a lady who has really mastered the art. May I?"

Nate handed over the chest. "Some kind of lady," he muttered.

"No, I mean it. Lady Abigail actually has the title."

Hardacre inserted the wire in the escutcheon and began working the lock.

"What's a sailor like you doing mixing with the gentry?"

Hardacre glanced his way in mute inquiry then continued his task.

"I saw the crossed-anchor tattoo on your hand," Nate continued, "so you were at least a bosun."

"Very good," Hardacre responded. "Go on."

The man was starting to rub him up the wrong way. Very well – he *would* go on.

"There's a war on and every abled-bodied sailor is being deployed against Napoleon's navy. You don't look ready to be pensioned off, and you seem able enough. So, what the hell are you doing here?"

"I'm here to talk to you."

"You said that last night. What about?"

He heard the click of the lock a split-second before Hardacre's soft "ah!" of triumph. The herbaceous aroma of tea leaves bloomed in the air. Now that the deed was done, there was nothing for it but to have a cup of tea.

Hardacre retrieved a teapot and two cups, then rummaged around until he found a tin that contained the remains of yesterday's bread. Nate shrugged and headed to the pantry to cut several large slices of ham and lumps of cheese. He also brought butter to the table.

"That's not a bad feast," Hardacre announced.

"Now you're begging the question." Nate filled his cup and sat at the dining table.

Hardacre acknowledged the observation with a salute of his own cup.

"Last month, you sent a strangely-worded letter to an aunt of mine in Truro."

Caution whispered in Nate's ear. He drew his tea closer on the table before sitting back, crossing his arms.

"From Felix," Nate confirmed. He watched the mysterious sailor's slight nod of confirmation before he stuffed a large slice of buttered bread and ham in his mouth. It precluded Hardacre from responding until he had finished chewing.

"Aunt Runella thanks you for the letter and has a question. Did the men who helped you escape from Fort St. Pierre give you anything to bring back?"

Nate made him wait by taking a bite of his own bread and ham, chewing slowly, and drinking a mouthful of tea before answering.

"What makes you think I wasn't simply released?"

Hardacre barked out a laugh. "Come, man, you know as well as I do that the only way an Englishman leaves St. Pierre is in a death shroud."

Nate's patience was at an end. "What the hell do you know about St. Pierre? Who are you? A revenuer?" He *knew* he was right to be suspicious.

Hardacre shook his head slowly in answer to each question. From within his shirt, he pulled out an envelope and slid it across the table.

"There's fifty pounds in there as a token of thanks from Aunt Runella. I'm also authorized to give you two hundred and fifty pounds for everything you brought back with you from France."

"Like what? What is your aunt hoping to find?"

"I'm not entirely sure."

It was Nate's turn to laugh. "Do you really think I floated in on the last tide? Either you level with me or I simply take my fifty pounds, and you can pass on my thanks to *Aunt* Runella."

Hardacre gave him a level look. Nate matched it, watching the man evaluate him.

Prince the dog nosed his way through the door that led to the mud room and looked at the two men before making his way to sit at Nate's side. The dog received a sliver of ham for his trouble and wolfed it down in one bite. The hound looked to Hardacre and, strolling to him, was similarly rewarded. Satisfied, the dog trotted to the fire and lay down before it.

There were sounds of movement elsewhere in The Queen's Head. Susannah and Peggy would be here shortly – and Nate determined he would tell them their pointer was a lousy guard dog.

"Well?" he prompted.

Hardacre gave a single affirmative nod of his head.

"Not here," he qualified. "Somewhere we won't be overheard. Now, perhaps we should finish our tea and make good in here before Peggy arrives and kills us both."

SUSANNAH MOPPED THE floors, humming idly to herself. It was Sunday, a day of rest. Well, half a day. The inn would be open after four o'clock in the afternoon for evening meals, but no hard liquor could be served. Even the ale served was small beer.

She had just spent the morning completing the books. Yesterday's fete had netted them a profit of twelve pounds. Six pounds each for her and Peggy. She had placed the sum in the strongbox hidden between two floor joists where a prospective thief would never think to look.

Peggy emerged from the kitchen with a tray laden with glasses. They rattled as she lowered the weight onto the bar. "You haven't told me how last night was with the pirate," she said.

"It was nice," Susannah answered, deliberately turning her back so Peggy couldn't see the color of her face.

"*Nice?* That's all you're going to say?"

"Thank you."

"*What?*"

Susannah took a shallow breath to hide the laughter that bubbled in her chest. It was rare she could bring Peggy to the point of exasperation. She decided to play on it and found her most priggish voice.

"Actually, the more I think about it, the more I ought to be cross at you, throwing Nate and me together like that – especially in front of a paying guest."

Peggy was silent, which was always a good sign. She turned in Peggy's direction to see her friend staring open-mouthed. Now, Susannah couldn't help the laugh that escaped her. It came so heartily, tears welled in her eyes.

A moment later, she felt a tossed drying cloth land on her shoulder.

"You're a cruel, cruel woman, Duch," announced Peggy theatrically. "Just a little romance, *that's all I want.*"

"You have a fancy man of your own, Miss Smith," Susannah retorted, clutching one hand to her breast and another to her brow, "and never once have you ever offered to share a crumb from your table to a poor lonely widow who was starving to know there was still such a thing as *love*."

"It's one thing with an ordinary man, Mrs. Linwood," continued Peggy in the same vein, "but it's not the same as making love to a *pirate!*"

Susannah heard the sound of slow applause from behind her. She wiped the tears of laughter from her eyes and turned to its source.

Lillian Doyle stood in the doorway of The Queen's Head, cutting a trim figure in a forest green riding habit. Her dark hair was pinned up to show off an elegant little black hat. The woman looked her up and down.

"My, I had no idea this was a meeting of the St. Sennen Theatrical Society, although you dress the part of *Cinders* quite admirably, Mrs. Linwood."

Susannah raised her chin. She refused to feel self-conscious in her old, grey, faded work dress.

Lillian spared Peggy a glance and walked into the bar. "I have to say, I don't recall there being a pirate in the story, but one can never tell with these pantomimes."

Susannah fixed a pleasant expression on her face and approached the woman, mop in hand.

"You'll have to forgive us, Mrs. Doyle. The Queen's Head is closed until this evening. Lemonade or ginger beer is the only cool refreshment we can offer."

"I won't put to you to such trouble, Mrs. Linwood. If you wouldn't mind letting Mr. Payne know I'm here..."

"I'm afraid he's out, but I'll be glad to let him know you called by."

She watched the subtle shift of expression move across the woman's face.

Lillian Doyle thought she was lying. But at hearing nothing more than the ticking clock on the dining room wall, she settled at last for a mildly put-out countenance.

"Do you know where he might be?" she asked with exaggerated

politeness. "I noticed his boat was here."

"My guests are free to come and go as they wish, Mrs. Doyle."

The woman raised a finely shaped eyebrow.

"And here I thought he was rather more than a guest."

Across from her, Susannah could see Peggy shift, ready to step in with her razor-sharp tongue if need be. But she'd been allowing her friend to do so for far too long now.

Susannah dipped her mop into the nearby bucket of soapy water and made a wide sweep close to the other woman's skirts.

"If you wish to wait for him, Mrs. Doyle, it's best to keep out of our way. You might get wet."

The woman seemed a little taken aback but recovered quickly. She swept her skirts back from the sweeping mop and made her way back to the front door.

"Then would you be so kind as to leave him a message?"

Susannah didn't bother to look up from her task. "Certainly."

"Tell him Mrs. Doyle awaits his pleasure at the usual place, at the usual time."

"Of course," answered Susannah. "The usual place, at the usual time – we'll remember that, won't we, Peggy?"

"The usual place, at the usual time," Peggy parroted, her eyes sparkling with merriment. "I can remember that, Mrs. Linwood."

Susannah continued to mop, listening to the stomp of Lillian Doyle's boots as she strode out of the building, and the jangle of the bridle as she remounted her horse. A moment later, the horse took off at a gallop.

Peggy went immediately to the door and looked out. "I think you've made an enemy out of *that* one. Um… Clem told me that Mrs. Doyle and your pirate were lovers once."

"I thought so," said Susannah.

It helped to carry on with her work and avoid looking at Peggy. While Martin Doyle's unexpected visit a couple of weeks ago had taken her by surprise, there was no missing the tension between Nate and the couple. Susannah had already suspected the cause.

"If it's any consolation, Duch, I did overhear him tell her ladyship that he never wanted to see her again."

"Considering how small St. Sennen is, I would think that's unavoidable, don't you?"

"You going to give Nate the message?"

She looked up to find doubt written all over Peggy's face. She stopped mopping.

"Of course I am. I'm not going to tell Nate who he may or may not see. I'll give him the message and he can make the choice for himself."

Her friend returned to the bar and, picking up a drying cloth, she started polishing the glasses.

"Well, all I can say is you're a braver woman than me, letting that she-wolf lurk about."

NATE LED THE way along one of the walking trails up to the headland on Arthyn Hill. The waves pounded on the rocks below them. Wind roared in their ears, making any kind of conversation difficult, even if Adam Hardacre had been in a mind to speak. So far, the man had said nothing during the brisk climb.

When he reached the top of the headland, Hardacre fell in step and they walked side by side.

"Hardacre... I've been wracking my brains trying to work out how I know your name," said Nate. "And now I've remembered. I heard some sailors talking about you in Newlyn. You punched out an admiral who refused to give you a promotion. But instead of throwing you in the brig, they paid you off because his daughter pleaded with him."

The man beside him laughed heartily.

"That's a new tale to me," he said. "Only one-fourth of it's true, though."

"Which fourth?"

Hardacre shook his head, unwilling to be drawn.

"You wanted me to speak candidly, so here it is," he said. "Felix was a spy."

Nate felt he ought to be more surprised than he was. He simply nodded. "Go on."

"His father was French and his mother English; but his loyalty was to his mother's family because they raised him. When he was caught, he was feeding us information about one of several plans Napoleon has for invading England."

They approached a clutch of large tumble-down boulders on the wind-swept bluff and sought shelter from the wind among them. It was so silent in their lee that Nate could hear himself breathe.

Hardacre picked up a small pebble and threw it beyond the cliff's edge.

"By the time our men discovered where Felix had been taken, it was too late. When they learned you were in the oubliette with him, they took a chance that he might have said something to you and they arranged for you to get out."

Nate closed his eyes.

You have friends, Nate Payne.

"Your letter confirmed it, and that's why I'm here," Hardacre finished.

"This is a jest," said Nate.

"I wish it was. There are French spies here in England, too. They nearly cost me my life – and that of my wife. We're trying to work out what Felix's message means. He didn't use our standard cipher, so it's evident he feared our code was compromised."

Nate frowned "So that gibberish actually meant something? It wasn't just the delusions of a dying man?"

"According to my extremely well-read wife, it's Greek mythology, so we know what it *says*, we've just still to work out what it *means*."

"I hope you haven't come all this way to ask *me*, because I haven't got a bloody clue!"

Hardacre laughed.

"Nothing so arcane, man. I simply want to pay you for the goods you brought back."

Nate bent down and pulled a long blade of grass from a tuft he'd nudged with his boot.

"What makes you think I still have them?"

"Well, God help us all if you don't because they might be the last best chance to contact our friends across the Channel."

"You don't know how to contact them?"

"After your escape, they went to ground. Disappeared without word."

Nate looked across at the blond-headed man who had kept his focus out onto the horizon. "And the price is two hundred and fifty pounds?"

"To start with."

To start with? Nate felt the question on his lips but didn't utter it. In his experience, a man who was too curious found himself with more trouble than he might be prepared to deal with.

At his silence, Hardacre looked his way. "The *Sprite* is a trim little boat. I could use something like that, and a man to skipper her."

The idea of returning to France made him sick, but he'd do it if Hardacre paid handsomely. And it would have to be *very* handsome.

"I'm sure we could come to some arrangement," Nate answered.

It was noncommittal, but it was as far as he was willing to go.

"And the contraband?"

"It's safe."

"Then we have an agreement?"

"Yes, I suppose we do."

Hardacre thrust out his hand. Nate took it and returned a firm handshake.

"There's just one more issue to be resolved," said the man Nate now knew to be a British spy.

"And that is?" Nate prompted.

"How much do you trust Susannah Linwood?"

Chapter Ten

SUSANNAH FLOURED DOWN the table and kneaded out another batch of dough. She worked it with her fingers and knuckles until it was pliable. She glanced at the half-dozen baking tins before her. This would be the last for tonight.

Just as she had done every night for the past eight months, she would set the tins on the shelf above the stove where they would prove overnight, ready to be freshly baked first thing in the morning.

On the stove, a large pot of crab and lobster bisque simmered away, the bounty of a successful day's crabbing by Clem and his son. She sampled a spoonful – it was delicious, fine enough to grace any grand table. She knew a moment of pride that such quality fare fed the ordinary folks who came through their doors.

"Hey ho!" called a familiar voice. "A man could die of thirst out here!"

She shook her head fondly at Clem's friendly impatience and headed to the bar. Without asking, she poured him a full pint of ale. He swallowed down a half of it in one drink before setting down the glass.

"Now, that's a beer! And the only thing to make my life a little sweeter would be a smile from my Peg. Is she in the kitchen?"

"She's around the back in the garden."

Clem finished the beer in another large gulp and rose from his stool.

"Well, I'm goin' to kiss the cook."

Susannah hesitated then spoke. "Clem, you haven't seen Nate around at all today, have you? He went out first thing this morning with Mr. Hardacre and they didn't return at noon."

Clem shook his head.

"No, love. Anythin' the matter?"

She shook her head. "No, I just have a message for him, that's all."

The crowd of regulars started arriving for dinner and, finally, Nate and the boarder returned.

Hardacre shared a meaningful look with Nate then trudged up the stairs without a word or a glance in her direction.

That little feeling of anticipating dread Susannah hadn't felt in more than two years returned. Mysterious comings and goings; the certainty something was happening around her; the knowledge she was purposefully being kept in the dark.

She had suffered the consequences once. She would not let it happen again. She touched Nate's arm to get his attention.

"Tell me what's going on."

"We need to talk. Privately. In your office."

There was enough gravity behind his words to bring long submerged dread to the surface. The anticipation was the worst, the trepidation when Jack returned from his trips and no one knew what mood to expect from him.

Susannah headed to the door marked *Private*, pulled a key from her pocket and unlocked the door.

"Adam Hardacre will join us shortly," said Nate, "but I want to talk to you first."

"I don't understand what's going on." Susannah forced the tremor from her voice.

"Remember the contraband I brought back with me a couple of months back?"

She nodded.

"I thought I knew who had commissioned the run, but it turns out

I was wrong."

"You thought it was Lillian Doyle, didn't you?"

Nate seemed taken aback.

"Why would you—"

"She came here today to look for you. She seemed most insistent on meeting with you. She said to meet her at 'the usual time, usual place'."

Nate's face darkened. She watched the play of expressions across his face as he seemed to consider then discard a response. When he finally answered, his voice was tight.

"I haven't been anywhere near that woman since I returned from France."

Out of long habit, Susannah lowered her eyes before she spoke. "I know we both have a past, and I have no right to pry..."

Nate took her hands. His were warm where hers felt cold. She had the sensation of withdrawing into herself once more.

"Susannah..."

One look into Nate's eyes forced her to fight it. He looked at her with a desperate want, and she felt the answering hunger in her own body.

His lips were on hers before she could form another thought. She responded with growing confidence, wrapping her arms around his neck to hold him close. He replied by sweeping his hands over her back, his touch through the fabric of her dress as sensuous a feeling as she had ever known.

She tossed back her head and his lips found her neck. She pressed herself to him more fully as heated desire shot through her body.

If she wasn't careful, she could grow used to being in this man's arms – having him touch her, bring her to the heights of passion she had heard existed between man and woman. She had every confidence a man such as Nate could bring her such ecstasy.

A knock at the door shocked them both back to their senses. Nate kissed her forehead and Susannah was pleased to hear his breathing as ragged as hers.

Adam Hardacre didn't wait for an invitation. He entered and closed the door behind him firmly. In his hand was a folded sheet of paper. If he noticed the tension in the air or the disheveled state of her hair, he was too polite to make comment.

He got straight to business.

"Mrs. Linwood, I don't how much Nate has told you, but I must ask that anything discussed here goes no further than the three of us in this room."

She was startled. Gone was the affable guest and, in his place, was a man whose manner exuded authority. She glanced at Nate. The set of his jaw was firm.

"Nate has told me nothing of your business together yet, and I will make no guarantees of secrecy regarding it," she said with an alacrity so forceful that the tall blond man was taken aback. Susannah was beginning to feel confident again. "The Queen's Head may have been a smuggler's den once but not since I've owned it. I will not have it turned into a meeting place for criminal conspirators."

Hardacre relaxed and tried to disguise his grin.

"You remind me of my wife, Olivia," he said. "The next time I visit St. Sennen, I should bring her with me. I think you'd like her, Mrs. Linwood."

Then his humor vanished once again. "I carry no credentials with me; only this," he said, raising the folded paper in his hand.

"But after I tell you the story I told Nate, I hope I will be able to count on your discretion."

SUSANNAH DID NOT reply but, with a sweep of her hand, gestured that they sit. Nate glanced about, taking in the room for the first time.

It seemed Susannah's parlor doubled as her study. At one end of the room, it was all business with few ornaments. Beneath the window was a small desk with a green leather-upholstered chair. On the wall that faced into the room was a bookcase. The middle shelf was half-filled with ledger books and accounts.

The rest of the room was distinctly feminine.

An embroidery frame, with a cascade of colored silks spilling down its face, stood on one side of the fireplace; a couple of books sat on a small side table. One was apparently only part read. It had a red strip of leather poking out of the volume like a reptile's tongue. A small clock cased in pale yellow alabaster stood on the mantel beside a white glazed vase filled with bunches of hollyhocks in several shades of pink.

Nate chose one of the tapestry-covered wingback chairs by the hearth. Susannah sat down on its twin opposite. Hardacre occupied the matching settee.

Nate remained silent as Hardacre related to Susannah the story he'd heard this morning. He watched the flutter of her eyelids as the man told her about the French prison and the fate of the agent, Felix. He regretted the fact that a man who was a stranger to them both was revealing something of Nate's own past that he should have told Susannah himself, but there it was.

Other than that, very little gave itself away in her expression, but he studied it closely. Studied *her*. Her face paled ever so slightly and, although both hands rested in her lap quite serenely, she fiddled with her gold wedding band, turning it around and around her finger restlessly, only ceasing when Hardacre handed over the paper in his hand.

He caught a glimpse of gold from an embossed crest on the letter.

"It is my letter of recommendation, signed by Sir Daniel Ridgeway on behalf of the Prince of Wales," Hardacre told her.

Susannah read it silently and returned it.

"Then what do you need of me and The Queen's Head?"

"Your discretion only, Mrs. Linwood, and that of your household. Can you vouch for Peggy?"

"She is my partner in the tavern, Mr. Hardacre," she answered firmly. "I will tell her everything and she will be discreet."

Nate felt obliged to add, "Clem as well. He's been a friend of mine for years. He and Peggy are courting. We should take them both into our confidence."

Both he and Susannah watched Hardacre consider before he gave a brief nod.

"Agreed – but no more than we five."

Outside the parlor, a door slammed along with the tinkling bell, accompanied by the sound of loud voices passing by the closed door.

Susannah rose from her seat. She'd taken to turning the wedding ring around and around her finger once again.

Nate and Hardacre rose also.

"Meal service will begin shortly," she said quietly. "I need to help Peggy at the bar."

Nate watched her leave and wanted nothing more than to go after her, to offer reassurance that however unusual this circumstance might be, there was nothing to fear and nothing he wouldn't do to protect her from whatever it was that worried her.

It had something to do with her past. He knew it to the depths of his soul.

And he knew just as well that he was powerless against it.

Despite bone-weary exhaustion, Susannah found it difficult to sleep.

She started awake with every sound, only to berate herself as she recognized it – the creak of the timbers as the inn settled, the pop from a coal in the fireplace, the hooting of an owl, the rustling of night creatures outside – at least she hoped they were outside…

She had worked hard to become accepted as a member of the community here without being forced to live a double life once again.

How she had hated being used as a veneer of respectability for her husband – and resented it even more so when she eventually learned the depths of his criminality.

She turned her head on the pillow and looked over to the bedside table. She wished for a bit of light now, a comfort in the dark, but she resisted lighting a candle. She was safe from the past, she was sure. It had been more than two years now since Jack Moorcroft met his end in the Denge Marshes and, in all that time, she had heard nothing from any of his business associates.

She sighed and looked up at the ceiling. Surely after so long her nightmare was over; her pleasant, peaceful life here in St. Sennen was the world finally put to rights. She prayed it was not a dream from which she would have to awaken.

Little by little, the creeping tide of her past recalled itself as Susannah drifted back off to sleep, pulled under the current of the dream...

SUSANNAH MOORCROFT HAD stumbled back into the house, midge-bitten, cut and bruised.

Of all the servants, Peggy Smith was the one who most had her wits about her. While Susannah sobbed hysterically, the housekeeper took her by the shoulders and led her into the drawing room alone and urged her into a seat.

"H... he... he's d-d-drowned... drowned," Susannah wept. "I couldn't save him. I... I didn't save him. I didn't *want* to."

"Shhhh, Ma'am."

She looked up. Peggy had poured a small glass of brandy and pressed it in her hand. She took a careless gulp. The liquor burned down her throat and she let out a gasp. Peggy took advantage of the silence.

"You listen to *me*, Mrs. Moorcroft," she said, her voice carrying an edge that went beyond the bounds of deference. *"You* were home *all* evening. *We* did not see the master return home at all. Do you understand what I'm telling you?"

Susannah felt her eyes widen. Peggy's words cut through her shock.

"Tomorrow morning, I'll send one of the boys out to the tavern at Lydd to see if the master is there and to raise a search party to look for him if he's not," she continued.

"But I *know* where he is... I saw—"

Peggy tapped her hand firmly.

"You saw *nothing.* We know *nothing* and neither do you."

Susannah nodded and took another swallow of brandy. When she next spoke, her voice was calm.

"He may not be dead."

Peggy shot her a look of visceral disapproval. "I'm sure he will be by morning. And good riddance, too."

A scant moment later, in the way dreams do, morning came.

Peggy sent one of the stable boys into the village looking for Mr. Moorcroft. The boy returned with two men, one of whom Susannah knew as Robert Lawnton, a business associate of her husband's. The other was a local farm worker.

She met with them in the parlor. She didn't have to feign worry – the tension of it ran along every nerve.

Jack was a harsh and unyielding man and so was Lawnton. She never did like him. His face was cruel and, unlike Jack, who could turn on charm in abundance, Lawnton never made a pretense of being a gentleman – at least not to her.

In the end, she could only manage being as polite to him as her role as wife dictated, but no more.

"You say Jack didn't come home?" said Lawnton. "His horse is here. The first thing I did was check the stable."

She bore the unsaid accusation of a lie without comment. She swallowed and fiddled with a piece of embroidery that she'd picked up to do something with her hands. Then she gave the answer Peggy had demanded she rehearse, over and over until it sounded like the truth even to her ears.

"That may be so, Mr. Lawnton. I was upstairs resting with a headache. Jack might have come home and gone back out without any reference to me. He frequently did so."

Lawnton gave her an assessing look. She waited for the denouncement.

"Mr. Moorcroft *did* come home, a little under the weather if you don't mind me saying so, sir."

All of them turned to Peggy who had arrived bearing a tea tray.

"When he heard supper wouldn't be ready for another two hours, he said he'd go for a walk," she continued, setting the tray down on a side table.

"Why didn't someone look for him?"

Susannah breathed a sigh of relief that it was Peggy he asked and not her.

Peggy shrugged. "Mr. Moorcroft is a man who knows his own mind, sir. He doesn't take kindly to being second guessed. If he's out, then he's good reason to be out, and it isn't for any of us to question."

It seemed enough to satisfy Lawnton who bid Susannah a curt farewell. She set down her needlework, went to the window and watched Lawnton approach a group of searchers preparing to leave through the side gate to the path that led to the marshes.

"The left sleeve on the green dress I wore last night is badly torn. The best thing to do is to unpick both sleeves – the bodice, too," said Susannah to Peggy's reflection in the glass. "There is some lace and ribbon missing. I'll have to refashion it."

"I can start on that now, Madam," said Peggy. "I'll burn the torn bits and no one will be the wiser…"

SUSANNAH AWOKE WITH a start just as the sky lightened and turned pink in the dawn. She must have slept some more, but the lingering tendrils of the dream still seemed real. They *were* real.

She left her bed and opened her wardrobe. The green dress was there, the damage repaired by a new white and green sprigged bodice. It was unrecognizable from the gown she wore on the evening of Jack's death.

Susannah touched it with relief; it had a new life as did she.

And when Nate promised it would be only a short association with Mr. Hardacre, she believed him.

But then there was still Jack's ledger…

Chapter Eleven

ANYONE WATCHING FROM the cliffs overlooking the stretch of sandy beach would see a grey horse harnessed to a trap with two men on the driver's bench and two women and another man riding in the back, sitting on blankets and guarding a large wicker basket.

They would rightly assume they were a picnic party, there to enjoy the bracing sea air for a few hours before the tide turned and covered the sand with water once more.

Down on the beach, outside a large cave mouth, Nate brought Sid to a halt with light tug on the reins. The locals knew this place well. Generations of lovers looking for privacy met there for their trysts.

Even at high tide, the cave was safe, though during the worst of storms and the surging spring tide its giant maw would fill with churning waves.

Further into the cave, hidden from a well-trod path about ten yards in and not visible from the beach, was another opening and another cavern. This too was a familiar place for certain men of St. Sennen – the smugglers who would hide their wares from the revenuers.

Clem held aloft a miner's lamp, the candle in it flickering wildly.

"Well, I give up Nate. Where did you hide the bloody thing? This is where we usually put the goods," he said.

"And that's exactly the reason why I hid it somewhere else," Nate replied drolly. "Wait here."

As long as there was light, he could deal with the confined space and the instinctive claustrophobic terror of being trapped underground. The truth be known, it had always bothered him, but it seemed worse now after being as good as buried alive in the French donjon. He'd showed Hardacre the entrance to the cave yesterday but there was no way he was going deep into it without a lantern, no matter how eager the spy was.

Now, he quelled his uneasiness to approach the side wall of the cave where there was a tumble of rocks. Here, there was a series of small crevices that could be used as hand and footholds, and he climbed up about eight feet before laying himself flat along a shelf hidden in the deep shadows.

"Pass up the second lamp, will you, Clem?"

It was Hardacre with his superior height who lifted the lamp. He then climbed to join Nate on the ledge.

"Well, I'll be damned," breathed Clem, looking up from below as the lamp revealed another aperture hidden in the dark.

It was a deeply cut niche, hidden well out of sight from anyone who stood on the cave floor, and, in it, were the goods, bundled in a fishing net.

"You got all of this up here by yourself?" said Hardacre.

Nate flashed him a grin. "I didn't say it was quick or easy."

Hardacre raised the lamp in the niche and examined the contraband more closely. He let out a low whistle. "Well, if nothing else, the two hundred and fifty pounds we agreed means I certainly got my money's worth. Let's get these out into better light and take a look at what we've got."

Together they dragged the goods to the edge of the shelf and grasped the rope that tied off the net.

"Ready below?"

"Aye-aye!" Clem answered, his voice echoing.

The two men sat back to brace against the weight and Nate, legs outstretched, nudged the laden net with his feet until it slipped off the shelf. He felt the weight through the rope. He and Hardacre controlled its descent until the line slackened.

A whistle from below told them the goods had arrived safely.

SUSANNAH EXAMINED THE charcoal sketch before her and rued her inadequacies as an artist. A skilled watercolorist needed to do it justice.

She really ought to have brought a book instead, but if she'd done that then she would have missed the magnificent scenery around her. The grey boulders, blackened and smoothed over time by the sea. Beyond the reach of the water, coastal plants took a toehold. Little pink flowers raised their heads to the cerulean sky. The beach and its gritty golden-yellow sand down to the water's edge. The clear water turning pale blue, then deepening to green and then a sapphire blue as the vista reached the horizon.

Peggy sat on a blanket-covered rock and knitted. Her practiced hands added row-upon-row of stitches while she, too, appeared mesmerized by the sea.

Nate and the others had left them at the mouth of the cave as lookouts, and they had been gone for nearly an hour. Susannah glanced at the small hand bell at her feet. She was to ring it loudly if someone showed themselves more than idly curious.

So far, she and Peggy had seen a small boat leave the St. Sennen estuary for parts unknown and two riders take their horses for a gallop along the shore, an impromptu race between two young bucks who were so fixed on their own enjoyment, they never once looked toward the cave.

Even so, Susannah breathed a sigh of relief when she heard the echoing voices of Nate, Clem and Adam Hardacre as they made their return.

Peggy looked behind her and set down her knitting.

"Cor, would you look at that? That's a right pirate's haul," she observed.

Susannah forced herself to look. Regardless for whom Hardacre worked, these were still contraband goods and too close to what her husband had done for a living to be comfortable. She scanned the crates and barrels as they were loaded onto the wagon.

Hardacre tapped the small barrels, listening for something, while Nate used a small pry bar to open one Hardacre selected. The rich, dark aroma of fresh tobacco filled the air.

"There's something else in here," Nate called, tension clear in his voice. Unwillingly, Susannah rose to her feet and approached.

From what she could see, it appeared to be nothing more than a notebook or a compendium of sorts.

Hardacre all but snatched it from Nate's hands. He flicked through it quickly at first, then went through it a second time more slowly and, to her surprise, the man's hands seemed to tremble a little.

"This is it," he said. "I've got what I came here for."

"Well that doesn't seem like much, compared to all those goods there," Peggy announced, verbalizing the question that Susannah had in mind. "The way you went on last night, I thought you were smuggling jewels!"

Like Jack Moorcroft.

"Excuse me," Susannah murmured before walking out of the cave and along the beach a little.

She raised her face to the wind, letting it cool her heat-stained cheeks, willing the salt-tinged air to settle her stomach.

I thought I was stronger than this... I thought I could leave it buried with Jack...

She started when someone touched her elbow. Nate stood half a pace away, concern written large on his face.

"Are you all right?" he asked. "I called after you..."

She shook her head.

"I didn't hear you... the wind," she finished lamely.

"You seemed well this morning," he said.

"I'm well now."

He frowned. He looked every inch the pirate now with the stern expression on his face and the wind plastering his lawn shirt against his chest.

How unfair that, even now, her attraction to him was undiminished.

"It's the contraband, isn't it?" he said.

Susannah closed her eyes, so he wouldn't see the truth in them.

"Even though you accept Hardacre's *bona fides*, the goods still trouble you, don't they?"

"It's not the goods themselves, Nate," she said after a moment. "If an agent of the Crown is a part of this, it's hardly contraband. I can accept that spies will have their schemes, but it just reminds me of..."

It was on the tip of her tongue to say his name, but to say it to Nate would break the wall between the two worlds she inhabited, and if she did that, how could she guarantee the nightmare of her past wouldn't leach into this one?

"Your late husband?"

Her eyes welled with tears. He pulled her into his chest. She accepted his embrace and felt his chest rise and fall with a deep sigh.

"What kind of bastard was he, to make you feel like this, Susannah?" he whispered against her ear.

"If I tell you, then it would be as though he lived again." She replied so softly, she wondered whether he heard her words. She drew in a breath and was relieved to find her voice didn't shake when she spoke again.

"Now that Adam Hardacre has found what he is after, he can be about his business and leave us alone to ours. No spies, no intrigue, Nate – that's the world I want to live in."

No spies, no intrigue… what about no secrets?

Hell, who was he kidding, they *both* had secrets.

Well, no, that wasn't entirely true. *She* had secrets; he simply had a past. And, yes, parts of it reflected poorly on him, but he would share even those to earn her trust.

Was he not good enough for her? Sufficient to flirt with, but not good enough to confide in? Was she just like Lillian or Yvette, but more skilled at pretending to be the ingénue?

He pushed the uncharitable thought down as he walked with Susannah back to the cave where Peggy had laid out a feast complete with a portable table and chairs. The other woman's expression when she saw them was full of contrition.

Interesting? What was it she'd said? Something about smuggling jewels?

Was *that* what her husband was? A jewel thief? A fence?

He watched Peggy draw Susannah away and the pair spent a moment in earnest conversation before Clem took Peggy by the hand for a walk along the beach. Now it was just the two of them – and Adam Hardacre who was so engrossed by his find that he might as well not be there.

Nate put together a plate of cold cut meats and cheese from the table and sat on the sand, his back against a boulder. He speared a slice of roast beef.

So what if Susannah's husband was a criminal? No blame attached to *her*.

He moved his head slightly until he caught her out of the corner of his eye. She sat as properly as one could on those canvas sling back chairs, as quiet and reserved as the day he first met her. She picked at the plate in her lap.

When she glanced his way, their eyes met. For a brief moment, he felt with a certainty that resonated through him that she was going to say something.

That's when he felt Adam's presence beside him and, not for the first time, he cursed the man.

"Nate, a word."

Shit.

Susannah's eyes blinked rapidly, as though she, too, had been surprised by the interruption. She turned her head away.

Nate stood, dusted himself off, and drew closer. In Adam's hand was an open notebook and drawn on a page appeared to be a map.

"Can you recognize where this is?"

The blue inked lines were not done by an expert cartographer by any means. This was a rough, hand-drawn representation of a coastal outline done in haste by an amateur hand. Nate followed the serpentine line from one end to the other, taking in marks that might represent habitations but, without scale or reference, it was impossible to say.

"It doesn't look like the Brittany coast," he said. "It could be anywhere along the coast of Cornwall, Dorset, Devon, or Wales. Or another part of France I'm not familiar with. Or even Ireland for that matter."

Hardacre straightened.

"Ireland? Can you be certain?" There was a note of agitation in the man's question. Nate turned to him and found an equal expression on his face.

"Not without consulting the maps on the *Sprite*. Why is Ireland so important?"

Hardacre stared back at him a moment, his expression closed.

"You already have us involved in your scheme, Mr. Hardacre." Susannah rose. She set down her plate on the table and approached.

"Susannah..." Nate started. The reservation earlier had gone and was replaced with a look of courage in her that filled him with unearned pride. She touched his arm and gave a smile.

"In for a penny, in for a pound," she told him. She looked at the map and frowned.

"This looks familiar," she said.

"Do you know where it is?" asked Hardacre, his voice softening.

"No, but I've seen something like it before..." She hesitated and drew a finger along the meandering line on the page. "It looks like something drawn in a document my late husband had." She withdrew her hand and it clenched, unconsciously it seemed, into a fist.

Nate felt the weight of Susannah's expression on him, her eyes telling him: *I'm ready to tell you about my past, if* you're *ready to listen.*

Mindful of the fact they weren't alone, Nate reached for her hand, holding it until her fingers unfurled like petals in his palm.

There was silence for a long moment, the roll of the waves on the sand, and a shrill cry of gulls wheeling across the cliff face.

"There is a man I'm after," said Hardacre quietly. "His name is Harold Bickmore, a lieutenant – *former* lieutenant – in the King's Navy. The man's a traitor. Once he was also a friend of mine.

"I've been trying to track him down for the better part of six months. Another man who was part of Bickmore's gang is an Irishman by the name of Regan O'Neill. If we can be certain this is Ireland..."

"Is there anything more in that book of yours?" Nate asked.

Hardacre shook his head.

"It's in code. I need to go back to Truro."

Chapter Twelve

NATE WAVED HIS hands. "Shoo! Go home."

A big pair of brown eyes stared at him. Prince proceeded to wag his tail.

"No," urged Nate, "you have to stay here."

Prince responded by dropping open his jaw into something that resembled a canine smile. Nate sighed. He had hoped to slip away to his appointment while Susannah was occupied in the kitchen, but now the woman in question had stepped outside to find out what he was yelling at.

Prince sat, looked at him, then to Susannah, and then back to him again, offering a whine and thump of his tail as though his loyalty was torn.

"He's really taken to you," she laughed.

"You don't mind if he goes with me?" Nate asked.

"It's clear *he's* made up his mind."

Nate nodded and offered a half-smile. Susannah's cheerful countenance sobered and returned the same uneasy half-smile.

Although he had not revealed his destination when he announced he would be out for the rest of the day, he suspected Susannah knew the reason for it.

Lillian Doyle.

He wanted to reassure Susannah, once more, that any attachment there once was had long been cut. But to do that required more explaining than he cared to do. Instead, he gave her a wave and crossed the road, cutting across the field and the hill to Trethowan House with Prince trotting happily alongside.

As he reached the headland, the dog ran ahead of him, scattering a group of terns as he did so. They took to the skies and squawked in irritation of their rest being disturbed.

The usual time at the usual place...

Yes, the boathouse at two o'clock on the days when Doyle was away on the judicial circuit.

Generally, her husband would be gone for three days, and Lillian would summon for him on the first day of his absence. Even if he hadn't been occupied with the journey to the caves yesterday, he would have ignored her. Now, it was the last day before the magistrate's return.

Nate reached a narrow path cut into the cliff rock. Prince ventured as far as the bluff and went no further. He barked once to get Nate's attention.

"Off you go home then," he called. Prince cocked his head as if he understood perfectly, then bounded away down the cliff path that would take him back to The Queen's Head, back to Susannah.

This time, the dog obeyed, Nate grumbled to himself. *Fine guard dog, you turned out to be... running off when I need protection from a she-wolf.*

The cliff path wended its way down to a large wooden boathouse tucked under a rock overhang. Across from the whitewashed structure and its grey slate roof was a wider, more cultivated path that led directly to the big house.

Not for the first time, Nate wondered what he was doing there. It certainly wasn't the promise of sex, though he was under no illusion that such was Lillian's expectation. After all, it had become quite the habit in times past.

No, he was there because Lillian had come up to The Queen's Head, as bold as brass, and spoken to Susannah.

That would not do. That would not do at all...

Whatever claims Lillian thought she had over him were long gone. Any flames of passion which had existed were extinguished in that hellhole in France.

Today would be a final and definitive farewell – and there would be no sex. Let the woman scream at him, if she must. Nothing she could say could possibly change his mind.

He breathed in, the fresh sea air clearing his lungs, the kiss of the sun on his cheek and his back reminding him of Susannah. And somehow, it happened that over the past few months, since his return, Susannah was the only woman he could now imagine making love to.

He reached the shore and picked his way across the shingle beach where the tide had only recently receded. Little pockets of water glinted and sparkled as he strode across to the firm plot of ground, safely above the spring tides. He reached the timber slipway and walked up it, using it as a path to reach the double doors before stepping around to the right and the smaller side door painted in a cheery blue.

He pounded on it with the flat of his hand and listened to the sound of movement behind it.

"It's open."

That might well be, but Nate was damned if he was going to make the first move.

He slapped his palm against the timber once again. This time, there was more movement, a rustling of fabric. After several moments, the door opened to a rather irate Lillian Doyle. She was looking back over her shoulder as she shouted.

"What the hell do you want? I gave orders not to be disturbed from my rest!"

The little tirade stopped when Lillian turned and finally saw him instead one of her household staff.

"Why didn't you come in when I told you?"

"Because I wanted to give you time to dress."

And indeed, Lillian looked as though she *had* dressed hastily. The ivory silk nightdress, so sheer that she might as well have been nude, lay over a chair. The pink and purple floral day dress had been hurriedly put on, the ties at the back only loosely laced.

"My undress never used to bother you," she said.

"Times change."

"Do they now? I wonder if something else hasn't changed..."

"You could be right there, too," he conceded.

Lillian beckoned him into the boathouse. He stepped through the door a few paces and stopped. He looked about. Little seemed to have changed since he was last there.

While most of the shed was still dedicated to the boat and its associated chandlery – ropes, sail canvas, tools, varnish, and the like – a quarter of the room was a cozy retreat. There was a small unlit stove and a kettle in the corner, a table with two chairs, a dresser with a display of plates, cups, and saucers of good quality, but not particularly fine. More impressive was an assortment of bottles – gin, claret, and brandy – clustered on top of a water-stained corner cabinet that was missing a couple of panes of glass from its leading.

Nate studiously avoided looking at the largest piece of furniture in the room – a large daybed covered in linens and pillows, a woman's boudoir transported to the most incongruous of locations where a man might rise and fall on the ocean of her carnal desires, far from the shores of her husband's vigilance.

Any vestige of seductive intent fell from Lillian's face.

"You'll at least take a seat, won't you?"

Her peevish nature was still intact.

He pulled out a chair, the one closest to the door, and sat down. He was willing to concede that much and no more.

Lillian made herself comfortable on the daybed.

"This is the last time we'll meet alone," he said.

With a put-upon sigh, she rose and turned her back to him to pour two large tumblers of brandy before coming over and setting them on the table.

"I had no idea she'd gotten her claws into *that* much… your *Mrs. Linwood.*"

He felt his lips curl in contempt at the emergence of the green-eyed monster. It was laughable in a woman Lillian's age.

"Where's the jealousy come from, Lillian? We've never had any claims over one another – and no love either. My visit here is a courtesy, to say in person there'll be no more assignations."

He rose to his feet. Lillian downed her brandy in one gulp like the practiced drinker she was.

"Well, they do say the quiet ones are the ones you have to watch out for."

It was a perfect actress' moment, a line delivered to make an audience gasp, but not him.

"I will not discuss Susannah with you."

"Ah… *Susannah.* How *intimate*… you don't have to *discuss* her," Lillian sneered. "I could tell you quite a few things I already know that your little paramour hasn't told you, no matter how close to between her legs you've gone."

He ignored the barb.

"I've said all I want to say – it's over between us. It was over before I left on that run to France. There's nothing you can say that will change my mind about you, or Susannah Linwood."

Lillian began to pour herself another large drink, despite Nate leaving his there untouched. He headed for the door.

"How about the fact her name isn't Linwood?"

The revelation surprised Nate less than it might, despite the fact he and Susannah had yet to talk in detail about her life before St. Sennen.

"So what if she chooses to go by her maiden name?" he shot back, belatedly realizing it was a mistake to engage in any way with Lillian Doyle.

She leaned back on the cushions and stretched her arm along the bolster and offered a slow, malevolent smile.

A gross mistake.

"Darling Nate… Linwood is not her maiden name *either*."

Nate turned to open the door and refused look back at her again. "I don't particularly care, Lillian."

"You should. You should ask yourself why a woman who appears to be the very model of propriety has gone to so much effort to hide her past," Lillian called after him. "It certainly makes one wonder if there was not more to the late Mr. Moorcroft than either of us know…"

Slam!

The front door to The Queen's Head was shoved violently closed.

Susannah started as the tower of glasses before her rattled but caught only a glimpse of Nate as he stormed past and stomped his way upstairs.

Behind her, the kitchen door opened and Peggy peered out.

"What on earth is going on?" she asked. "It sounded like a herd of cattle going up the stairs."

"Nate went to see Lillian Doyle today. I suppose the interview didn't go well."

"Are you going up to talk to him?"

She felt her brow pucker into a frown.

"Why?"

Peggy looked at her as if she were some kind of half-wit.

"He's just gotten back from the home of that Jezebel in a temper. Trust me, he'll want to talk to a sympathetic face."

"Whenever Jack got in one of his tempers…" She suppressed a shudder.

"Do you honestly believe that Nate Payne is anything like Jack Moorcroft?"

She was forced to shake her head.

No, Nate wasn't *anything* like Jack. Not even his display of anger a few moments ago filled her with the roiling dread that accompanied her husband's arrival home in a temper.

Peggy pulled a bottle of brandy down from the shelf next to Susannah.

"You promised you were going to tell the pirate about Jack. Take this up and gauge his mood. If he growls, leave him with the bottle. If not, have a drink with him. Go on Duch, perhaps he'll tell you about his Mrs. Doyle. Let me put it this way, he couldn't get in a worse temper."

Susannah accepted the bottle and took two clean glasses from her stack. She headed for the stairs, where she hesitated at the foot.

"Go on," Peggy urged, peering around the corner of the bar and waving her on her way.

Susannah wrinkled her nose and started up but, before she could take more than a couple of steps, she heard the sound of feet coming down the stairs two at a time.

Nate cleared the landing before he spotted her and came to a stop. He searched her face a moment before spotting the liquor and glasses in her hand. Surprise ebbed to wry amusement.

"You thought I needed to drown my sorrows?"

"I thought... maybe... um... yes?"

She examined his face thoroughly, looking for a hint to gauge his mood. Perhaps she had made a complete cake of herself. She held her breath waiting for him to say something, *anything*.

"We need to talk," he said suddenly, as though he had come to a conclusion. "We can decide whether we need to have a drink afterwards."

SUSANNAH WORKED HARD to keep up the same swift pace as Nate, making conversation impossible as they walked over the Arthyn Hill headland down to the beach. It was early afternoon and the sun was still high in the sky. To the south, thick grey clouds gathered.

As they drew closer to the caves they had visited just a few days before, their pace slowed and the urgency to speak became greater.

What if she was wrong to believe that to talk of Jack and her marriage would conjure back up the darkness? What if saying the words could break the spell of her nightmare years?

"There's something you should know about me," she began, walking beside him but not looking at him. "My name is not Susannah Linwood. My legal name – my married name – is Susannah Moorcroft."

He remained silent. She risked a glance sideways and saw the corner of his mouth twitch, but didn't know the cause of it.

She returned her gaze straight ahead. It would be easier to tell him the truth if she did not have to look at him.

"My husband, Jack, was a criminal receiving stolen goods. But I didn't realize how involved he was until after his death when I was going through his papers." A shell in the sand caught her eye, one perfect half of a bivalve. She stopped to pick it up, pleased to have something to occupy her fingers other than turning her wedding band round and round.

"I didn't know Mr. Gilliam turned a blind eye to smuggling until you arrived," she continued, "but I couldn't be involved, no matter how benign it might seem. Everything I owned was suspect, bought with the proceeds of crime. I wanted a fresh start – to get away from everyone and everything that my husband's memory tainted."

"Including his name," said Nate.

"*Especially* his name."

"And Linwood was your maiden name?"

"No, it was the name of the cottage where I grew up. It had so many happy memories, I chose it in the hopes it would bring happiness for me here."

Now that she had started, the words came easier. The storm clouds stayed out on the horizon and the creeping dread of her fears disappeared in the beautiful summer's day.

"I had to use my legal name for the publican's license, but when we moved to St. Sennen, I made Peggy vow to never tell anyone my name or my past. When we were here a few days ago, I gave her permission to tell Clem, and I told her I would tell you.

"I hope... that is... if you think there is a chance for something more than friendship between us, then I thought you deserved to know."

They walked in silence for a few yards more. Nate put a hand on her waist to steer her away from the shore and up toward the caves until they were in the lee of the wind.

NATE WAS GLAD Susannah had fixed her attention to the beach ahead as she spoke. The last thing he wanted was for her to see his face and the relief he knew was written on it.

Lillian's words had bothered him more than he wanted to admit and, during his angry walk back to The Queen's Head, he cursed the woman for planting a seed of doubt in his mind.

He hadn't appreciated how cynical he had become of women and the notion of love until he met Susannah. Because of her, he was changing and, hopefully, for the better.

He was beginning to fall in love with Susannah, and the thought of any part of her was an artifice jabbed like a knife in the ribs. Even before she had told him, he knew she must have good reason for keeping her past to herself. Knowing she entrusted him with her secret was a gift.

"I'm honored that you trust me," he said.

Susannah briefly dabbed her eyes, whether from the wind or from burgeoning tears, he didn't guess.

"It's taken me such a long time to trust," she said. "When Jack died, I was numb. I spent the first three months afraid I'd only dreamed it. Every male voice I heard, I thought was his returned."

Nate swallowed against the bile that rose in his throat.

She rolled the seashell over and over in her hand and he was glad for the silence to give him time to fight the boiling fury in his veins.

"I have another confession to make," she whispered. "After those three months, I became glad he was dead."

He pulled her into his embrace, holding her close until her silent sobs subsided and his hammering heart slowed enough so the sound of it didn't fill his ears, and the visceral violence that welled from within settled back under the control of his rational self.

Susannah shifted in his arms. He looked down at her beautiful blue eyes staring back at him, sparkling with unshed tears.

You're safe with me.

It seemed right to whisper the words in her ear. "You're *safe* with me."

And it seemed right to put his lips to the lobe of her ear and listen as she took a shaky breath. The press of her body against his shot a bolt straight to his groin.

"I'm safe with you," she whispered back.

He embraced her fiercely, his eyes screwed tight and his jaw clamped firmly shut to prevent a surge of emotion from breaking him completely. Then when it became too great to contain, he channeled it into kisses across her face, her hair, her cheeks. His hands roamed her back until they cradled the back of her head. His fingers wound their way through her hair, now loose from their pins.

"Nate, please." Her voice was breathless. She wanted him. He was sure he was not mistaken in her desire for him but, nevertheless, she pulled away. And, being the male he was, his attention was fixed on the rise and fall of her breasts as she sought to control her breathing.

"This is too fast," she said, panting as though, indeed, they'd each run a mile.

He couldn't deny he wanted to make love to her and, if she had been willing, he'd have taken her there on the sand. He squeezed his eyes tight to force the vision of it from his mind.

"I know widows are supposed to have a reputation," she added with forced humor, "but nothing I experienced with my husband makes me keen to repeat the experience."

The confession, lightly delivered as it was, sobered him. *He was a cad.*

He breathed in deep and nodded. A gentle touch of her hand on his reminded him his eyes were closed. He opened them to find Susannah looking back at him.

"Be patient with me, Nate, please."

Chapter Thirteen

SUSANNAH CONTINUED CHOPPING vegetables while watching through the kitchen window as Nate split firewood for the stove.

He removed his shirt in the heat of late afternoon sun and her body reacted, knowing how his muscles felt under her hands.

"Enjoying the view?"

Peggy's question may be innocently phrased but Susannah knew her friend well enough to know it was laden with additional meaning.

"It *is* very pleasant," she said, unable to hide a knowing smile.

"Aye, and I see that it is, you saucy minx. Will there be chimes of wedding bells in the near future?"

Susannah set the knife down before she dropped it and chopped off a finger.

"What? Of course not!"

The question was startling. What on earth did Peggy think? That a little flirtation with an attractive man was more than what it was?

Jack had accused her of being frigid, which was his excuse to seek his release elsewhere. A mistress or a prostitute, she didn't know who exactly. All Susannah knew was that he would come to her bed wearing a shirt that smelled of smoke and a cloyingly sweet perfume.

I know widows are supposed to have a reputation. But nothing I experienced with my husband makes me keen to repeat the experience.

She'd meant every word she'd said on the beach, but Nate's kisses had helped her uncover a desire she didn't know she owned.

But, in truth, she could be nothing more than a diversion to him. A man like Nate was too full of passion and adventure to stay in one place for too long. Eventually, he would sail away on the *Sprite* to whatever quest awaited him with Adam Hardacre.

"Well, it would be a shame to let a good man like that get away, that's all I'll say on the matter," Peggy sniffed.

Susannah glanced back at her friend with a wry smile.

"I hardly think that is up to me. I'm content with life as it is. I promised after we moved away from Lydd, I would be grateful for today and little else. Nothing more has changed. Let's see you well married to Clem first before we start thinking about me."

Peggy harrumphed and went back to her cooking.

"I NEED YOU to remember."

Nate stared at his fresh pint rather than at Adam Hardacre, watching the thin layer of froth sink back into the dark liquid. The man seated opposite had been strung tighter than a violin ever since he returned from Truro two nights ago.

"I've spent the past three months trying for forget."

But the truth of the matter was, he *couldn't* forget. Fragments of memories surfaced – emaciated faces, festering wounds turning black and gangrenous from poor treatment.

Damnation.

Forced to look at them in his mind's eye, it would a long time before he would sleep tonight.

Adam knew all this and yet the man looked implacable. Nate shook his head and let out a put-upon sigh.

"I was there for a month when they brought in sailors from the *HMS Starbeck*. Two hundred of them. Three months later, seventy-five were dead. Another fifty wished they were. The French had little enough for themselves so the prisoners were down to quarter-rations."

"When was this?"

"November. I can't give you an exact date. Each day felt very much like another in that place. Although I do remember one day there was a bit of agitation amongst the officers. We figured some important people were expected and it turns out we were right.

"Three men came into the barracks but they were in civilian dress, not uniforms. They were very specific about who they were looking for."

"How do you know?"

"We were made to line up by our bunks for an inspection."

"Did you recognize these men?"

"No, but they were recognized by at least one prisoner. He started to say the man's name when one of the French guards pistol-whipped him. After that, everyone held their tongues. If anyone else knew them, they kept it to themselves. The visitors pulled three of them, petty officers I suppose, and took them away. I never saw them again."

"Can you remember the name the man said?"

"No. It began with the letter 'B' but that was as much as he could get out before he was cold cocked."

"Describe him. The man he recognized."

"About our height, brown hair, a younger man, aged mid to late twenties. And I'm pretty certain he was English."

"What makes you say that?"

"His French was very good but formal, mannered. He didn't speak the language of the working Frenchman. And he just *looked* English."

"What happened after that?"

"I never saw them again – nor the three men they took with them."

"Could you identify him again if you saw him?"

"I would."

Nate had watched Adam's face carefully during their exchange. *He* knew exactly who 'B' was and God help whoever it was because Adam Hardacre looked like a man who was ready to kill the bastard where he stood.

Then the pieces fell into place.

Harold Bickmore. The traitor. The former friend...

He took another gulp of his beer. He felt he was standing on the edge of a cliff, one step beyond and he would plunge headlong into Hardacre's intrigue. He didn't want to do it. There was a very nice life – a *safe* life – emerging for him right here in St. Sennen.

But his goddamned curiosity got the better of him. One question was enough to nudge him over the edge.

"So, I take it finding Bickmore is more than professional?" said Nate.

A light of surprise flared in the other man's eyes before he picked up his own glass and saluted him.

"Until my dying day. Have you ever thought you knew someone? Someone you could trust with your life?"

Lillian Doyle's face passed before him. Nate nodded but didn't volunteer his experience.

"I would have put my life in Harold's hands willingly – in fact I did, many a-time at sea when he was my commanding officer," said Hardacre. "At first, I didn't see his betrayal. I refused to see it, even when the evidence was right before my eyes."

Adam lowered his voice. "Even when he had my wife hostage, he had such a way that a few well-chosen words would have me believing the opposite to be true," he said.

"It was only afterwards, when I followed the line of inquiry for myself that I could see the depths of his deception. So yes, it's personal and, yes, I have no doubt his intent was to hold my wife to ensure my cooperation."

"Cooperation for what, exactly?"

"That's what I want to find out, because it was one hell of a set up," said Adam, pitching his voice low. "Sir Daniel Ridgeway is convinced that Harold believes I have the key to something, some information, but I'll be damned if I know what it is."

Hardacre pitched his voice even lower. The only sign of his agitation was a rough hand through his fair hair, the tattoo on his hand standing out against it.

"That's why I'm pushing so hard for information about your time in France. I know you're not willing and I know the questions I ask may not make sense, but none of this does when there are pieces missing."

A group of men barreled through the front door of The Queen's Head. Nate watched as they made their way to the bar where they were served by Susannah.

"You need to come to Truro with me."

Nate wasn't sure he heard properly. He turned back to Adam.

"We could do with good men like you," Adam continued.

"Thanks, but I already have a job."

Judging by the tic in the man's jaw, Nate's answer wasn't well received.

"Look, I'm happy for you and your band to hire my boat, but that's all. I played my bit. I'm no spy and I'm not sure there's enough gold in England to get me to go back over to France again."

Adam's eyes lowered to the table a moment. When he raised his head once more, his face was a mask.

"Agreed – a boat and a skipper," he said. "And if France is out of the question, then what about Ireland? You don't have any objection to *that* do you?"

Nate sat back in his chair, drained the last of his pint and set the glass down with a thud.

"Not in the least. When do you want to go?"

"I don't know yet. I'm waiting on a messenger from Truro. But when the call comes, we'll go on the next available tide."

SUSANNAH HAD ONLY half a mind on her work. Out of the corner of her eye she watched Nate and Adam Hardacre at a table in the far corner of the dining table. They'd been in earnest conversation for more than an hour.

"It all looks rather serious over there," whispered Peggy in passing on her way through to the kitchen. "What do you think Hardacre and the pirate are talking about?"

She had no answer for that. Whatever business brought Hardacre back to St. Sennen, she hoped it would be concluded soon. As much as she liked the man personally, he brought with him the unpleasant reminder that England was at war.

And soon, Nate might be caught up in it.

For so many years, she had kept her thoughts and feelings to herself. She'd become quite practiced in life behind a façade of serenity, of doing and saying the expected things regardless of how she truly felt.

She recalled the conversation with Peggy this afternoon. She wanted it to be different with Nate and she couldn't deny the way he made her feel, a visceral desire she never thought she possessed. But it was more than that, Nate Payne was the first man who saw *her* as she really was.

Several times during the day he would catch her eye and her body would heat under his gaze. What would it be like to give herself completely to this man? Would he hold her heart with as much care and tenderness as he'd done when he held her at the beach?

Peggy tapped her on the shoulder and glanced at Nate meaningfully.

"It's still light out, why don't you step outside and get some fresh air," she said. "I can take over at the bar."

"Are you sure? What about the kitchen?"

"Tressa's doing a good job. I thought I'd give her a bit more responsibility," said Peggy.

Peggy, too, was beginning to change and adapt. Initially, she had been resentful of the idea of someone else in *her* kitchen, but the truth of the matter was she needed assistance; she couldn't act as cook and maid-of-all-work forever. Susannah knew she'd made a good choice in Tressa, a local girl recommended by Clem. The girl had proven herself smart and willing to learn.

Susannah cast her eyes across the bar and dining room. In summer, the customers came later in the evening. She took off her apron and laid it on the bar just as Nate looked up.

He gave her that look again. And there must have been something in her own expression because he left his place at the table and approached.

"I'll be back in time for the last rush at the bar," Susannah told Peggy.

"Go on, enjoy yourself," Peggy urged with a wink.

Nate met her at the door.

"A fine evening for a walk. May I accompany you?" he inquired.

"I was hoping you would."

Those few simple words brought a smile to his face and Susannah was glad to put it there. They stepped outside. He offered his arm and she accepted it.

Outside, the world was touched in pink by the setting sun and seemed so much hotter for it, like the glow of a furnace. Above her, the sky was filled with thin high clouds like small waves on the ocean, except these were the most fantastic colors – purple, vermillion and a marigold shade so vivid it hurt to look at it.

They continued hand-in-hand in silence along the path that led them down to the water's edge where the creek met the estuary. Overhead, seagulls took advantage of the twilight, calling out to one another before they settled for the night.

They reached the end of the path which mated with the old stone seawall that protected the land from the powerful push and pull of the sea.

The breeze that came up from the estuary cooled her heated cheeks. She sat on the wall and removed her shoes and stockings, raising her skirts to lower her legs into the ankle-deep water. She wiggled her toes into the sand and sighed.

Nate made a throaty chuckle and Susannah couldn't help but grin in return. He, too, sat down and removed his shoes and let out a welcome groan as his feet joined hers in the water. Susannah's grin became a giggle. She took in a deep breath of sea air as Nate placed his arm around her shoulders and drew her to his side.

The stroke of his hand along her arm below the short sleeve of her dress was achingly sweet. Susannah leaned into him and closed her eyes, allowing his hands to wander. Her arm was left in gooseflesh, surely only a result of the zephyr as his fingers grazed the length of her waist and, if she was not mistaken, he had touched her ear with his lips.

Susannah hadn't even been aware that her right hand had been rubbing the top of Nate's thigh until he stilled her restive hand with his own.

"I have to go away," he said.

Susannah opened her eyes and fixed her attention on the view ahead, the sun catching the creek and turning it bronze in hue.

"With Adam Hardacre?"

She felt Nate nod his answer as his fingers started stroking her hair. She thought she ought to ask more questions – *Where are you going? Why? How long will you be away? Are you sworn to secrecy?*

Out of habit, she asked none of those things. Jack would either lie to her, tell her to not worry her pretty little head, or, if he was in a foul mood, would shout at her for prying. He told her only what he wanted her to know and nothing more.

She turned herself around, dried her feet and slipped her stockings and shoes back on.

Nate stood before her.

"Susannah?"

She looked up at him and found his expression confused. Had he expected her to say something? To ask those questions? She didn't have the right. He was as free as the birds wheeling in the deepening sky overhead.

"How soon?" she asked.

"I'm not sure," he answered. "In a couple of days maybe."

She allowed him to take her into his arms and kiss her slowly on the earlobe. The sensation shot like a lightning bolt straight down to her feet. Her sigh was instinctive, as was the need to put her arms around him in return.

"I want you to come home to," he said in her ear.

She pressed herself to him more fully to stop him from seeing the pinprick of tears in her eyes.

"I want that, too," she whispered.

He held back no longer. His lips claimed hers swiftly, his tongue teased her until hers responded in kind. She gave herself to the sensation of it, noting how her body reacted to his touch and how he made her skin come alive, making *her* come alive. The more he touched her, the more she wanted of him. All of him.

She allowed her imagination to take flight. Nate's bare body against hers, flesh to flesh, making love to her with the same confident passion he showed now. As though he could read her thoughts, he brushed his fingertips down her throat and lower, to the top of her breasts, then pulled her firmly to him. She felt his own desire press against her.

Chapter Fourteen

August 1805

NATE RAN THE wide blade along the line of the hull. Barnacles and green algae slid off the scraper's keen edge, exposing the dark blue paint beneath. The *Sprite* lay careened on the low-tide sand in the Pengellan estuary.

Adam Hardacre had departed for Truro two days ago after his messenger arrived and, during that time, Nate had made up his mind. He had already committed to Ireland. Now, despite his deep misgivings about ever setting foot on French soil again, he had to go there, too.

Not because he had any special love of King and Country – no more than any sensible man at any rate – but there was no denying that two others, possibly more, had risked their lives to save him, a stranger.

Sure, they'd also wanted to learn what he knew about Felix, but he was deeply grateful that they had saved his skin. And there were new stakes revealed by Hardacre's messenger. Now those very men were missing.

He knew what the consequences were for them. Nate had seen for himself how prisoners of war were dealt with, and traitors fared so much worse. He squeezed the handle of his scraper and worked with renewed vigor.

Last night, he had told Susannah of his decision to throw in his lot with Hardacre. It meant having the *Sprite* ready in seven days' time to sail around to Truro. He could be gone for months.

Unspoken between them was the fact that should things go wrong, he could be gone for good.

In his experience, women reacted in one of two ways to such news. An insouciant woman like Yvette would simply shrug her shoulders; *c'est la vie* – easy come, easy go. Lillian would be less sanguine; she would sulk and pout in an attempt to get him to change his mind. And when he refused, he would see the savage demon anger that lurked beneath the practiced manners and fine clothing.

Susannah was different. She did not dissuade him from leaving yet he was sure indifference was not the cause. She spoke with her eyes instead of her tongue, and Nate was both humbled and concerned by it. She had feelings for him, he knew that. Perhaps she was already in love with him, but couldn't allow herself to break out of the prison her brute of a dead husband had put her in.

If the man still lived, Nate would have killed him and happily worn the consequences.

"Hey ho!"

He looked up at Clem's cheery greeting. With him was young Sam and both were dressed down to their shirtsleeves.

"Nice day for it," Clem said as they got nearer.

"Nice day for a hell of a lot of work," Nate responded. "You wouldn't care to give me a hand, would you?"

He hadn't expected his friend's answer. Clem picked up two more scrapers from among the tools and tossed one over to his son. Nate gave a grateful nod. The young man responded with a cheery wave and got to work at the bow of the boat.

Clem started work near the keel, not far from Nate.

"Since we're here, I've got somethin' to get your thoughts on."

It was on the tip of his tongue to make a jest but he glanced over at Clem to find him diligently working away.

"I'm thinkin' of askin' Peggy to marry me."

Nate ran a hand over the freshly exposed paint, pleased to see it had held up well. A repaint would have delayed him nearly a month.

He nodded over at Sam. He had his father's easy-going temperament, but in looks and height he took after his mother. In fact, Sam was at least three inches taller than his father already. A true blessing to be sure, Clem had said on more than one occasion over the years.

"How does Sam feel?"

"He likes Peggy, so good-o there. And there's somethin' else which may have swayed him, too, and that's Tressa. You know? The new maid at The Queen's Head? Sam's rather sweet on her. I *suppose* he's now of an age where he appreciates the merits of courtin', if you know what I mean."

This time, Nate *did* laugh.

"I can't think of any two people better suited to being shackled than you and Peggy."

Clem's sigh of relief was audible.

"You're not just sayin' that, are you? I've thought about it a lot, you know. I loved Sam's mother for the longest time and still do in a way. But she's long gone, and there's just somethin' about my old Peggy that makes a man feel alive again."

Nate didn't hide the delight on his face. "I mean it, Clem, I like Peggy a lot. She's a good woman and she deserves a good man like you. When are you going to ask her?"

"In the next few weeks; maybe an October weddin' if she'll have me."

"Well, you have my congratulations. Now all you need is for your intended to say yes."

Clem chuckled. "No fear of that, old man. Then all we need to do is for you to wake up to yourself and ask Susannah to be your bride, and we'll have a double weddin'."

"Ah, you cheap bastard, you're only saying that in the hope of paying half of the wedding feast!"

Nate was rather pleased that the words slipped effortlessly from his mouth and, better still, Clem's reaction – a mock annoyance at his perceived parsimoniousness – meant that he wasn't expecting him to give a serious answer.

Marry Susannah...

The idea had occurred to him in the abstract. Whenever he held her in his arms, he thought how nice it would be to wake up every morning with her in bed beside him. But that was as far as his thinking went. Besides, everything he had learned of her disastrous first marriage gave him the distinct impression she would not want to be so bound again.

Right now, their arrangement was fine just the way it was. And, if he didn't think too hard, he could just about convince himself he wasn't falling in love with her.

No. Better he remain here, in the moment, with the wind and the sun in his face, the feel of mastery whenever he was at the helm of his boat. This he loved, all of this within his control. Over everything else, he had none.

THANKS TO THE additional pairs of hands, the antifouling work on the *Sprite* had been completed early.

Nate had refloated her on the incoming tide and secured her at anchor. Now with the dinghy half-full, he was readying a return journey to his boat with equipment he would need if he and Adam planned to spend more than one night aboard.

Across the street, he spotted a group of women leaving the rectory at St. Catherine's. His eyes slid away from Lillian Doyle to Susannah who was among them, wafting the painted fan he had given her as a gift. She was in animated conversation with a couple of members of the village committee, planning good works of one sort or another.

A wave of tenderness came over him. He loved watching her

when she was not aware of being observed, like the first time he watched her in the field when he was building the chicken coop.

Carefree and unreserved – the true self she kept hidden. He found himself once more imagining making love to her, savoring those uninhibited moments that would be for him alone.

He had no doubt Susannah was a passionate woman, but she fought it, hiding it from herself.

Would it be wrong to seduce her before he left?

His body responded enthusiastically to the idea, but his rational mind forced the urge down. He had made a promise to be patient and allow her to set the pace for their relationship.

Would marriage be so bad? Would Susannah even agree?

He came to a decision. He would broach the notion of marriage when he returned from his excursion with Adam Hardacre. Hopefully, the old saying of absence making the heart grow fonder was true.

Nate shook his head and turned his attention back to his task. He was letting Clem's sentimentality get the better of him.

"You ought to be kinder to me."

He hadn't even seen Lillian Doyle approach.

"Is there a reason why I should?" he asked, deliberately turning his back to her and loading another crate into the dinghy.

"I can think of many reasons, my pet. For instance, your Mrs. Linwood relies on her good reputation, but whispers that her services include more than a bed and board could see her license revoked."

He looked at her for the first time since she had approached, not hiding his expression of contempt.

"You're resorting to blackmail? Is that how low you've sunk, Lillian?"

She gave a delicate shrug and traced a finger down his arm.

"Consider it a measure of how much I've missed you."

"That you would do anything to have me back?"

"I fail to see why things can't go on as they were. I never complained about Yvette; why should Mrs. Linwood complain about *me*?"

"Because I don't want you."

"But you do want *her*."

Over Lillian's shoulder, he saw Susannah approach. He shook off Lillian's arm and returned to loading the dinghy.

"I already said I won't discuss her with you."

"Fair enough, my pet. Let me do you and Mrs. Linwood a good turn. One night with you and my solemn vow to never cause trouble for you and the innkeeper again." She leaned forward to effect a stage whisper. "I'll make you a present of her."

Nate let out a humorless laugh and walked away, shaking his head. He untied the dinghy and used the oar to shove away from the dock. He locked the oar in place, picked up its mate, and rowed.

Two women stood on the dock watching him leave, but he only had eyes for one of them. Elegant Lillian, with her striking black hair and expensive gown, barely registered. It was only Susannah he saw – the way strands of her brown hair escaped their confines and the hem of her faded pink day dress rippled and danced with the breeze.

Lillian turned and said something to Susannah before walking away. He watched for Susannah's reaction. There was none. Should he go back?

He was moving away. Every necessary stroke of the oar was taking him away from her.

If she raised her hand to beckon, he would return. But she did not. He glanced behind him to see how close he was to the *Sprite*. He corrected course just as a cloud crossed the sun, throwing the estuary into shade, sharpening the chill of the breeze. He shivered.

Then he looked back to the shore.

Susannah was gone.

HE CURSED A superstitious dread all the way back to The Queen's Head. Nate dropped anchor just as the last of the daylight faded. The lights on the ground floor of the inn were a beacon that drew him in.

He entered by the kitchen. Susannah was there alone, kneading out dough, looking deep in thought.

He drew close enough to touch her and he did, to briefly touch her neck with his lips. Her sigh was arousing and he continued with kisses down her neck and across her shoulders.

"Please... we can't," she whispered. "Not here."

He breathed out a frustrated sigh and took a step back.

Yes, her reputation and that of The Queen's Head... God, he hated that the smug voice in his head sounded so much like Lillian Doyle.

And, without knowing why he did so, he stepped back and dropped to one knee.

"Susannah, will you marry me?"

The words were out of his mouth before he fully considered the import of them and his prior intent to leave a proposal until he returned.

He caught her momentary surprise in a small lift of her shoulders. She bowed her head a moment before raising it. Not once did she stop kneading the dough. What exactly had Lillian said to her?

The longer it went without an answer, the worse he felt.

After half a minute, Nate got to his feet.

"If you're going to refuse me, at least have the courage to say so."

And it was only then he saw the line of silent, silver tears running down her cheeks.

He swallowed against the worst names he could call himself. He was the cause of those tears. Never did he feel so low.

"It's a kind offer made of pity, of chivalry, and I thank you for your regard for my reputation," she whispered.

"Oh, for God's sake..." he began, hating himself because he knew she was right.

"I cannot accept on those terms, for your sake as well as mine."

The rejection stung as much as his own self-loathing.

He turned and walked out of the kitchen, unable to stop himself slamming the door behind him. He stalked back to the *Sprite*.

By God, he was angry, and just as well that he was, otherwise he'd find the better part of himself who would turn back and wipe away the tears of the woman for whom he would give his life, the one he knew with shocking clarity that he loved without reservation.

Except she didn't love him in return.

Chapter Fifteen

THE MORNING BELLS of Truro chimed five o'clock and Nate found himself outside Charteris House. The door was locked, so he pounded on it with the heel of his fist.

He knew what a stranger must see – a man unshaved and somewhat disheveled making a racket. Nate knew he had enough of the madman in him.

The front door was soon opened cautiously by a little man wearing a dressing robe. He stood not much over five feet by Nate's reckoning. The man adjusted his thick glasses and peered up at him as he barged through the door.

"You'd better come in, Mr. Payne," the little man said as Nate pushed past him. The man's voice hinted at boredom rather than sarcasm or annoyance. "We don't want to attract unnecessary attention, do we?"

Nate wasn't sure what he was expecting as he entered the shop, but he was pretty sure a chandlery was not it.

Opposite the door was a wall full of clocks, all keeping metronomic tempo, all dials bearing the same time: three minutes past five. The little man, too, didn't miss a beat. He walked round the counter and fiddled with something behind a large map hung between two rods on the wall. Suddenly, a panel moved away from the wall, revealing a narrow staircase up to the next floor.

"You'd better come upstairs while I send a messenger out. I imagine it is Lieutenant Hardacre and Sir Daniel Ridgeway you've come to see. This way, Mr. Payne."

"You know my name."

"I know everyone's name," he said as they reached the top of the stairs.

Here, it looked like an architect's or cartographer's office. The room was large enough to house four drafting tables and it was filled with light from the large windows even at this early hour. In the corner, opposite the stairs, was an oak desk and a side table with an ornate silver tea service that was decidedly out of place.

"Wait here, will you?"

The man, who had yet to introduce himself, disappeared into one of the adjoining rooms. Nate heard voices then the sound of a pair of feet bounding down another set of stairs.

The bespectacled little man returned.

"Well, it will be at least a couple of hours before we can expect visitors. I suggest you freshen up so you don't look like a vagabond. Then we shall have some breakfast."

"Excuse me, but who the *hell* are you?"

"All in good time, Mr. Payne. Sir Daniel will be the one to tell you what you need to know."

Nate followed the man down the corridor. He opened a door to a room. It was small but comfortably furnished with a single bed, a mirror, and a washstand.

"I'll be back in fifteen minutes with hot water and shaving accoutrements. And tea."

Nate sat on the edge of the bed, weighted by exhaustion. He scrubbed his bristled face. Adam would think he was a lunatic. Hell, he *was* a lunatic.

He'd worked himself up into a lather over the day and night it took to sail to Truro. Susannah's face flashed before him now and his shoulders slumped. There was little he could do on that score no matter how overwound he got about it. Still, it frustrated him. He offered her everything and it still wasn't enough to convince her of his commitment.

Did she truly believe he offered marriage out of pity? Had her villainous lout of a husband poisoned the very notion of marriage? Or was the inn worth more to her than him?

Or perhaps it was just *him*.

Time away from her was the only thing he could think to do and Adam Hardacre promised one hell of a distraction from romance.

Nate clung to it desperately.

The door to the room opened. He started, surprised to have slumped into a half-doze on the edge of the bed.

"Wakey, wakey, my good man."

Nate's sour temper was sparked again and he snarled at the odd balding man who simply chuckled as he set down the tray on the washstand and closed the door behind him.

The aroma of brewing tea finally pulled Nate from his stupor.

It was time to put thoughts of Susannah aside. He needed more than just a distraction, he needed to push himself and deal with his dread of going back to France as he now must. The thought of that, and its reminder of his fear of dark, enclosed spaces was never far from his mind while he'd been sailing, a strong undercurrent to his present bad mood.

Nonetheless, compared to Susannah's demons, dealing with France and what Hardacre wanted to do there seemed a much easier quest.

TWO HOURS LATER, Nate entered the cartography room feeling rested and refreshed. Three men were waiting. There was the strange man from this morning, Adam Hardacre, and another man, older but tall and broad-shouldered, golden-reddish hair partly gone to silver.

Adam undertook the formalities.

"Sir Daniel, I'd like to introduce you to Nathaniel Payne, Nate to his friends. Nate, meet Sir Daniel Ridgeway."

Nate nodded in deference to the man's title. Then his eyes slid across to the other man whose name he did not know.

"Would you mind introducing me to the dwarf while we're at it?" he asked.

Adam laughed over the small man's indignant interjection.

"Bassett didn't introduce himself?" asked Ridgeway. "He is our master forger and chief procurer, so we forgive him his peculiarities."

Bassett gave Nate a smug grin, folding his arms to boot.

"As you've probably gathered," Sir Daniel noted, "we don't usually entertain unexpected guests, so may I ask what brings you to Charteris House today?"

Nate turned to Adam Hardacre. "I've had time to consider your proposal. Count me in. France included."

Hardacre's expression became one of surprise. "You seemed quite adamant to the contrary just a short while ago. What happened to change your mind? Susannah Linwood?"

"Does it really matter? I'm ready and the *Sprite* is ready, that's all you need to know."

Sir Daniel was the first to move, heading to his desk.

"Do you realize this is not a pleasure jaunt? If this all goes balls-up, you'll be back in a French prison once again. *If* you're lucky."

Nate ignored the attempt to dissuade him.

"I have nothing to come back to here, so it's a risk I'm willing to take."

He saw Adam's look of further surprise in his peripheral vision, but kept all of his attention on the peer of the realm in front of him.

"Well, Adam here has already vouched for you, so there's only one thing to do," said Ridgeway. He thrust out a hand. "Nathaniel Payne, welcome to The King's Rogues."

Nate returned the handshake with equal vigor.

Sir Daniel pulled out a slim gold pocket watch and glanced at it. "I'll leave you in Adam and Bassett's hands for the next few days. When we reconvene, I want a full plan."

And, like that, the man departed.

Hardacre now took Nate's hand and shook it, clasped in both his own. "At this point, I don't particularly care what rush of blood caused you to change your mind, but I'm glad you did. I just hope it didn't cost you too much."

Nate pushed any reservations he had to the back of his mind. If there was a plan, he could force down the fear of returning to France. He would worry about his relationship with Susannah, what there was of it, later.

"So what's the plan?"

Hardacre glanced to Bassett. The man lost his impish humor and was suddenly all business.

"Thanks to the information you brought back from Brittany, we've been able to make contact with our agents in France. We've also learned Harold Bickmore has made an attempt to contact them using old codes. And, not too long after, there was a raid on their rooming house. We have to get them out as soon as possible."

Nate found himself drawn to a large map of the Brittany coast that Bassett unfurled.

"How many of them are we picking up?"

"Two," said Bassett. "But we have to find them first."

"You jest."

Bassett gave him a look of indulgent exasperation.

"Mr. Payne, you'll learn I *never* jest."

September 1805
St. Sennen

"Now, the harvest markets."

Mrs. Johnston, the vicar's wife, looked down at her notes and addressed the assembled group of half a dozen women.

Susannah set down her cup of tea and opened the small journal beside her. She smiled at Miss Wood, the late rector's spinster sister who ran the local Sunday school, as she reached out to help herself to one of Mrs. Baumann's spiced ginger biscuits.

On noticing her, Miss Wood gave a small wink and pushed the plate closer to her.

"There has been a request to hold the apple bobbing as the first activity of the afternoon," Mrs. Johnston continued. "And that will require extra apples. We went through three bushels of them last year..."

Mrs. Johnston delegated tasks with the efficiency of a general, but not stinting on taking on work herself.

Such a pity that Lillian Doyle didn't make herself as useful.

Susannah pushed the uncharitable thought down and wrote notes to take back to Peggy. Judging by Mrs. Johnston's ambitious plans, they'd do a roaring trade on the apple sponge Mother Eve's pudding.

Discussion about the harvest markets continued until everyone agreed that all the logistics they could think of had been taken into account, and tasks allocated.

Susannah relished the extra work. It was good to be busy. She could collapse into her bed every night and fall into a dreamless sleep. That's what she wanted when she came to St. Sennen nearly a year ago and that's what she wanted now that Nate was gone.

At the sound of her name being called, Susannah drew her attention back to the meeting.

"And finally," Mrs. Johnston announced, "I think I speak on behalf of St. Sennen's Ladies Guild to offer our congratulations on the upcoming marriage of your friend Peggy Smith to Clem Pascoe before the end of the year."

The ladies politely clapped in agreement.

"I was sworn to secrecy until the first of the banns was read out at the pulpit last week," the vicar's wife confessed. "We were all wondering whether that dear man would walk down the aisle again."

Susannah accepted the good wishes and readied herself to leave the rectory for the walk back to The Queen's Head. She declined the offer of a ride back to the inn. It was a pleasant late afternoon and, although it was late in the season, there was enough twilight to walk home if she didn't tarry.

She followed the road as it rose up out of the village and turned back to look at the view. The estuary and the sea beyond were silver. The hills were the deepest shade of green, almost black. But, by contrast, the whitewashed walls of some of the cottages glowed, reflecting the last of the sunlight.

It had been three weeks since Nate stormed out of the kitchen – and out of her life. She had awoken the next morning to see the *Sprite* was gone. More startling was her own reaction. She was bereft, carved hollow. It was as though the past four months had been naught but illusion.

But try as she might, Susannah couldn't forget him. But how could she have done anything different? Words of love spoken in the heat of passion are too easily regretted.

You're a fool if you think he will stay. The past always catches up with one, don't you agree?

Lillian Doyle's words were as true as they had been poisonous.

If Susannah had accepted Nate's proposal, would he have stayed? Would he come to regret his choice and chafe at a quiet life? She imagined he would. There was no denying he was one of Hardacre's men now. He could not resist the pull of adventure the man promised.

And she recognized now that she loved Nate more than she loved her own happiness. As much as it had cost her, she knew she had made the right choice that night.

Unbidden, her imagination planned a happy reunion, where he would confess that he loved her, too, with his whole heart and without reservation. She would accept his proposal and they would be as happy as Peggy and Clem.

But now it was time to make a clean break from her old life as she had determined to do twelve months ago. There was only one thing of those days that remained – the ledger; the final legacy from Jack. She had thought to use it for insurance in case any of his associates returned but, having seen no one for over two years, maybe it was time to finally cast off that weight.

She would burn it into smoke and ashes; a fitting representation of hell if there ever was one. It was something she no longer needed. No one would find her now. No one *could* find her.

She quickened her step. The light was disappearing faster than she had counted on. Instead of continuing along the road, she would take a shortcut along the path that ran by the creek.

There was much to do before Peggy's wedding. For nearly a year hers and Peggy's partnership existed on a handshake. It was time to make their business agreement official.

She smiled. It would be their wedding present.

The late afternoon darkened into early evening, the sky dulling from blue to grey. The sound of the day birds finding their roosts mixed with the sound of the waking night animals. Behind her, there was a crack of a twig and the birds around her quietened a moment, leaving only the sound of croaking frogs.

Then there was the rustling of grass that caused her to pause.

A hare? A goat that had gotten loose? Or something larger still?

The birds resumed their chorus and she continued.

Crack!

The sound was closer and louder.

She turned around, looking for a figure in the gloom but saw no one. She quickened her steps, but the rustling continued, the sound of brushing against bushes beside the path, something pushing through. It was getting closer and would overtake her at this rate. She bent over to pick up a large stick to brandish as her pursuer emerged from the bushes.

Woof!

Prince barked once but his tail kept wagging furiously as he barreled toward her.

"So much for a guard dog," she told him. "You're supposed to bark at strangers, not me!"

The pointer moved to her side and sat down. He looked up at her, panting, until she patted his head.

"Come on, let's go. It's time to help Peggy with the supper."

Chapter Sixteen

"WE DID WELL tonight," Peggy announced, throwing a tea towel over her shoulder. "The cooler weather is bringing them in, you know."

Susannah offered an *uh-hmm* in reply while she dried the glasses.

"I'm working on a new menu," the woman continued. "A rich beer pie and a pudding with the extra brandy that Lieutenant Hardacre gave us. We have some left over after we finished those brandied apricots. We don't tell the folks the secret ingredients. That's what will make it special."

Susannah simply nodded. Peggy offered a mild frown in return.

"What's up, Duch? I'd have thought after getting that letter from Sir Daniel Hobnob or whatever his name is, and the lieutenant, you'd be happy to know that the pirate is getting along all right in his new employment."

She shook her head. This was difficult enough without being distracted by thoughts of Nate.

"It's about you and Clem."

That kept her quiet. It was Peggy's turn to frown.

"A year ago, we arrived here in St. Sennen and this tumbledown inn," she said. "Look at the place now."

And, indeed, Peggy looked about, casting her eyes around the bar and the dining room. "You've done a fine job."

Susannah shook her head.

"No, it's not me alone. It's never been me alone these past two years. It's been *us*. We're partners, especially since we came here. We split the profits half and half. The Queen's Head is as much yours as it is mine. Do you remember what I said when we first arrived?"

Her friend stared at her a moment, as though Susannah had taken leave of her senses. "I thought you said that because you couldn't afford to pay me proper wages."

"Well, yes, that was true in part. But I also knew I couldn't make this place work without you. *You're the finest cook this side of Bath.* And now that you're getting married, one of the things I would like to do is make it official. A contract between the two of us."

"Blimey."

Peggy turned over one of the newly dried glasses and poured herself a small brandy. She lifted the bottle and raised her eyebrows. Susannah nodded. Peggy poured a measure into another glass.

"I don't understand," she said. "What does me getting married have to do with anything?"

Susannah smiled, picked up her glass, and shared a salute with her friend. "Well, it is customary for a wife to move into her husband's home."

Peggy gaped at her as though the thought had never once crossed her mind.

"Equally, Clem would be welcome to live with you here, but he does have a business of his own and a son to consider."

Susannah sipped the liquor and savored the heat as it traveled down her throat.

"Which means you've got yourself a very nice nest egg," she continued. "I never mentioned it, but last month I received an offer on The Queen's Head two and a half times the amount I paid for it. That would leave you with a very tidy sum which is yours alone to decide what to do with."

Peggy looked horrified.

"You're not going to sell her are you?"

Susannah shook her head vigorously. "No, not at all! But that's my point. I couldn't even if I wanted to. You'd have to agree to it, too. Now that the inn has been cleaned up and is profitable, you're within your rights to capitalize on your investment. Perhaps you'd like to become business partners with Clem and expand his ironmonger business to other towns."

Susannah took another sip. Peggy showed no such restraint and downed her brandy in one gulp.

"The profits over the past three months have been more than I would have earned in wages," she said. "I've already got a tidy sum put away. You're not asking me to *leave* are you?"

"No! Not if you don't want to! I just wanted to look after your interests. We're friends, but marriage does change things."

"I... I don't know what to say."

Susannah set down her glass and gave Peggy a hug.

"You were the only one who stood by me when Jack was at his worst," she whispered. "And when he died, you were the one who kept your head and helped me keep mine. I owe you a lifelong debt."

Susannah kissed her on the cheek and felt the salt of Peggy's tears. "Whatever you decide to do, you have my full support and blessing. You and Clem both."

"I need to sit down," Peggy whispered. "There's too much to take in. I'll have to talk to Old Boots first. I never even thought past getting him down the aisle..."

"Of course you should talk to Clem. In fact, I insist."

"Peggy, have you seen my gloves?"

Susannah looked at her hands and rubbed some more lanolin onto them.

"No, I haven't," Peggy called back from the kitchen. "When did you last see them?"

Susannah grimaced ruefully at her reflection in the dressing table mirror. If she knew *that* she wouldn't have to ask. "Not since last Sunday. They should be in my glove box."

"Try somewhere else!"

"My glove box is gone as well."

She let out a frustrated sigh. She couldn't wait any longer; she would just have to buy another pair of gloves in Truro.

Susannah looked at her small packed case. Not only did it contain clothes and toiletries for an overnight journey, there was also a pouch containing nearly one hundred pounds. Peggy was not the only one who had been frugal with her share of the profits.

There was a coach departing St. Sennen at seven o'clock. She would meet it at the crossroads soon after for a trip that would take more than half a day. It would put her in Truro just after lunch, which would give her time to conduct some of her business. The rest she would do the next day before taking the late coach back to St. Sennen.

As she secured the latches on the case, it occurred to her this was the first journey she had undertaken on her own. How strange that she had reached the ripe old age of twenty-seven and not once traveled further than a few miles on her own.

Soon she would have to get used to doing a lot of things on her own.

Peggy had yet to tell her the outcome of the discussion she'd had with Clem but she knew it went long into the night. Getting Mr. Craddock, the solicitor, to draw up a contract of partnership was the first point of order.

Wearing her green walking dress, Susannah made her way to the crossroads. How much easier and more pleasant it would have been to sail in Nate's boat. She missed the little *Sprite* anchored at the jetty. She wondered how Nate fared. Perhaps she should pay a visit to Lieutenant Hardacre and ask whether he would be so kind as to pass on a message to him.

Well, she would have more than enough time to think about it on the journey.

THE TRIP FROM St. Sennen to Truro was wearying even with an hour to rest at Bodmin. She booked a room at the White Hart Inn before heading to her solicitor's office.

She outlined the arrangements she wished to make to formalize the partnership between herself and Peggy. Mr. Craddock reminded her she would have to get Peggy to sign and have someone witness both documents. Susannah decided to see Martin Doyle for the task when she returned.

Then she handed over the purse containing her savings and obtained a receipt to keep it in the solicitor's care to save and invest on her behalf. If Peggy decided she wanted to be bought out of The Queen's Head, Susannah would need more than just that tidy sum.

They concluded their business. The solicitor rose to his feet and held out his hand. He shook hers vigorously.

"If only all of my clients were as prudent as you. It's a pleasure doing business with you, Mrs. Moorcroft."

Susannah inwardly winced at his use of her legal name.

"And before we wrap up today, there is just one more thing. Your old solicitor in Kent has forwarded a letter to you.

"I thought I'd forwarded it on to you in St. Sennen but as it so happened, it returned here two days ago. But since I knew you were coming into Truro to see me, I've kept it unopened here for you instead of trying a second time."

Susannah frowned. "A letter from Kent? I can't think of anyone I know who remains there. What does it say?"

Mr. Craddock handed over the envelope. She didn't recognize the writing. There was no return address on the back and the seal was plain red wax. It didn't have the look of anything official about it.

"Perhaps a long-lost friend writes to wish you well."

She stared at the address.

Mrs. J Moorcroft
Seamist Cottage
Lydd

A cloud of dread began to settle over her. She broke the seal and unfolded the paper.

Mrs. Moorcroft,

Do you remember me, Robert Lawnton? Your late husband and I were business associates. You're making it difficult for me to track you down, but I do have ways and means.

I believe you have something of Jack's that's mine by rights and I very much want it. If you'd be so good as to let me know whether you have the item of which I speak – a ledger. On receipt of it, I can be persuaded to leave you well enough alone in the future.

You can reach me at the Red Lion Inn in Hastings.

Pay heed, Mrs. Moorcroft – failure to respond will force me to make further inquiries. And by God, if you're still above ground, I will – this word was underlined three times – *track you down and make you rue the day you ever crossed me. There are many ways I can make your life very unpleasant.*

The paper shook in her hand. Spots danced before her eyes and blackness edged at her vision.

"Mrs. Moorcroft! Are you well?" asked Mr. Craddock. He called to his associate. "Atkins, bring some water for Mrs. Moorcroft, will you?"

She responded only when the solicitor tapped her hand. She folded the paper hastily and gripped it tight. When she looked up, she saw the concerned faces of Craddock and Atkins.

"No, everything is quite well," she answered quietly. "I'm just tired from a long journey."

"Was there something in the letter to disturb you?"

She shook her head. "No! No, it was just... an old friend of my husband's who wished to be remembered."

She hid her still shaking hands behind her satchel and thanked the solicitor. When she returned to the White Hart Inn, she placed the letter on the table in her room and stared at it as though it were poison.

"Help me! Don't just stand there like an imbecile, help me, you stupid bitch! Pull me out! What are you waiting for?"

It had been months since the memory of Jack's drowning came back as vividly as it did now. She kept her eyes wide open. If she closed them, she would see that night in the Denge Marshes so clearly and hear his terrified screams as he slipped under and she did nothing.

She fought the panic brewing inside her until her heaving breaths became even once again.

"Think! Just stop and think," she told herself aloud.

The letter was not dated but it looked travel-worn. It was addressed to her at the house near Lydd. Whoever had bought the place must have sent it on to the solicitor who handled Jack's estate and her purchase of the inn. And he, in turn, must have forwarded it to her new solicitor here in Truro. She trusted the two solicitors well enough for them not to breach the confidentiality which was a condition of their trade. She had to – it was her only hope.

And it meant Lawnton did not know where she lived.

She let out a shaky breath. She *was* safe. Why should she fear a man who lived so far away and who had no power to harm her anymore? She opened her eyes and looked at the letter once again. It was just a piece of paper – only a piece of paper.

The temptation to set it alight in the fireplace and let it burn was strong. Instead, she folded up the wicked missive and placed it in the folds of a small diary she'd brought with her.

She examined her reflection in the oval looking glass in the wardrobe. Her face was flushed. Indeed, when she put her hands to her face, she felt the heat of them. She returned to the washstand and splashed cold water on them. Panic rose again...

Stop it!

She needed a distraction.

Out of the corner of her eye she spied a bundle tied in a piece of plain linen. That was one of the things she had come to Truro to do.

Among the items she brought with her from St. Sennen was a beautiful bolt of silk from France. It was part of the smuggled treasure that Lieutenant Hardacre insisted she accept as recompense for her inconvenience. The color was like nothing she had ever seen before – neither purple, nor red, nor pink, but somehow a combination of all of those shades as it shimmered in the light; perhaps the shade of fuchsias she'd once seen in a grand garden, or the particular shade the sky became in the mornings ahead of a spell of bad weather.

Red sky in the morning, sailor's warning.

Having a dress made of it was an extravagance she would never have considered for herself. She had it wrapped in clean paper and plain linen to sit on the shelf above her wardrobe. Where would she find such a place to wear a gown of that shade?

And yet, as she took out Jack Moorcroft's cursed ledger from its hiding place to withdraw her savings from the hidey hole in the floor, she had reconsidered her situation and came to two conclusions. She would burn that hideous reminder of Jack in celebration when Peggy signed their business partnership papers.

And she would have a dress made of the fabric. It seemed apt. Red, the color of passion; red, the color of atonement.

They were both starting life, renewed, rediscovered. So, it was purely on impulse she brought the fabric with her to find a dressmaker.

Susannah was directed by the innkeeper's wife to the salon of Madam Lefanu. The woman and her apprentices, too, had gasped over the color and the fineness of the fabric.

The dress was an indulgence. And she had Nate to thank for helping her see there was more to life than the small existence she had created.

Despite her best efforts, she found her thoughts drifting back to him. Was he here in Truro? Should she call on him?

Recalling the name on a card Hardacre had given her, she walked past the White Hart Inn instead of going in and, instead, crossed into Wharf Street. She found the name – Charteris House – on a row of terraced shops, whitewashed but mostly unassuming. Two of the three shopfronts had brightly painted signs advertising their wares. The middle shop, over which the Charteris House sign sat, was devoid of such promotion.

She crossed the road and peered through the window. It appeared to be a chandlery, filled with bright brass bits and pieces she didn't know the names of, with a back wall filled with clocks. It looked like a charming place.

"Can I help you, miss?"

Susannah hadn't seen the shopkeeper emerge.

"Oh! I'm sorry. I… it's just I heard a friend mention this place once and…"

She backed away and the little man with the thick glasses offered a smile.

"Is there anything in particular you're looking for? We're specialists in finding unusual wares."

"Oh, ah, well, nothing in particular… I should get going."

This was foolishness. What was she expecting? To see Nate Payne working in there – in a shop? More foolishness. She glanced across the street to see if she could make a successful dash with her dignity intact.

The shopkeeper bowed and reopened the door on which a brass

bell tinkled merrily. She had heard *that* now, so why hadn't she heard it when he came out?

"I need to go."

The man smiled. Susannah stepped off the pavement.

"Then come again," said the little man, pleasantly. "Goodbye for now, Mrs. Linwood."

It wasn't until she reached the White Hart Inn again that she realized the shopkeeper called her by name.

She shook her head.

Surely, she had been mistaken.

Chapter Seventeen

September 1805
Ascorn, Brittany

NATE AND ADAM Hardacre walked into the *Le Pomme d'Eve* early in the evening and immediately caught the attention of Yvette Piaget.

"*Mon cher*! I never thought I would see *you* here again."

She offered him a subtle welcoming smile which lasted only until she saw he was not alone. Then the smile broadened. She squared her shoulders, presenting her bosom to its best advantage.

"I see you bring a friend with you. That's very generous, *n'est-ce pas?*"

Nate chuckled.

"Put away your charms, Yvette. My friend here is married – happily so."

The woman's brows rose in speculation, unabashed in her perusal. "That in and of itself makes him an interesting specimen. Is there a reason why he doesn't speak for himself?"

Nate shook his head. "His French is terrible. Where's Claude?"

"He's with the fishmongers."

"We need a place to stay for the next few days, somewhere discreet... out of the way. After last time, I'm keen to avoid the *soldats*, you know what I mean?"

"You and me both, *lover*. But I think I have a place for you. Are you sure there is nothing else I can do to help two weary travelers?"

He kissed Yvette on one cheek, then the other.

"A good meal to start with, yes?"

Yvette nodded and headed for the kitchen. Nate followed her as far as the bar.

Meanwhile, Adam found a dimly lit corner which afforded them the best view of the tavern, Nate noted it was no coincidence that it was close to a window *and* the kitchen door – two means of escape if they're needed.

It hadn't taken them long to settle into a routine. Adam's sailing experience made crossing in the foggy, moonless conditions far less treacherous than it ought to have been. Now on dry land, they'd fallen into step as though they had known each other for years.

He'd wondered if the man would try to take command of the mission but, so far, Adam watched more than he spoke which, considering his command of the language, was a blessing.

Nate returned with two mugs of local cider.

"So, how do you want to play this?" he said under his breath.

"We'll be patient," Adam answered. "I'm hoping that our friends are still free enough to get a message to us."

Nate nodded, recalling their meeting the day before last. A mix of anticipation and dread made him restless and uncharacteristically short-tempered.

He forced himself to sit through Bassett's frustratingly detailed preparations until he could no longer hold back from the one question that had to be asked and no one yet had.

"How, exactly, are we supposed to find them? Go door-to-door?"

Bassett shook his head and looked to Ridgeway. That man looked mildly amused by his outburst.

"Word will reach them. I've arranged for a ship to traverse fifteen miles of coast at night and send a coded lantern signal every five minutes. The patrol will do that for three nights only. The message is to make contact with you via your old haunt, *Le Pomme d'Eve.* It's enough of a criminal haunt that unfamiliar faces won't attract the attention of well-meaning *citoyens*.

"You and Adam will have one week to get in and get out."

All traces of amusement were gone from Ridgeway's eyes as he directed his next comments to Adam.

"If you find Bickmore, bring him back if you can, or kill him if you must, but take no unnecessary risks. We don't know what resources he has at his disposal or how well connected he is with Napoleon's inner circle."

Adam responded with a curt nod, but said nothing. It was clear as the nose on his face that his wounds of betrayal by the former friend were felt deep.

Nate took a sip of his cider, the sharp, crisp taste reawakening memories. It had been some time since he awoke from nightmares of being buried alive in the oubliette; he suspected they would return tonight.

"If we're going to be here a while, we might as well look like we're here for the night." He nudged Hardacre with his elbow and nodded toward a newly abandoned game of pallets. "Have you ever played this?"

Adam shook his head and cracked a grin. "No, but I'm a quick learner. Let's see if you're as good as you say you are."

Nate responded in kind. "Care to make a wager on it?"

"Not me, but them," said Hardacre, indicating the patrons now filling the tavern. "Encourage an audience, but play it straight, we don't want to attract the wrong kind of attention. I can slip into the background which should make it easier for our friends to make contact."

A plan that kept him active, and kept his nerves under control, was one he could get behind.

Nate quickly outlined the rules of the game. It was similar to boules but using painted iron discs instead of balls. A player tossed painted iron discs, concave on its underside, onto the wooden board. The board they examined was scarred with crescent shapes made by the edge of the disc which bit into the wood after being tossed.

Adam nodded his understanding and picked up six discs, the chipped red paint showing the patina of pitted iron beneath. Nate picked up six green discs and tossed the smaller yellow painted jack onto the board to start.

Nate found Adam to be a quick study and a good aim. Within a few rounds, they were evenly matched – and beginning to draw a crowd. Some started making bets on the side.

At the beginning of a new round, Adam gave Nate a particular look. His first throw was right off. Nate quickly took advantage to win the round in spectacular fashion.

Adam threw his hands in the air. "Bah! *J'ai fini!*" he announced in his basic French.

Nate laughed. He knew what to do. He thumped his chest and yelled boastfully: *"Je suis invincible! Qui va me prendre?"*

ADAM WITHDREW FROM the crowd and reclaimed the back table near the window and the kitchen once again. *Payne's quite the showman*, he mused. *Let's see how long he can entertain a crowd.* He ordered another cider and observed the people.

He quickly identified the regulars; they were garrulous but stayed in their own groups. Then there were the strangers – newcomers into port who were here only long enough to fill their bellies with food and drink, and perhaps to take a bed either alone or in company.

A whoop from Nate suggested he had won another round. Adam looked around for the clock. It was getting toward eleven. He would only risk staying for another hour before he'd pull them both out for the night.

The later the hour, the greater the risk, as men grew more drunk and tempers frayed.

He had just finished his beer and risen from his seat when a group of five men, all the worse for booze and two of them singing a bawdy song, carelessly careened into him. For a moment, they were a stumbling tumble of arms before the drunks recovered and went on their way. But Adam was near certain his pocket had been dipped.

If that was the case, they would be disappointed. He only had a few copper centimes in a leather pouch. He touched his coat pocket. The pouch was still there. He reached inside to confirm it and found a slip of paper that had not been there before. He glanced at it.

Tante Hilda, nous sommes prêts à rentrer chez nous.

He knew enough French to roughly translate.

Aunt Hilda, we are ready to come home.

THE FOLLOWING AFTERNOON at *Le Pomme d'Eve,* they were joined by two men. The pair seemed comfortable with Adam but they regarded Nate with suspicion. Dark rings around their eyes and thinned lips hinted at the strain they were under. How ironic that they had to listen to him as he translated instructions.

And they weren't too happy about what they heard either. They would sail out close to midnight. The men, Ignace and Guillaume, wanted to be away from Brittany right away. Their disappointment was ill-disguised but, being disciplined men, they said nothing more.

"You may as well get some sleep," said Nate. "It's going to be a rough crossing when we leave sail."

Yvette had found them a disused warehouse to hide out at. One by one, over the space of two hours, they left *Le Pomme d'Eve,* watching for anyone taking special notice of them.

Although Nate was one of the first to leave, he was the last to arrive near the warehouse in the late evening. Before going there, he ran a check across the *Sprite*. Again, the activity kept him focused. When he returned to the deck, he cast his eyes out across the wharf. Braziers every thirty feet kept the chill away and provided light to the fishermen who would soon be going out for a night's haul. And the *Sprite* would be hiding among the fishing fleet.

So far so good. They had seen nothing of the soldiers from Fort St. Pierre. Years of smuggling had made Nate cautious, aware of anyone who followed or who stared for too long. So far, he had experienced nothing of that. So why did he feel as edgy as a cat?

He started whistling along to a folk tune he could hear being played in one of the taverns and disembarked the *Sprite*.

He walked along the waterfront mindful of a group of men some distance behind him. Out of an abundance of caution, he slipped down an alleyway between two warehouses well short of his destination.

Below him, he could hear the gentle lapping of the water on the pylons. The faint strains of a violin from the tavern reached him even here. The men who had been following slowed as they approached his hiding place.

"Where did he go?"

"*Merde!* He must have gone down one of the alleys in the darkness."

"Never mind, we know which boat is his. We will wait for them there."

Nate heard three distinct voices, but it was the last one in particularly formal French which stood out. He never thought he would recognize a voice heard only the once, but now, as he closed his eyes, he knew not only did he know the voice, but he could also see the speaker in his mind's eye.

It was the man who had been at the prison fort. The Englishman. The man he was certain Adam was looking for. He returned to the warehouse at ten o'clock to find it in total darkness and silence.

Was he too late? Had Adam and the spies been captured? Had they been forced to relocate?

He continued whistling the *chants de marins* quietly and worked his way around the warehouse until he approached a pile of crates and barrels in one corner.

"Come out, come out, wherever you are…" he said softly in English.

A lamp, which had been hidden, emerged and spilled light, revealing the shadows of spectral figures emerging from their hiding places.

"I have some bad news," he said in English.

"What is it?" answered Adam, his voice grim, matching Nate's in tone.

"I think your friend Bickmore is on to us."

"Are you sure?"

"I heard a voice, and I'm certain it was the man I heard in prison. They have the *Sprite* under watch."

"How many?"

"They were at least three, including Bickmore."

Hardacre looked thoughtful. "They're odds we can work with. Tell our friends here we may need to fight our way onto the *Sprite*."

The translation was quickly made and the two men grunted their assent.

"They'll be waiting for us at the dock."

He turned to Guillaume who was about his height with dark hair.

"Have you ever sailed a boat?"

"We both have," the young man replied, "we're old hands."

Nate nodded. "That's good. You and me – let's exchange clothes. At a distance, you'll pass as me. Get on board and pretend you're making ready to disembark. That will keep the attention of at least one of them on you. They won't try anything until they think they have all of us. We three should be enough to deal with them."

After he had finished, Nate belatedly realized he should have deferred to Adam. After all, this was his operation. He explained what he'd said – this time in English.

The blond-headed man simply nodded in agreement. "Then that's our plan. But remember, Bickmore is *mine*."

WHEN THE FOUR of them returned to the dock around midnight, they saw a group of about a dozen men huddled around the brazier closest to their berth, close, but still fifteen yards away.

"Damn," Nate grunted. "I thought they were only three."

"Wait," said Adam as they hung back in the shadows. He watched them intently for over a minute, then nodded toward the group. "See the three with their backs to us? See how they're standing slightly apart from the others? One of them keeps looking about. They *are* only three. The rest are probably just workers and fishermen."

Nate pointed out the *Sprite* to Guillaume and the young spy, dressed in Nate's clothes, made his way down the pier to the vessel, hands in pockets. One of those hands clutched a knife. He stepped over onto the *Sprite* and lit a lamp, taking it with him below deck.

Nate held his breath. There was a chance the men looking for them were already on the boat. But a few moments later, Guillaume emerged onto the deck. He whistled along with the tune that spilled out from the tavern. It was their prearranged "all clear" signal.

Nate watched him go down into the body of the boat.

The three men Adam had pointed out now started to peel away from the group of others at the brazier. As they did so, the fire showed one man's face clearly. Adam muttered a curse under his breath.

"That's your friend?" Nate asked.

Adam nodded the once. Nate didn't need to look any closer to see the hostility radiating from the man.

"Ready?"

Adam stayed his hand. "I want to take Bickmore with us."

Nate nodded. "It will be crowded onboard, but we'll manage."

"Thanks."

"Save it until we're back in England."

Nate slapped Ignace on the shoulder.

"Your turn, *mon ami*. Walk confidently as you approach the boat. Don't run. As soon as you get to the *Sprite*, you and Guillaume loosen the lines and prepare to weigh anchor."

"*Oui, merci beaucoup.*"

The man did as instructed. As he neared the boat, the trio near the brazier unexpectedly began to walk quickly after him.

Adam and Nate broke cover. Coming up behind the men, Nate grabbed the shoulder of one and wrenched him around. He punched him in the face and a fist fight ensued.

Ignace turned at the sounds behind him and faced the man who advanced on him.

ADAM HARDACRE'S ATTENTION remained solely on the third one – Bickmore.

His old lieutenant was startled at first, but smiled as Adam closed on him.

"Well, if it isn't the old man," Bickmore sneered. "Are you going to beat me up like your thuggish friends over there?"

Adam caught a glimpse of Nate kicking his man as he cowered on the ground. Ignace was raining blows on the other and clearly establishing the upper hand.

"Don't tempt me. All I want are answers."

"Who I'm working for? Why the hell did I involve you in *The Society for Public Reform*? Why I wanted you in France?"

"They'll do for starters."

"What Wilkinson told you was right, Adam. You were going to be a clarion call. Men would have rallied around you. Men *were* beginning to rally. I do have to say this for the English, their sense of justice is very well developed."

"And you have no qualms about using mine. For what end?"

Adam glanced over at the sound of a splash as Nate rolled his man off the wharf and into the water. Guillaume had joined Ignace beating the other man.

Adam yelled. "Get on the boat! Get ready to sail!"

He then addressed Harold. "Tell me. Why?"

"Do you remember a shore leave two years ago? We stayed at a tavern in Corsica and we caroused with one of the local men."

"We were dicing as I recall."

"You won a particular bet."

Adam shook his head. His memories of that night were foggy. "Did I?"

"I'm sure with a proper incentive, I could make you remember."

Bickmore's calm cruelty chilled him. "You're not the man I thought you were, Harold."

"You think you will shame me? Remember my duty to England? I hate my country, an evil pox and stain on the world. Napoleon will have her on her knees soon enough, and in a way you will never conceive."

In the distance, a whistle blew. Most of the locals around the brazier had merely watched the fight between these strangers with interest but no desire to get involved. But someone had called for the guard.

"Come on! Let's go!" Nate yelled from the *Sprite*.

The sound of the whistle grew louder, and the fishermen, emboldened by the arrival of the authorities, were more attentive.

"*Le garde va vous battre bien, rozbif,*" called one man with a smirk.

The guard will beat you well, 'roast beef'.

Damn! The chance to subdue and take Bickmore with them was gone. Oh well, there was still time for this…

Adam slugged Bickmore in the jaw. The traitor went down like a sack of potatoes. He looked up at Adam, obviously hurt by the blow. But instead of looking rueful, he simply rubbed his jaw and sneered as Adam started to back away.

"Leaving are you?" he said thickly, blood on his lips. "Do say hello to that lovely governess of yours for me, won't you? I still have that fantasy about her, you know."

Adam took a step back toward the man and spat on him.

"Come *on!*" shouted Nate.

Adam turned and sprinted. He leapt aboard the *Sprite* as it was shoved away from the dock.

"Keep your eyes to the skies, *mon ami*," Bickmore yelled after him. "We'll be seeing each other again soon. Sooner than you think."

Chapter Eighteen

SUSANNAH TRIED ON a new pair of brown leather gloves lined in cashmere. They were just the thing to keep her warm this coming winter. She added them and a new glove box to her purchases.

By the time she finished her errands, the sky was closing in. There would be rain before the end of today. As she was preparing to make her way up to the third-story room at the White Hart, one of the maids dropped a curtsy and told her there was a letter waiting.

For her *here*? The only people who knew her plans to come to Truro were back in St. Sennen.

From Robert Lawnton? The thought was fleeting but it was enough to send chills through her.

She made her way up to her room and opened the curtain to allow the light from the clouded-in sky to spill across the desk and the floor.

But this letter was not travel-stained and the paper itself was heavy, expensive stock in the brightest shade of white she had ever seen.

Susannah snatched it up and even though her hand shook, she could see the address was in a distinctly feminine hand and sealed with red wax impressed with a crest of some sort.

Then who? Surely not Lillian Doyle.

She broke the seal and unfolded the letter.

Lady Abigail Ridgeway cordially invites
Mrs. Susannah Linwood

to join her for an at-home
Bishop's Wood
Tomorrow, the 15th-inst. At 11am
If convenient, leave an acceptance with the innkeeper of the White
Hart Inn.

Lady Abigail Ridgeway? The wife of Sir Daniel Ridgeway?

She recognized the Ridgeway name, of course. Adam Hardacre had used Sir Daniel Ridgeway's credentials to enlist their aid but that was no reason why the peer's wife should take an interest in her.

She was barely above the notice of someone like Lillian Doyle – and even that was only because of *her* interest in Nate.

When she informed the innkeeper of her acceptance, she was told a carriage would be sent to pick her up.

The following day at the appointed hour, Susannah saw the liveried driver enter the White Hart Inn. He stepped into the waiting room, smart in his uniform of forest green, and glanced down at a card in his black-gloved hands.

"Mrs. Linwood?"

"I am she."

Susannah duly followed him, not out to a coach, as she thought would be the case, but to a rather impressive-looking curricle with two matched white horses in harness.

They made an easy pace through the streets until they left the outskirts of town. Here, the driver urged the handsome white beasts to a canter. The acres of farm land whizzed by, slowing only as they crossed a creek downstream of a mill on a tributary.

Not long after, the curricle passed beneath a stone archway. It opened up to a wide gravel drive and sweeping lawns designed to showcase an impressive-looking building, a perfectly formed Georgian house rendered in a cream wash. A peacock idly crossed the path in front of them, unconcerned about the oncoming vehicle.

As the curricle slowed toward the front entrance, Susannah patted her hair, shoving in a few pins that had worked loose from her chignon, and dusted down her skirts. She had been perfectly happy with what she had put on this morning, but now she doubted herself.

After all, it was not every day one was invited to tea with a titled lady. Or driven there in such a smart and speedy vehicle, for that matter.

The large entrance doors to the house were opened immediately by a man and a woman – a butler and a maid, she assumed by their uniforms.

The butler gave a small bow and the maid a curtsy.

The butler was an imposing man, tall and large of build with hair as black as the ace of spades.

"Welcome to Bishop's Wood," he said. "I am Musgrave and at your service. Molly here will show you where you may wish to repair yourself."

"Thank you, that would be most kind," replied Susannah, feeling a little breathless from the journey.

The anteroom, just off the impressive entrance hall with its marble-tiled floor, was painted in a soothing seafoam green. A chaise longue in a complementary blue and silver brocade beckoned. As did an iron and marble dressing table on which was set a selection of cosmetics.

She availed herself of a spritz of lightly scented toilet water and addressed her appearance in the mirror. When the maid returned about ten minutes later, she felt presentable once more.

The maid escorted her across the hall and knocked on the ajar door of what appeared to be an elegant drawing room in lavender, white, and green.

"Mrs. Linwood, my lady."

The maid stepped aside.

There were three in the room, but Susannah didn't need to be told who was her hostess. The elegant woman in her early forties rose from her chair. Her white-blonde hair was, surprisingly, not her most striking feature; rather it was her grey-green catlike eyes. The day gown she wore was simple in style, but made from expensive cream fabric and was expertly styled for her.

Susannah curtsied to her hostess.

"I'm so pleased you accepted my invitation. I imagine it would have come as a surprise, but you'll soon get used to the way I do things. Susannah – Mrs. Linwood – allow me to introduce my daughter, Marie."

The pretty girl, with light brown hair and slender build, was aged about sixteen by Susannah's reckoning. The young woman bobbed a curtsy.

"And I'd like you to make the acquaintance of Olivia, Mrs. Adam Hardacre."

The woman, aged in her late twenties, extended a hand. She was smartly dressed but nowhere nearly as expensively as their host. "It's a pleasure to meet you, Mrs. Linwood," she offered.

Suddenly the sound of her assumed name didn't seem right to Susannah's own ears.

"Please, call me Susannah."

"Then you must call me Olivia."

From the corner of her eye, Susannah saw Lady Abigail nod to the maid and request tea be served.

"Adam tells me that you run a lovely little inn on the north coast," Olivia Hardacre continued.

Susannah was startled that this woman, a perfect stranger, should know anything about her. And yet, why wouldn't a husband tell his wife about his work?

Jack didn't. The thought came to mind unbidden, although she supposed it wouldn't be fair to judge all marriages by her own.

"Yes, at St. Sennen. It's a lovely village and we've grown very fond of it."

"We?" Lady Abigail asked. "You mean yourself and Mr. Payne?"

"No..." Susannah replied, somewhat nonplussed by her ladyship's inquiry and the look of surprise on Olivia Hardacre's face.

The arrival of the tea at that moment was welcome. The three returned to their seats and Susannah took a spare velvet upholstered seat next to Marie Ridgeway.

The moment her cup was poured, Susannah brought it to her lips even without sugar and milk to give herself time to decide how to elaborate on her answer.

"I arrived at St. Sennen with my housekeeper after I was widowed. I decided we should run The Queen's Head together. As partners."

Lady Abigail saluted her with her cup. "An enterprising woman! I'm beginning to like you more and more, Susannah. You will be a lovely addition to our circle."

Susannah frowned. Lady Abigail ploughed blithely on.

"Olivia was a governess before she married Adam nearly a year ago," she continued. "Sir Daniel and I were wed twelve years ago on, shall we say... a *visit* to Paris. You see, my dear, we are all married to spies."

It dawned on Susannah there was more to the introductions than met the eye.

"I think there has been some kind of mistake," she said. "You've been kind enough to extend an invitation to me on the belief that I have some kind of attachment with Nathaniel Payne."

"Don't you?" Lady Abigail inquired mildly.

Susannah could not help quickly rising to her feet, nor the words she blurted out. "Most certainly not!" Their shared intimacy – their kisses and caresses – did not in any way constitute the promise of an *attachment*.

"I'm sure that will come as a surprise to Nathaniel," the older woman added.

Olivia Hardacre shifted in her seat uncomfortably to look at Susannah directly and with no small degree of sympathy.

"Susannah, I can understand your confusion. This *is* a rather unusual situation, and I'm sure Lady Abigail doesn't mean to offend by making assumptions about your relationship with Mr. Payne."

"Quite so..." offered Lady Abigail, but her solicitous tone was betrayed by the slight upward quirk at the corners of her mouth.

"If I might clarify," Olivia continued, "England is in great peril. Greater than has been publicized in the newspapers. There are men who are tasked with identifying and dealing with specific threats."

"You mean Sir Daniel and your husband?"

"Yes. And now your Mr. Payne."

Susannah lowered herself back into the chair.

"Adam invited him to join the organization when he was in St. Sennen but Nathaniel refused. Not in so many words, but I believe he did indicate *you* were one of the main reasons why he declined."

"Three weeks later, he arrived on the doorstep of Charteris House to throw his lot in with The King's Rogues." continued Lady Abigail. The woman watched Susannah keenly, but also with a hint of sly amusement.

"The King's what?"

The woman shrugged, a small smile in her striking eyes. "*Rogues.* That's what Daniel calls their league. They don't have an official title or designation in the Home Office. They work...*off the books,* you might say. I rather like the name though – it adds a bit of dash and élan, don't you think?"

Susannah turned to young Marie Ridgeway, who was the only person yet to say a word. She returned a sympathetic look.

"I'm afraid I cannot offer you any comfort here, Madame," she said with the slightest hint of a French accent. "My adoptive parents have been spies all my life."

Susannah was vaguely aware that her jaw had dropped. "Both... your..." She turned back to Lady Abigail whose mirth was barely contained.

"I have a mind to create a little 'league' of my own," she offered with humor before her expression sobered.

"Nonetheless, even if we have been premature in assuming your relationship with Nathaniel," she said, "we would still like you to join us."

"I… I can't. I have a business to run, responsibilities. I don't have time to be a lady of leisure."

"Who said anything about leisure? This is all business. And that's why you interest me, Susannah. You are a woman of discretion and strength of character. You have a good head on your shoulders and can keep a confidence.

"Furthermore, the fact The Queen's Head was once a smuggler's inn with its own tributary to the Irish Sea is opportune. It would be an ideal base of operations."

"I beg your pardon?"

Lady Abigail picked up her cup and took a long sip. She was deliberately slow in putting the cup and saucer back down onto the low table before her.

"I'm sorry to insist, but information Nathaniel and Adam have brought back from Ireland has forced Daniel to reassess his planning. The threat of invasion from Napoleon is not necessarily going to come from France. It could very well come from Ireland.

"I'm not suggesting taking over your inn, just that you take in some additional guests from time to time. Paying guests, of course."

Susannah started fidgeting with slim gold band on her finger, rotating it round and round. Nate had been furious when he left. How cruel would it be to force him to be in close quarters with her again, knowing what had gone on between them?

Besides, she had been successful in hiding herself away in her own quiet little corner of Cornwall. Getting involved with Lady Abigail's "league" – whatever *that* was – would ruin everything. Who knew what attention it might attract? And Robert Lawnton was looking for her. What if he managed to find her?

"No. I cannot. I have Peggy to consider."

Marie discreetly excused herself, leaving her with Olivia Hardacre and Lady Abigail.

"Do you think your friend would refuse?" Olivia asked gently.

No. And *that* was a problem, too. At least she had Clem to look after her.

Susannah forced herself to stop playing with her ring.

"No, I suppose she wouldn't," she conceded, "but Peggy will ask questions and I won't lie to her – or put her in any danger. The Queen's Head may have the reputation as a smuggler's tavern, but Peggy and I have cleaned it up, made it a respectable place."

"And we wouldn't dream of asking for it to be otherwise," said Lady Abigail. "Nor would we ask you to do anything that would put you or Peggy at risk. All we need is a place that is discreet and quiet for our men to spend a night or two. They will not draw attention to themselves and they will not draw attention to you."

The request seemed so perfectly reasonable that it made it near impossible to refuse, but there was still the matter of her husband and the shadow cast by Robert Lawnton.

Susannah shook her head. Then she drew a deep breath.

"There is something about my past that only Peggy and her fiancé know that makes it impossible for me to help you."

"Oh, tosh!" answered Lady Abigail with a flick of her hand. "We *all* have a past, some less savory than others."

Olivia gave the titled woman a mildly exasperated glance and leaned forward.

"I can promise you that whatever you share with us will be kept in confidence," she said. "And we promise not to press you further on your involvement with us."

"We're a talented bunch, you know," Lady Abigail offered cheerfully. "Olivia has quite a gift for ciphers. And I have particular talents for finding out information. I know all about your late husband, Susannah."

The offhand way the woman revealed *that* tidbit of information, as through it were merely some drawing room *on dit,* was simply beyond the pale. Susannah had to look away. In her lap, she saw how her fingertips were white at how tightly she gripped her wedding ring.

Before she could mount a protest, Lady Abigail continued, but more softly. "I can guess at the pain you've been though, but I won't presume to give you sympathy. You're a resilient woman, Susannah – perhaps even more than you know."

"And love is worth the risk," added Olivia. "Take it from someone who knows. My husband has a particular enemy. That man's scheme put both his life and mine in mortal danger, but I couldn't stop loving Adam, even if I'd wanted to."

She reached across and put a hand on Susannah's.

"Adam tells me that Nate still cares for you deeply."

Susannah felt her throat constrict. "He said that?"

"Not in so many words. You know how men are. But there *are* signs."

Susannah felt her wall of reserve continue to break down. The question was past her lips before she could stop herself.

"How *is* he?"

Olivia looked to Lady Abigail. The two women seemed to communicate silently a moment. Olivia answered the question.

"He was well when I saw him. He stayed with us when he and Adam recently returned home from an excursion into France."

France? He went back to France? She recalled the first time she saw Nate, starved and bruised. The ordeal had taken a toll on his mind as well as his body but still, he went back...

"Is Nate still in Truro?" she asked.

Olivia Hardacre shook her head. Disappointment cut the tender shoots of hope to the root.

"He and Adam departed yesterday on a scouting mission along the east coast of Ireland."

Susannah swallowed against a rising tide of emotion of fear, regret, but also love. Now she prayed it wasn't too late to tell him.

"May I leave a message for him?"

Lady Abigail smiled gently. "You may. In fact, I insist upon it."

Olivia Hardacre touched a hand to her arm. Looking into the other woman's warm brown eyes, Susannah finally understood. The hollow feeling in her chest ever since Nate left was a sensation shared by Olivia. She loved her husband deeply and she worried for him.

"I MUST SAY I'm grateful to Lady Abigail for encouraging my involvement," she said. "When Adam is away, I'm not alone. And knowing I'm doing something to aid his work gives me additional comfort. That's really what we're offering, Susannah – friendship, support, and camaraderie. And that won't change, even if you decide to play no active part."

Susannah sighed. "I need time to think about it. I need to speak to Peggy."

"Then I thank you. We—" Olivia nodded to include Lady Abigail, "—thank you."

Lady Abigail cleared her throat. "Well ladies, now that the introductions are out of the way, we should find something to occupy our time until luncheon is served.

"My husband has forbidden me from playing Faro and, since Olivia doesn't play whist, shall we take a turn about the garden? I think some fresh air will do us a world of good."

Susannah found it hard to believe that Sir Daniel could successfully forbid his wife anything. Her expression of disbelief obviously showed itself because the blonde woman laughed.

"Let's get to know one another better, Susannah, then I'll tell you how I met my husband while cheating at cards."

Chapter Nineteen

SUSANNAH FOUND IT strange she should feel energized rather than exhausted after her trip to Truro.

Despite her reticence in giving a commitment to Lady Abigail's league, she allowed herself to be persuaded to make a return to the town in a month's time. After all, she had the final fitting for her gown then.

Peggy's wedding was two weeks away and, in her valise was the partnership deed her solicitor had prepared.

You are more resilient than you know.

Lady Abigail's words stayed with her throughout her time in Truro – as did Olivia's assurance that Nate cared for her still.

It seemed vaguely surreal that two women she had never met before, who seemed to know *all about her*, had reassured her so deeply.

She disembarked from the carriage at the coach stop, using the mounting stone to aid her descent, then waited for the postilion to unstrap her baggage from the back.

As she turned away from the departing coach, Susannah saw something catch the light in the tall grasses at the roadside. It glinted in the early morning sun. She approached it to find a broken sliver of polished and painted timber.

She picked up the piece and turned it over. A fleck of paint came off on her finger, a pale pink. She stared at it a moment, the shade familiar, then she spotted another larger piece of wood another yard beyond. The shape of it made itself known to her.

Recognition cut deep in her chest. It was *her* wooden glove box and it had been destroyed.

She clutched the pieces to her chest and looked down the road to where the slate grey roof of The Queen's Head was just visible over the trees. How long had her box been here? Had anything else been taken? If it had, surely she and Peggy would have noticed.

Prince, the lovely but useless guard dog he was, hadn't raised a hue and cry either.

Susannah shuddered. Who would do such a thing? She and Peggy were cautious and in such a small community there was very little real trouble. Occasionally, someone would be worse for the drink and lash out, but a stern lecture from her or Peggy, and a week's ban from the inn was enough to sort out most ill manners.

But this was different, *much* different.

Peggy!

In a sudden panic, she hurried down the road toward the inn as fast as she could go while lugging her bag. About one hundred yards away, Prince came bounding toward her, circling around and bounding at her heels.

She did not slow.

"Peggy!"

Susannah called out for her a couple times more but there was no answer.

Susannah barreled through the door. A few familiar faces turned from the bar to look at her quizzically.

"Glad you're back, Missus," said Farmer Rowe. "We missed your smilin' face we did."

Peggy entered the bar from the kitchen.

"You're back!" she greeted warmly, words tumbling from her mouth. "I was wondering why Prince shot out of here so excited. How was your trip? You must be exhausted. Go and put your bag away, then come on through to the kitchen and tell me all about it."

Susannah blinked rapidly. The men in the bar didn't look worried, neither did Peggy. But the longer she stood there unmoving the more the other woman's smile faded.

"Are you all right, Duch?"

Susannah shook herself.

"Yes, a little tired from the trip, that's all."

SUSANNAH CHANGED FROM her traveling dress, hanging it up to air and later brush down, into one of the dresses she normally wore while working in the tavern. As she changed, she glanced across to the pieces of her ruined glove box.

Odd. Why would anyone destroy a box? It may not have been worth much but it still had value. Such wanton vandalism made no sense.

When she returned to the kitchen, she decided to come directly to the point.

"Did you have any trouble while I was gone?"

"Trouble?" Peggy shrugged as she bustled about preparing a plate of cold cut meats for her. "Old Jago got himself a little argumentative last night if that's what you mean. Oh, and we'll have to follow up with the vintner's again; they were one barrel short when they delivered this morning…"

Her voice trailed off when Susannah said nothing.

"Tressa," Peggy instructed, "would you please mind the shop?"

The young maid left her place at the stove to go out into the bar. Then it was only the two of them in the kitchen.

"What's going on, Duch?"

Where to start first…

"Is there anything missing?"

Peggy frowned. "*Missing*? The occasional glass and fork, no more than usual."

Susannah took a deep breath. "Remember when I left a couple of days ago, I couldn't find my gloves?"

Peggy nodded.

"I found my glove box. It was smashed near the high road."

The other woman's eyes widened.

"What?"

Susannah nodded.

Peggy shook her head vigorously, understanding Susannah's question at last. "No, there's nothing else been stolen. I would have known. Who do you think it was?"

Now it was Susannah's turn to shake her head. "I'd hate to think it was someone local. We know everyone around here."

Peggy's face was red with ill-concealed anger.

She went to the barroom door and stuck her head through. Susannah heard her address the late afternoon drinkers.

"Right, you lot! Someone's been a-thieving in these parts and stolen personal things from Mrs. Linwood's room."

Even from a distance, she could hear a murmurs of disbelief and dismay from the regulars.

"So keep your eyes open, fellas," said Peggy.

"You're both safe as houses with us, luv," someone called.

"We'll make sure you're all right," said another.

Peggy returned to the kitchen.

"Right. Now we have some proper guard dogs on duty," she said.

"There's something else, too..." said Susannah. "I received a letter from Robert Lawnton."

Peggy sank down at the dining table, her ruddy complexion paling.

"Where? Not here, surely."

Susannah swallowed her own apprehension. "He sent it to the house at Lydd. The solicitor in Kent sent it on to the one in Truro. It looked months old."

"You don't think he's the one who stole..."

Having someone ask the question out loud coalesced the issue in Susannah's mind. The answer came to her swiftly.

"No."

Susannah shook her head, now more sure of her answer and her reason for it.

"No, he doesn't know where we are. How could he? The fact the letter reached me at *all* was only happenstance. And Robert Lawnton didn't strike me as a man who'd skulk in the shadows and play games."

"He's a nasty one, Duch. Your husband was bad enough but Lawnton has a cruel streak."

So, she hadn't been the only one to notice.

"He's looking for the ledger."

Peggy squared her shoulders. "Well, he can't find it if it doesn't exist."

The avowal bolstered Susannah's own confidence – after all, she and Peggy had been through much more trying times than this.

"That's exactly what I was thinking. I want to burn it tonight. I want to make sure not even ashes remain."

"Then that's what we'll do, Duch." Peggy looked at her sympathetically. "You look like you need a cup of tea."

As Peggy busied herself with the teapot, Susannah took a deep breath and tried to sound lighthearted. "I promised you a wedding present."

"I know," said Peggy over her shoulder at the kettle. "A partnership in The Queen's Head."

"Have you given any thought as to how you'd like your dowry?"

The trouble of the stolen glove box aside, now was a time for celebration. The woman who had become her dearest friend in the world was getting married.

Susannah's smile broadened when Peggy turned and had a healthy blush instead of the angry red of a few minutes earlier. She looked girlish.

"Yes, I had a quick word with Old Boots. Neither of us are in the first flower of youth and we're both set in our ways. So we've agreed Clem can run his business his way, and leave it to his son, and I can run my half of *my* business in the way I see fit. It'll need a few changes though."

Susannah's smile broadened.

"You said you had a *quick* word?"

Peggy gave her a look that said her pointed tease had not gone unnoticed. She came to the table with the teapot.

"Tressa's proven herself a good little maid-of-all-work – and she's got a friend in need of employment as well."

"An extra set of wages, Peggy. Have you thought this through?"

"Indeed, I have," she replied, pouring their tea. "With me living in the village, the two girls could share my old room. I'll still come in every day and do my other work but I'll teach the girls how to cook. That'd mean we have more time to make preserves. It's a good side business, we know that already. Well, Clem says the pirate knows a provedore in Newquay who'll take a regular quantity..."

Susannah wasn't sure what expression she had on her face, but Peggy halted.

"I'm sorry, I didn't mean to bring up his name."

Forcing a nonchalant set to her shoulders, Susannah shook her head. "No, that's fine but that's another thing I need to tell you. I... I don't think Nate is going to come home."

Susannah picked at a scar on the table to avoid seeing Peggy's expression.

"He's going to continue to work with Adam Hardacre out of Truro now."

"Ooh..." murmured Peggy doubtfully. "I suppose it's honest business in a way. But if you ask me it's barely different from smuggling."

"So how would you feel if some of Mr. Hardacre's... *friends* came to stay every now and again?"

"And they'd be paying guests?" asked Peggy sharply.

"Yes. According to Lady Abigail."

"Lady who?"

"Sir Daniel Ridgeway's wife. I met her. She runs some of their... *business interests.*"

Peggy raised her eyebrows then shrugged. "Well, as long as they're paying, they're welcome, because I have a *business* to look after, too."

THE MONTHLY MARKETS in St. Sennen were where Susannah and Peggy did their best trade. They sold a fine quantity of cordials and preserves. It added finely to the income from the bar, guests staying at the inn, and those who came for meals.

It was also at the markets where ideas were shared and deals struck for future business, so it had been the habit for Susannah and Peggy to attend together.

But not today.

Peggy had been fighting a cold bravely for days now. Susannah insisted that not only could she do the markets on her own, but she'd also make supper for their evening patrons.

"I may not be as good a cook as you, but I have been paying attention," she said, touching a hand to Peggy's forehead. It was warm.

"It's not right," she croaked. "I never get sick."

Susannah shook her head indulgently.

"You've been working hard every day since we arrived here. Besides, you're getting married soon – you want to be completely well. Sleep, and I promise you won't even notice I've gone."

An attempt to "harrumph" ended in a series of hacking coughs. Oh my, but Peggy was a dreadful patient.

"There, I've left you a small crock of chicken soup and some lemon tea."

"Don't fuss, I'm not a complete invalid."

"I'm glad to hear it!"

Susannah looked at her friend. "Besides, there's a method to my madness. If you let me take over the duties for the next couple of days, you'll be well enough for Friday and Saturday which you know are our biggest days. And don't forget, we're expecting four new guests to stay with us for the next two weeks shortly after that, and we have yet to prepare their rooms."

Peggy offered a resigned nod of her head.

"I suppose you're right."

Susannah accepted that as a victory.

"I am, you'll see."

"You'll send Clem or Sam with a message back to me if you need anything at the markets?"

"I promise faithfully," she said.

ON THIS CHILLY late September morning, Susannah set up her display of bottled brandied apricots and rosehip cordials, and nodded at familiar faces among the stallholders as they set out their wares.

She would miss Peggy's company. She was far more attentive to gossip than Susannah, and her asides about people who came and went during the day always made her giggle.

Susannah and the other stallholders chatted business for a while before Simon Sitwell, the rounded, grey-haired owner of The Rose and Crown, drew her to one side just as the church bells chimed eight o'clock.

"I heard about the break-in at your place, Mrs. Linwood," he said. "I wanted to let you know one of my regulars caught the cove what done it. You can rest assured it won't happen again."

Sitwell placed a pair of black leather gloves in her hands and, indeed, they were hers.

"Thank you!" she exclaimed. "How did you come by them?"

"Pettigrew caught young Joe Stapes clambering through my office window the other night," Sitwell continued. "He was looking for the cashbox and admitted he tried your place first. He swiped your glove box because – in his words – 'something that pretty should have something expensive inside it'. He's not the brightest boy God ever made."

Susannah knew Joe's family, although not well. She tutted her disappointment.

"He's not a bad 'un really," said Sitwell. "A few of the boys took him outside to, er, straighten him out. He'll get another hiding if he doesn't apologize to you in person."

Susannah thanked the innkeeper warmly and returned to her stall ready to serve her first customer. She was relieved to find the theft and destruction of the glove box was not as malicious as she had feared. She'd even entertained the thought that Robert Lawnton had stolen the gloves. Between the theft and Lawnton's letter, she had been jumping at shadows, afraid that if she turned around Jack's associate would be there.

Three hours later, Susannah gave in to her aching feet and resorted to using a shooting stick to rest upon instead of remaining on her feet. Beneath her skirts, she rolled one ankle and then the other, flexing her toes to rid them of an ache.

A figure caught her eye, a stylishly dressed woman in a dark blue riding habit and an ostrich feathered hat. It was Lillian Doyle.

My, the peacock is up with the hens today, thought Susannah uncharitably, in a voice that sounded too much like Peggy. Worst luck, Mrs. Doyle approached her.

"Good day to you, Mrs. Linwood."

"And to you, Mrs. Doyle, a pleasant day, indeed," she replied.

That was best. Keep the conversation agreeable.

The woman stepped closer and picked up a jar of brandy preserved apricots.

"I rather thought Moorcroft was a perfectly serviceable name," she said casually.

Susannah rose to her feet, ignoring their aching and the sudden tightening in her chest.

"I beg your pardon?"

"Just making conversation."

"With all due respect, Mrs. Doyle, you are not the type of person for whom conversation is an idle pastime."

Someone else approached the stall. Susannah give her attention to an *actual* customer who bought a selection of preserves and marmalades. But the other woman didn't take the hint and remained.

"I've started to wonder why you're really here, *Mrs. Linwood*. St. Sennen is such a backwater. Your manner and your speech suggest you're a lady of some quality, so it makes me curious."

Susannah rearranged her display of goods, trying her best to ignore the woman without seeming too rude. "I regret that I've occupied so much of your thoughts. I would have expected someone as important as you to have much more interesting things to do with your time."

"My time is my own, my dear, and I choose to spend it in the ways I found most... stimulating."

A sly dig about Nate, no doubt.

How was it that she could never think of anything clever to say back? That was why she needed Peggy by her side. Her friend could snap out a stinging riposte faster than anyone she knew.

In her case, silence served her best.

"And by the way, how is your houseguest?"

"Are you thinking of anyone in particular?" Susannah responded with mock sweetness. "After all, I *do* run an inn and we have any number of guests."

Lillian Doyle put down the apricot preserve.

"I think you and I know exactly who I'm talking about, *Mrs. Linwood*."

Susannah pulled together every ounce of self-possession she owned and pinned the woman with a direct look. *This* response came easily from her lips because she had rehearsed it often enough.

"If you're inquiring about Mr. Payne, then I'm afraid I'm going to have to disappoint you. He moved away over a month ago and left no forwarding address."

She watched the look of surprise flash across the woman's face before her self-assured mask slipped back into place.

"How disappointing."

Those two words were layered with meaning. For the first time, Susannah thanked her years with Jack Moorcroft for teaching her the ability to give nothing away on her face. No hint of emotion. Nothing.

"Well, it's been delightful chatting with you, Mrs. Doyle," Susannah said brightly.

If Lillian Doyle doubted her sincerity, then let her.

"Please do let your cook know the relishes he ordered are ready to pick up from The Queen's Head, if he cares to send someone down."

She had to give Lillian Doyle some credit, too. The woman did manage to keep her composure well.

With a condescending incline to her head, the magistrate's wife looked every inch the lady of the manor.

"And a good day to you, *Mrs. Linwood.* By the way, a word to the wise – once something piques *my* curiosity, I don't stop until it's satisfied."

Chapter Twenty

Early October, 1805

SUSANNAH GLANCED OUT the kitchen window, and the dishcloth stilled in her hand.

A trim white sail was appearing over the tops of trees along the banks of the Pengellan River.

Her heart stilled a moment, then continued in double time.

She recognized it. It could belong to only one vessel.

The *Sprite!*

She turned back to the kitchen, willing her heart to slow to its regular pace. Peggy caught her eyes, glanced out the window herself, then took the dishcloth from her hand.

"You'd better go and see what those smugglers are after, Duch," she said softly.

Susannah shot her a melancholy smile and walked unhurriedly across the field. Six months ago, it had been fallow; now part of it was an orchard beginning to thrive, and in another corner a couple of goats ruminated. Secure, now that the chickens had a run of their own, was their vegetable patch where long runs of vines had produced bright orange pumpkins nearly ready for harvest.

Perhaps she should greet Nate as she had done all those months ago. Would he remember he had confused her for a housekeeper? Would he find amusement in it now as he had done then?

The cat got your tongue?

Surely, she was forgiven if he had returned.

Or should she greet him with an apology on her lips? She was ready to move forward now. There was nothing of her past that could hurt her; hurt *them*.

Lawnton would surely have given up searching for her by now, and Lillian Doyle's knowledge of her real name was easily explained by her nosing through Magistrate Doyle's records.

And now, even the wedding band she'd worn as a reminder of her past – and her penance – was gone from her finger.

There was a moment when she and Peggy burned the ledger that she was tempted to throw the ring in the fire along with it, but she put it away instead. Gold was gold after all.

As slender as the band had been, her hand felt lighter without it. *She* felt lighter without it. And, for the past three weeks, she had considered Olivia Hardacre and Lady Abigail's words.

Nate *cared* about her.

Did he love her still?

She stopped at the boatshed, its deck out to the jetty now fully repaired. The shed was also completely weather tight and white-washed. It would welcome Nate's chandlery and supplies. And she would welcome *him*.

The first person she saw was Adam Hardacre. He dashed across the deck to throw a line to moor the *Sprite* and, with his back to her, threw out the anchor into the creek.

That was her first hint something was wrong.

Susannah's eyes swept across the deck to the helm.

There was no one there.

Nate wasn't there.

She climbed the steps and ran out to the end of the jetty.

"Lieutenant Hardacre! Adam! Where's Nate?"

The man pivoted around to look at her. Susannah took a step back. His bewhiskered face was grim.

"Get a man out here now to help me get him inside."

She put a hand to her mouth to cover an involuntary sob.

Hardacre's expression softened immediately. He stopped what he was doing and jumped onto the jetty to give her a quick embrace.

"Is Nate…"

She couldn't finish her words, let alone try to articulate them.

"It's all right, Susannah. He's just concussed and has a badly sprained ankle. We had a narrow escape from a French patrol. We fled into some bad weather to evade them. We had a devil of a time to make it back here."

Susannah nodded her understanding, then took a deep breath to calm her jangled nerves.

"And *you're* unhurt? I know Olivia worries about you, too."

The name of his wife from her lips had the most remarkable effect on the man. He picked up her hands and kissed them.

"You've met her! I hoped Lady Abigail would arrange something. That you speak of Olivia warmly makes me happy. As The King's Rogues, there are few we can trust. Knowing we are not alone in this enterprise brings more comfort than you can imagine."

Susannah swallowed and nodded, offering a wan smile in return. There was a noise from the cabin, a stumbling. Nate appeared, holding on to the roof of the cabin for support.

He looked horrible. Half his face was black and blue. Anywhere not covered in bruises was covered in cuts and scrapes.

He managed to cant a corner of his mouth upwards in an approximation of a grin. "Good morning, Miss. I've not seen you around here before. Are you one of the maids from old Gilliam's inn over there?"

Susannah's heart leapt. *He remembered!*

But his attempt at a jest seemed to drain his last reserves of energy. He took another stumbling step forward and swayed. She and Adam reached him at the same time.

"We're going to arrange a stretcher," said Hardacre.

SPYFALL

"Like hell," said Nate through gritted teeth. "Find me something to use as a crutch. If I can't walk two hundred yards unaided, I may as well be dead."

"Really? Because you were doing a good enough impression of that two nights ago."

Nate snarled. Adam ignored it.

Susannah retrieved one of the paddles from the dinghy.

"Will this do?"

"Just dandy," he bit out, but the look in his eyes conveyed his gratitude.

She stepped back onto the jetty to give Adam and Nate room to make their egress from the *Sprite*.

"He's not going to be able to make it up stairs," she said. "Take him through to my room."

Adam gave her a quick nod. Nate's face contorted with pain as he shuffled forward to make the step across off the boat.

Susannah hurried back to the inn ahead of the two men.

"How's the pirate?" Peggy asked.

"Hurt. Get some water on, Peg. We're going to put him in my room."

She continued through into the bar and unlocked the connecting door that opened onto her parlor. She entered her bedroom and pulled down the blankets on the bed before gathering a selection of bandages and bottled ointments.

From the kitchen, she heard a cry of pain and her heart clenched in sorrow.

Things will be *different*, she vowed. Things between them will be much different now.

She would not squander a second chance.

The two men, both dirty and disheveled, made their way through into the bedroom with Peggy following up behind.

Susannah opened up her linen chest and pulled out two blankets.

199

She folded them neatly into squares. They would help cushion his ankle while they addressed what to do about the swelling.

"I'm making up your old room upstairs, Lieutenant Hardacre," said Peggy. "There'll be hot water waiting for you."

"I'm much obliged, Miss Smith," he said as he walked Nate to the bed. "Susannah, I need to borrow Sid for a few hours if I may."

"Of course, whatever you need," she said. "We're all part of The King's Rogues now."

THE ROOM WAS warm, uncomfortably so. Despite the coolness of the autumn night outside, Olivia unlatched the sash window, propping it open a couple of inches with a block of wood.

A lamp burned low and, even in the dim light it cast, she could see the sheen of sweat across Nate's forehead.

With as much quiet as care, Susannah set down the tray. She touched a cloth to the water scented with a drop or two of lavender oil and dabbed it over his brow. His right leg was exposed at the knee, elevated on the folded blankets. His badly sprained ankle was wrapped in bruised cabbage leaves and bandaged.

She contemplated changing the dressing, but he seemed to be sleeping so peacefully, even without the dram of whiskey he'd asked for. She decided to let him sleep. That and time would be the best healers.

The cool air from the open window brought with it the smell of damp earthiness. The rain would be here soon.

It was very late and The Queen's Head was quiet. Peggy had gone to bed an hour ago. Adam Hardacre had popped his head in when he returned from his mysterious errand and, apart from his meal, spent the rest of the night in his room.

Speaking of which, she should find her own place to sleep tonight.

The room on the second floor near the door that led to Peggy's attic domain was vacant and had last been cleaned a couple of weeks earlier. She could put up with a bit of dust.

But, with a blanket, she could sleep more or less comfortably on the settee in her parlor. Yes, that would be better. She would be close if Nate needed anything and still remain within the bounds of propriety.

No sooner had she put a hand on the doorknob to leave, she heard the bedclothes behind her shift.

Susannah prayed he slept.

"You're not leaving on my account, are you?"

No such luck.

"You should be asleep," she told him.

"I've slept."

"Then sleep some more. It's only just gone past one o'clock."

"Only if you join me."

"No... I don't think that's a good idea."

"C'mon, I'm an invalid. I'm damned near helpless."

Susannah couldn't help an unladylike snort.

"Nathaniel Payne, I don't think you've been helpless a day in your life."

The sound of more rustling bed linen caused her to finally turn around. It would be just like him to get out of bed.

Fortunately, he hadn't made it that far – he'd moved only enough to sit up in bed. She saw the flash of his white teeth as he hissed in pain attempting to move his foot.

"Well, I can't sleep now, so you *have* to keep me company for a while." His reply was so near to a pout that Susannah lowered her head to hide a smile.

"*You* might be wide awake, but I need to sleep."

Her hand covered the brass doorknob that separated her room from the parlor.

"I've taken your bed."

The playfulness left his voice, the simple sentence sounding like the grumble of distant thunder.

Why did he have to make this harder than it needed to be?

"You may have it until you can stand on your own two feet – and climb those stairs."

"It's big enough for two."

"Goodnight, Nate."

"No… gah! Goddammit!"

She turned to see him struggling to get up. He knocked his hip against the nightstand and clutched the brass bedpost with both hands to haul himself upright.

She hurried to his side. To her surprise, Nate didn't say anything. Instead, he accepted her assistance to pivot around on his good foot and sit on the side of the bed. She sat alongside him.

His shoulders slumped. His head remained lowered. In all, the man looked defeated, no longer was there the luck-of-the-devil charm.

"I regret the night of our parting from that moment to this," said Nate, his voice low. "I should never have stormed out on you the way I did. I meant it when I asked you to marry me. I still do, but I don't know where I stand with you. One moment I think you believe this is just some fling, and the next I believed you might even be falling in love with me, too."

She chanced a glance at him. He offered a rueful smile and reached out, taking her hand in his.

"But I need to know, once and for all," he continued. "Here, now, while we're both calm and sober. I want you to tell me, Susannah. Be honest with me – but, more importantly, be honest with *yourself*. I'll respect your decision, whatever it is. But if your answer is no, then I can no longer stay because my feelings for you have been unchanged from the beginning."

Susannah looked away and squeezed her eyes tight but tears

SPYFALL

leaked from them anyway. She fought a hitch in her throat but forced the words out.

"I've spent too many years of my life living in fear. I thought getting away to St. Sennen would be enough distance, but where can one escape from one's own thoughts? There was many a time I wished my husband dead. I would dream of finding him dead on the floor after a fit of apoplexies or knifed in the back by one of his accomplices."

Susannah felt her hand squeezed and she returned the squeeze in full measure, grateful that, here in the darkness, Nate was her lifeline.

"And sometimes, I'd imagine wielding the knife myself. I resented Jack so much for the way he made me feel and, in the end, I hated myself as much as I hated *him*. I was impotent, useless. I wanted to fade away until I was nothing. I watched him drown in the marshes. I murdered him, Nate. In my heart I murdered my husband."

Susannah accepted Nate's arm around her. She leaned into him and breathed in the lavender and the arnica ointment she'd used to treat the bruises on his body.

"Here," she whispered, "I could be the widowed Mrs. Linwood, a woman with no past, nothing of interest, nothing to commend or condemn. I wanted to hide from myself, but I couldn't do that either. You made that impossible."

"Do you really need me to tell you what an incredible woman I believe you to be?" Nate asked, his voice barely audible.

Susannah hiccoughed a sob.

"I'm afraid I am not the woman you believe me to be."

"How about you let me be the judge of that? How about you lean on me, just as I have had to lean on you?"

She rested her head against his shoulder. Light fingers brushed her hair, comforting, soothing.

"Sometimes," Nate continued, "sometimes when things are so dark you can't see, you have to take a step forward and trust there is solid ground underfoot." He turned himself with effort to embrace her in both arms. "Call it an act of faith. Do you have faith in me, Susannah? Are you willing to trust in something you cannot see? Can you put your trust in *me*?"

She could not answer. Instead, she wept openly with deep soul-shaking sobs as though she were crying an infection out of her system as one might sweat out an illness. In the end, she was drained and her limbs felt weighted with lead.

NATE WAITED UNTIL her breathing slowed, the rhythm of it deep and steady against his chest. He began to wonder if she slept in his arms.

He ignored the incessant throb of his ankle and the weariness that seemed to be bone deep. And yet, it was enough to stroke her hair in the stillness of the night.

It still surprised him how much her rejection had wounded him.

He'd more or less parted on good terms with all the other women he'd known. *They'd* not wished for commitment, and *he'd* never offered it. Once upon a time, he couldn't imagine being tied down to a life where one day seemed very much like another.

But now, with Susannah in his arms, he wanted days upon endless days of nothing but her beside him.

He fought a yawn and acknowledged his sudden burst of movement. Even just sitting up like this had exhausted him.

She also hadn't given him an answer…

The longer she remained silent, the more certain he was she would refuse him once again. Perhaps it would be better if she went and he just went back to sleep and forgot the whole embarrassing thing as a bad dream. And as soon as he was recovered, he could go away and…

"I trust you."

The three small words she whispered gladdened him as much as if she'd said she loved him. For as dense as he was, he'd realized over the weeks of their separation that to win Susannah's love was one thing. Winning her trust was quite another.

"Then I'll find a place to sleep and you can reclaim your bed."

"Please…" she whispered. "I want to stay with you."

Nate swallowed against a lump in his throat.

"I have come to accept the fact I love you," she said, "but, in fighting with myself, I've hurt both of us. I thought I had lost you for good, but when Olivia and Lady Abigail suggested there might be hope, I prayed for your safe return. I didn't dare hope there might be anything more."

This was too much for him to take in. He was dreaming this, surely. He nodded, or at least he thought he did. His mind was adrift in utter fatigue.

He had a vague recollection of Susannah rising from the bed and encouraging him back into it. He did not resist; he no longer had the energy for it. And he was asleep as soon as his head fell into the pillow.

He found himself floating on the waves, and he welcomed the familiar feel of the sea beneath him. A hand touched his, and he was no longer alone.

Susannah stood at the wheel of the boat, directing it confidently, the bright gold rays of the morning sun illuminating her with a radiance like a goddess – like a sprite. He reached out a hand and she met him partway, twining her fingers through his, a splicing of two lives as well as two hearts and two hands.

At some point, in the hour before dawn, he woke and found her hand in his, exactly as in his dream, before he plunged deep into another, dreamless slumber.

Chapter Twenty-One

Mid-October, 1805

ADAM HARDACRE DRUMMED a restless tattoo on the table with his fingers.

"We need to go back to France."

Nate looked up from his coffee. It was a beverage he rarely partook in but its scalding black bitterness was just what he needed to wake himself more fully.

The swelling on his ankle had gone down substantially in the last two weeks thanks to Susannah and Peggy's treatments, although he had balked at the idea of a garlic and onion poultice.

"For any particular reason?" he asked.

"I want Harold Bickmore."

"The man is really worth dying for, is he?"

"Better one man than tens of thousands."

"Does Ridgeway know about your plans to be a martyr to the cause?"

The man grinned. "He does and he *wasn't* terribly happy."

"And that makes *you* happy?"

"Upsetting the boss? No. Wringing that bastard Bickmore's neck would though. Seeing him in irons on his way to a traitor's death is the next best thing."

Nate reached for his coffee once more. "Hung, drawn, and quartered?"

Hardacre's grin turned savage. "I'd gladly wield the blade myself."

"Well, you'd better have a plan, I'm best man at a wedding next week."

"I will have. You can be sure of that. But today, I'm intending on returning home and spending some time with my wife."

Nate nodded. "I know how much getting Bickmore means to you. Whatever you need is yours."

Hardacre rose from the table and clasped Nate on the shoulder but said nothing. Indeed, nothing further needed to be said.

He started to move away from the table but seemed to have a second thought. He turned back. "Join me in Truro after Clem and Peggy's wedding. You'd be welcome to bring Susannah with you, too, if you like. I know Olivia would be pleased to see her again."

Nate put on what he hoped was his most noncommittal face and gave only a nod in acknowledgement.

"Susannah and I still have a lot of things to work through," he said.

"Love is never easy is it?"

Nate shook his head.

"Well, if anyone can work things out it's you and Susannah. Sometimes you have to trust that love is enough and everything else in the world be damned. Not that there's anything you can do about the rest of the world anyway."

Nate chuffed. "Thanks."

Adam nodded and slung his satchel across his back and left by the inn's front door. From his place by the window, Nate turned to look out. He saw Adam's figure distorted through the glass as he made his way up the path to the crossroads and the mail coach direct to Truro.

His new friend's endorsement was welcome, but not so surprising considering the man himself was somewhat newly wed. It was Sir Daniel and Lady Abigail's little operation which still had him shaking his head. Deadly serious espionage on one hand and jolly families on the other. And yet, somehow it worked.

All *he* had to do was persuade Susannah to accept his proposal.

He could do that. At least, he was *sure* he could do that...

IN DEFERENCE TO the superstition of not seeing the bride a day before the wedding, the groom, his son, his best man, and a few close friends drank in The Rose and Crown in the heart of St. Sennen until Sitwell yelled for the third time that the bar was closed.

The band of a dozen wove their way through the darkened streets of the village and Clem broke into song.

The very notion of it very nearly made Nate stone cold sober. In all the years he had known the man, he had no idea he could sing – and sing so *well!*

Come live with me and be my love,
And we will all the pleasures prove
That hill and valley, dale and field,
And all the craggy mountains yield.

There we will sit upon the rocks,
And see the shepherds feed their flocks,
By shallow rivers to whose falls
Melodious birds sing madrigals.

Unable to resist, one, and then another of their band took up the song.

There I will make thee beds of roses
And a thousand fragrant posies,
A cap of flowers, and a kirtle
Embroidered all with leaves of myrtle.

Nate joined in halfheartedly. He was not a tuneful man. And after his recent experiences in France, he was also a cautious man.

A gown made of the finest wool
Which from our pretty lambs we pull;
Fair lined slippers for the cold,
With buckles of the purest gold.

Nate considered what was the worst thing that could happen to them here in the village. Probably an irate home owner dumping a chamber pot over them to silence the caterwauling. Nevertheless, he kept his eyes attuned to the shadows where, in larger ports, footpads and cutpurses lurked – sometimes in gangs – to confront the ill-prepared and inebriated.

A belt of straw and ivy buds,
With coral clasps and amber studs:
And if these pleasures may thee move,
Come live with me and be my love.

Nate shook his head in a vain attempt to sober up. He was being overcautious. This was St. Sennen for God's sake, a village of three hundred in a district of more cattle than people. And yet he saw a figure in the shadows following them.

The band of revelers thinned as they peeled off to their own homes. Now they were four.

They crossed the green to be only a block away from Clem's shop. Under the guise of stumbling, Nate bent and took a look behind him.

"That ole ankle of yours still givin' you grief?" Clem slurred.

"Yeah," he replied. He glanced behind once more. The shadow was a lot closer than it was a couple of moments before.

He got to his feet and made as if to hurry off after his companions. They stumbled into an alleyway between the two buildings that Clem and his son Sam used as a short cut to their shop in the next street. But Nate lingered in the shadows just inside the alley and waited.

The street returned to silence, apart from the purposeful steps of the man who trailed them.

Nate estimated the man's distance and counted down his footfalls until he turned into the alley.

He sprang at him, shoving him until his back collided against the stone wall.

"Why have you been following us?"

"Um... me? I'm on my way home to my bed!"

The accent was wrong for these parts despite the man's attempt to disguise it. In the shadows, he had difficulty making out the man's features. Out from under his cap hung hair gone to grey but there was nothing frail about him.

"Then you're a long way from home, my friend."

The nervous voice disappeared.

"Then let's say I'm looking for a place to stay in these parts."

"And you thought you'd follow us home and knock on the door looking for a place to sleep... or try to rob us?"

The man shrugged Nate's hands off his lapel and offered a sour grimace.

"Whatever it is you think you're after, you've picked the wrong night and the wrong man," he said. "I'm nothing to you and you're nothing to me and I'd like to keep it that way because I'm not a man you want to get on the bad side of."

Nate felt the switchblade lightly sweep across his chest in warning.

Bloody hell, he'd never even seen the knife! He brought both fists down and his right knee up to meet them, trapping the man's knife hand between them and catching his assailant by surprise. The knife clattered to the ground.

Nate followed up with a left hook across the jaw and a right fist into the man's solar plexus. He wheeled him around by the shoulder and lashed a booted foot against his arse, kicking hard.

The man tumbled out onto the street, gasping. Nate kicked his knife after him.

"A world of advice," he said. "Find another village to stay in. I don't know who the hell you are, but you're not welcome here."

The man retrieved his knife and folded the blade. He got to his feet slowly and slipped the knife back in his pocket before dusting himself off.

He glared at Nate. "Mark my words. I'll deal with you…"

He turned and began to walk away, muttering something more that alarmed Nate. For a split second, he almost went after the man to demand to know what he meant. Then better sense prevailed – Nate was still drunk, the man was armed, and the advantage of surprise was gone.

He couldn't be sure what the man had said anyway.

It sounded like "as soon as I've dealt with *her*".

AS FAR AS places to lay low went, this was not a bad one, even though it had been the devil to find – and get to – in the dark.

Robert Lawnton found the boatshed door unlocked, just as the letter said it would be. He found a flint and striker on a small stove. He lit it and coaxed the coals to life. It shed enough light to help him find a lamp.

He lit that, too.

The inside of the shed had been whitewashed, an extravagance only the wealthy would indulge themselves in. A daybed large enough for two was in the corner farthest away from the boat and its gear – a perfect location for assignations.

He grinned to himself. He was beginning to get an idea of what his mysterious benefactress was like.

And he was in no doubt it was a woman who wrote him.

The whole thing was the devil's own luck. He hadn't intended to return to the house at Lydd after learning the little bitch had sold it.

But after four months of dead-end inquiries, he returned there on a whim to find a letter written in a feminine hand waiting for him.

To his surprise, it wasn't from Susannah Moorcroft.

Lawnton,

I have come to learn that you are seeking a mutual acquaintance. I may be able to assist. Come to St. Sennen and spend one night at The Rose and Crown giving the name of McAllister. Do not ask for your quarry by name. You will only be disappointed.

You will receive a further communication from me there with instructions.

A friend.

A lifetime in society's shadows had taught him caution. Two years in Causton Prison reinforced it. So he'd thought long and hard before following the letter's instruction.

He'd pondered if it might be Susannah drawing him into a trap but, no, the stupid bitch didn't have the guile for it. All the same, it could be any of his enemies – and there were many – trying ensnare him. But the lure of Jack Moorcroft's ledger could not be ignored so he'd determined to advance with extreme care.

He had, indeed, received another communication to "McAllister" at The Rose and Crown, this time a crudely drawn map from the inn through the village to a path that would take him over the headland and down to the boatshed by the sea.

It had been a mistake to follow the drunken men from the pub, but the map was crap and the village a rabbit warren. He'd thought to let the drunks lead the way through the unfamiliar streets until one of them, obviously not as soused at the rest, clocked him.

Whoever *he* was, Lawnton planned to find the man later and make good his threat.

Mark my words. I'll deal with you as soon as I've dealt with her.

His jaw and gut still hurt from the man's blows. On top of that, he was exhausted from being so long on the road. He glanced around and found a bottle of spirits. He uncorked it and took a swig. Brandy – and good quality at that!

He grinned. There was active smuggling going on in these parts. He'd put a hefty wager on it.

He dropped his satchel and unlaced his boots. He lay down on the bed and listened to the sound of the lapping water on the wooden slipway. He speculated on the identity of the woman and the thought it might be a set-up came to him again.

This place was so isolated that a gang could jump him, slit his throat, and dump his body in the sea.

He sat himself up onto his elbows and looked about. The boathouse double doors were chained. He set one of the wooden chairs under the unlocked side door.

That would have to do until morning.

LILLIAN SURPRISED HER maid by waking early and insisting on being dressed in her walking dress. The servant was wise enough to never question her mistress' decisions or activities and was well compensated for her lack of curiosity.

"Ma'am, a reminder that Mr. Doyle expects your company in hosting a luncheon today for the meeting of the bankers' board," she said.

"Yes, yes, I haven't forgotten," she said impatiently, although she had.

Of all the impositions!

Lillian pulled herself out of bed. She slipped on a sky blue silk wrapper before sitting down at her dressing table and pulling forward a small writing box.

"Set out my rose gown and the cultured pearls that go with it.

Then I need you to run an errand. Take this note down to the boathouse."

Lillian ignored the maid's lip twitch reflected in the mirror.

"Am I to wait for a response, Ma'am?" she asked.

The question was mild and deferential, but Lillian knew better than to take it at face value. Sloan's silence was best fed from time to time, and this was one of those times.

"No – but bring out my jewelry box."

Sloan went to the wardrobe and drew out the ebony box Lillian rifled through it until she found what she had in mind – a pair of silver and amber earrings a lover had once given her as a token. She hadn't liked them at the time and had never worn them. *They* would do.

She held them up momentarily as though she was considering wearing them herself, then held them out to the maid.

"Here, let me make you a present of these."

Sloan's avaricious, little piggy eyes lit up.

"For *me*, Ma'am?"

Lillian forced a pleasant smile onto her face.

"Yes, for you. You're such a faithful servant, *Agnes*." It nearly pained her to use the girl's first name. "So faithful. And *discreet*…"

The heavy-set maid dropped a curtsy and accepted the trinkets.

Lillian wafted the lightly scented paper until the ink dried and folded it in half. Let Sloan believe it was an assignation. It wouldn't have been the first she'd covered for Lillian, and the little miss had done quite all right out of it over the years.

LAWNTON AWOKE AT dawn. He didn't like the idea of being cooped up in a shed until someone deigned to call on him. He'd had enough of confined spaces in his prison cell.

He shaved and dressed, supposing to take on the role of an eccentric rambler if anyone looked at him. He would explore the region until he knew it as well as a local.

He had plenty of experience playing whatever part was required for the job. That was the difference between himself and Jack Moorcroft.

That man had been a crafty bastard to be sure, but was more a blunt object than a clever operator. Robert Lawnton, on the other hand, had coolly walked right into the fanciest houses in London and Brighton in the guise of a vicar, a brush salesman, a rag and bone man, an itinerant scholar, a collector of subscriptions, a handyman. Once he had impersonated the long-lost son of a marquis. Mind you, *that* had only fooled a poor ignorant maid, but it had been enough to learn the layout of the house from the inside-out.

He was a master at his craft, often imitated but never beaten. Why? Because he was patient, he was thoughtful, and he was thorough.

Lawton returned from his walk and spied a stout figure making her way down a manicured path. He had avoided that one because he suspected it belonged to the big house on the headland.

Keeping his distance, he followed the woman, a lady's maid, judging by her attire, and watched as she walked right up to the side door and knocked.

Surely this was not the woman who had contacted him? There was something a little tentative about her actions that suggested not. Coming here on behalf of her mistress perhaps? Yes, much more likely.

"You'll find no one's at home," said Lawnton in his most charming voice.

The woman started and turned. And, indeed, her face was as plain as her figure suggested. That told him something about the mistress. No woman with a philandering husband would hire an attractive female as an intimate servant. And no unfaithful woman would take one either lest she turn her lovers' eyes.

The maid looked him up and down but said nothing.

"Is there a message for me?"

The woman glanced at the closed door as though she might see through it and know there was no one inside. Then she turned back to him. He kept his distance and a pleasant demeanor, lest he be considered as a threat.

"I was told to wait here and a message would be waiting," he offered.

Satisfied he was the right person, the maid held out a note. Lawnton accepted it, but before the woman could withdraw her hand, he took hold of it. Today he would play the part of a poor but deserving gentleman.

"Thank you... may I know your name?" he asked with earnestness.

"Sloan, sir."

"You must have a first name."

"Agnes, sir."

He bent over her hand in a practiced, courtly gesture, then released it – just enough to keep the woman unsettled but not arouse too much suspicion. He held the letter to his nose to breathe in the perfume.

"Tell your mistress I await her at her convenience – and thank you, Agnes."

The message duly delivered, there was one more thing the maid could do for him.

"Agnes... I... well, I don't wish to create an inconvenience, but I have a favor to ask."

Her face remained blank.

"Is there a chance you could bring back some food? Of course, I wouldn't want you to get into trouble..."

The maid sighed ever so slightly with relief, it seemed. Obviously, she had expected a task much more difficult.

Interesting...

"Of course, sir, I should be able to slip something out of the kitchen before the master's guests arrive."

"Thank you, my dear. You've been more than kind."

He offered a small, friendly wave as the woman ascended by the path again, then he looked at the note.

Stay where you are. I will come to see you as soon as I can.

The perfumed paper suggested a woman of great wealth and whose maid was well used to being a go-between for her lovers.

Lawnton tapped the paper. He'd really like to get a look inside that lady's boudoir and not the one set up in the boatshed. A decent haul of jewelry and silver would set him up in business again quite nicely. Quite nicely, indeed.

This was just the stroke of luck he'd been waiting for.

Chapter Twenty-Two

THE WARM, PLEASANT sunshine of autumn lingered the next morning. The air was crisp, but the sky was completely blue.

Susannah and Tressa were up at dawn, decorating their wagon with sprays of greenery and bunches of stock with flowerheads in pink, white, and purple. Swags of pink and green fabric decorated the cart. Even Sid sported a double row daisy chain collar, that he wore with much forbearance.

A few other ladies from the village had arrived early to help prepare the bride for her big day.

"My dear, you look a treasure," said Miss Wood.

Peggy burst into tears for the second time since rising, and Susannah nearly joined her.

Indeed, her old friend did look a treasure in her wedding gown of ivory and pink stripes worn beneath a woolen spencer in russet. It showed the highlights of red in her brown hair and brought out the warm shade of her eyes.

"Well, stop that crying or he'll wonder who the red-faced harridan is," Mrs. Baumann joked. It was just the right thing to say.

Peggy's tears became a howl of laughter instead.

Mrs. Baumann rounded up the rest of the bridal party to herd them down the stairs and into the wagon, giving Susannah and Peggy a few precious moments alone.

"Oh, Duch, I didn't believe a day like this would ever come for me," she said. "I've never been a picture, I know that. After a while you leave the idea of marriage behind. And as you're getting older, you think falling in love is something silly young people do. But now I know love can come your way, no matter what your age."

Susannah hugged her friend gently by the shoulders as not to crush her gown. "And it's well deserved," she said. "I've never seen anyone look so much in love as you and Clem. I'm delighted for the both of you. I must say, Clem has become a dear friend."

Peggy accepted Susannah's kerchief to wick away the moisture from her eyes. "And you know how quiet young Sam is?" she asked Susannah. "Well, yesterday, he welcomed me into the family and asked what he should call me after I marry his pa. Bless him, I told him that he should call me Peg and I'd be honored if he considered me a friend."

Now it was Susannah's turn to search for a kerchief to wipe the tears away from her eyes.

"Well, let's get you wed!" she announced. "Everyone is waiting downstairs. But before we leave, I have a gift for you."

Susannah picked up the box from the dressing table and opened it to reveal a little hair comb. Set above the gold teeth was a pretty enamel bluebird and, in its beak, a white rose made of mother of pearl.

"I found it in Truro. It is your 'something blue'."

Tears started to well in the middle-aged woman's eyes once more as Susannah lifted a lock of her hair and set the comb.

"There, it's perfect."

The two friends embraced.

WAITING FOR THEM outside the church were Nate and Clem's son, Sam.

Nate was dressed in a frockcoat of dark blue. Against his black hair, the color was striking. There was never any doubt in Susannah's mind that he was a handsome man, but seeing him dressed in finery she never knew he possessed made him even more arresting.

Sam looked more like an adult than a youth dressed in his Sunday best waiting to play a father's role by giving away the bride. The youth had even had a haircut which made him look more mature than his years. Sam said something to Nate which caused him to flash a smile. Susannah's heart tumbled a little with the sight of it.

As much as she tried denying it, the fact was plain. She *was* in love with Nathaniel Payne and it appeared he was sincere when he said he loved her.

For one brief instant, she could see herself as the bride with Nate waiting inside at the altar of the old Norman church as Clem did now. She mentally shook her head. This was Clem and Peggy's big day.

She turned and helped Peggy down from the wagon. Her friend squeezed her hand and leaned in.

"Perhaps mine won't be the only wedding before the end of the year," she whispered.

Dismayed her thoughts were so transparent, she was about to fashion a denial when Peggy nodded over to the actual subject of her observation – Sam, whose gaze had followed Tressa, also part of the bridal party.

"Really?" she whispered. "I hadn't noticed."

Peggy touched a finger to her nose. "A housekeeper always knows, and it's not escaped the attention of his dad either."

From inside the church, the first notes of the organ tumbled out and voices rose for the first hymn.

Miss Wood shepherded in those who tarried, leaving just four at the entrance. The bride was suddenly looking nervous. Nate stepped forward and took Peggy's hand.

"I've never seen a more radiant bride," he said.

Peggy slapped his arm. "Ooh, you saucy pirate! The cheek of flirting with a girl on her wedding day."

Nate held back a laugh and kissed the back of her hand, then presented it to Sam.

"I've never seen Da look so happy since he met you," he said. "Thank you, Peggy."

"Ooh, dash the lot of you! I shall be cross if you make me cry," she exclaimed.

The hymn came to an end, and the organ took up the processional.

Nate offered his arm to Susannah. He had a wry smile on his face. She was dying to know exactly what the look was all about, but he said nothing. He escorted Susannah down the aisle to their positions either side of where Clem waited for his bride.

"AND THE LORD God said, 'it is not good that the man should be alone; I will make him a help meet for him'."

Nate gave a sideways glance at Susannah as Reverend Johnston delivered the homily. The pink gown she wore brought warmth to her cheeks. He liked it a lot.

It was not good for man to be alone.

For a long time, he had been alone out of choice. To be married, he thought, would be an anchor dragging on the sea floor, slowing him down or even stopping his progress completely. For a long while, being alone suited him. But, more recently, Nate had begun to appreciate the true meaning of the words.

When he thought perhaps he might die in the French prison, he'd pondered who if any outside would mourn his passing. Perhaps Yvette, a little, for a short while, but what they had was just a dalliance. Certainly not Lillian. *She'd* just shrug her shoulders and move on to the next man. In truth, the only person he could think of who would miss him was Clem, as a man misses another man he has called friend.

Then it struck him clearly a few weeks ago when he awoke in Susannah's bed with her beside him while he was recovering from his latest injuries. There was something about being able to simply hold her that warmed from within.

He had never experienced anything like it before, and he wasn't quite sure what to make of it. He'd experienced overwhelming desire for a woman before and, indeed, considered himself in love once or twice in his youth, only to later learn the rush of blood went not to the head, but to another part of his anatomy.

And yet, in the early hours of that morning, he found himself profoundly grateful for the chance to just hold Susannah and watch her sleep. She had slept in her shift that night, hardly at all undressed. And while the thought of making love to her stirred his body, he knew he wanted something more from her than a bedmate.

He wanted to cherish her. He wanted to be the one who made her feel safe, and was fulfilled in the knowledge that she did with him. But more – he wanted to be the one she could turn to share her innermost dreams, desires, and fears.

He *loved* her.

And it was not just a feeling, a whim of his emotions. It seemed to him that it just *was* – a state of being like being awake or being asleep. It had no beginning and no end.

He simply *loved* her.

Their hands touched as he passed the pen to Susannah to sign the register. The awareness that flowed between them was palpable.

He couldn't wait to get Susannah alone. He needed to talk to her.

THE WEDDING BREAKFAST was under a marquee on the headland. It was an informal affair, even though it seemed all of St. Sennen was there. Tables groaned with dishes brought by everyone who attended.

A couple of villagers had brought fiddles and tin whistles, and they started a lively tune that immediately brought dancers to the fore.

Susannah surveyed the scene, feeling quite relaxed. She did not have to play hostess today. Their friends entertained themselves. She remained quite content watching Peggy and Clem be the center of attention.

Nate caught her eyes as he made his way toward her.

With just a look, he could make her blush and think of nothing but being in his arms.

When he reached her, he took her hand but, instead of bowing over it, he wound his fingers through hers and drew her close.

"You and I are going for a walk," he said.

"Are we now?" she replied, allowing a little tease to color the question.

Although they were a good decade or more younger than Clem and Peggy, neither were they inexperienced youths. He wanted her and she wanted him in equal measure.

That they had already established. Did they need more?

She allowed him to lead her away from the crowd and down toward one of the grassy hollows where eons of water had eroded away part of the rock on which they stood. Over time, earth and grass had reclaimed it. The sound of the revelers was muted here as was the sound of the ocean not so far away. At this point, the hill descended down into St. Sennen. The Pengellan River glittered like a cloth of gold between where they were and Trethowan.

Nate spread out his coat and encouraged her to sit.

"It's been just over a year since Peggy and I moved to St. Sennen," she said. "When we arrived, I thought it looked like a piece of Eden. I thought I could start over again without being judged for who my husband was. I could be part of a community and build my own reputation. I wanted nothing more. In fact, I dared not hope for more. On that alone, I could have been content for the rest of my days, until you came and turned my world upside down."

She reached out and touched Nate's arm. He seemed to realize she needed to talk so he simply kissed her hand and listened.

"I hadn't appreciated how much of myself was trapped in my past, separate from the side I showed the world. After you left, I knew I was a thief, little better than Jack was.

"I stole from you time you might have spent rebuilding a life here in St. Sennen after your ordeal in France. I drank in your attention like a plant starved of water but offered you precious little in return. And when you did me the honor of offering marriage, I stole from you the joy that should have been my truthful answer if I had not still been afraid."

She seemed to run out of breath. She breathed in and glanced Nate's way. His attention was fixed on the view ahead. The breeze ruffled his dark hair but otherwise he sat as still and motionless as the boulders strewn about these parts.

"If you had the chance to change your answer, would you?" he asked.

"Yes."

He faced her slowly. The expression on his face was difficult to read. Closed off.

Was she too late?

He nodded his understanding and slowly lowered his eyes before raising them to hers again. Susannah found her heart tripling in its beat, her breathlessness increased.

"Last time, you gave me plenty of reasons why you would not marry me," he said. "This time, let me give *you* plenty of reasons why you shouldn't marry me."

He looked back over the landscape before them but seemed to be looking within himself as he spoke. "There are things I've done that have not exactly covered me with glory. I've been unfaithful to all the women I've been with in the past. I've lied and cheated my way into trouble and had to lie and cheat to get myself out of it again.

"Yes, I *am* that unrepentant smuggler you showed such contempt for at our first meeting. Does it make a difference to your answer?"

She shook her head. "No, it does not. I see another side of you – a man who is generous, kind, brave, and loyal. You are a good man, Nathaniel. You regret your sins. You don't revel in them as my late husband did."

Nate covered her hand in both of his, brought it to his lips and held it there. His brow furrowed and head bent deep in thought.

"Then let's consider something else," he said. When he raised his head, he looked like a man going to his execution. "I've swapped a life of lying, cheating, and smuggling for that of spying – a no less desperate and morally questionable profession, and a thousand times more dangerous. I could be killed in a heartbeat and you'd never know my fate. I could be tortured by the French but released and return to you a broken, changed man.

"Let's not forget the sea. Tens of thousands of sailors have left widows and fatherless children. Have you considered you may have to raise a child on your own? Does that make a difference to you, Susannah? Do you give me a different answer even knowing, wherever the road takes us, it will not be easy?"

Susannah turned toward him and raised her chin with far more confidence, now sure in her love – and his. "No. It still does not make a difference."

"Then I shall ask you again. Susannah, will you marry me?

"Yes. The answer is yes. Without doubt or hesitation."

With her hand in one of his, Nate reached for her with his other hand, cupping the back of her head, and he kissed her. Susannah drew close to him, giving him her answer with her body as well as her words. Thorough, demanding kisses were taken and given in return, but she wanted more still. Eventually, she broke free, gasping for air and savored the way he kissed her neck and caressed her cheek.

"We're going to make it, beloved," he said. "One day at a time."

She knew the expression in his eyes and wanted nothing more

than for him to make love to her without hesitation or reservation. Instead, he got to his feet.

"Come," he said, extending a hand down to her. "We'd better return to the party before we're missed."

They walked hand-in-hand back to the gathering. Once, Susannah would have been embarrassed by such a display of affection in public, Indeed, she had not done such a thing in her entire adult life. But now she didn't care who saw her. Let them speculate on the nature of their relationship – most likely they'd be correct.

Mrs. Johnston said something to the musicians, who played a flourish to win everyone's attention.

"Now the bride and groom wish to take leave of us, but there is one more service they need to perform," she said. This was followed by a typical amount of whistles and teasing. Clem cupped his hands and answered back. Although Susannah was too far away to hear his words over the ballyhoo, the resulting laughter suggested the rejoinder was very well received.

Peggy, the radiant bride, blushed and looked ten years younger than her age. She waved over to them.

"Now, all the unmarried ladies," said Mrs. Johnston, "come to the front here. Don't be shy, you might never know your luck."

Tressa grabbed Susannah's hand as she and Nate came alongside. The girl started to pull her forward to the front of the line.

"Oh no, Tressa, I don't think it means someone like me," she said, but the girl would not be daunted. Nate released her other hand. Susannah looked back to see his grin of amusement.

Peggy waited until all spinsters had assembled – the girls too embarrassed to even look at the boys they had their hearts set on and young women who gave their beaus a significant look before joining the group. Susannah found herself in the middle.

Peggy surveyed the crowd and caught Susannah's eyes once more, giving her a wink before turning her back.

"On the count of three," said Mrs. Johnston.

Peggy raised and lowered the arm that held the bouquet in time with the count.

One – Two – THREE!

The toss was high, sailing over the heads of those who jostled toward the front. The bouquet appeared to be heading directly for Susannah – a very unsubtle sign from Peggy. Oh well, she may as well accept it in good grace. She stepped onto her back foot, ready to catch it when Tressa jumped high, intercepting the arrangement.

She squealed at her success and became the center of attention in a clutch of her friends.

Sam, who had remained on the sidelines, received a good-natured jostling from his friends and didn't appear at all dismayed.

Clem left to arrange their horse and trap. Peggy called Susannah over.

"I knew Tressa would do that. You should have got in with your elbows, Duch," she joked. "But, seriously, I've left instructions for her in the kitchen and I've written down the recipes for the week. Now, mind you and Tressa don't go altering them because they won't work..."

Susannah silenced her with a hug.

"Don't worry about us. The Queen's Head will be closed tomorrow and we can survive for the rest of the week. Nervous?"

"Yes... no..." Peggy let out an exasperated sigh. "I don't know! I've never been married before..."

Susannah kissed her friend on the cheek. "You and Clem will be blissfully happy together, I know it."

"What about you and the pirate?" Peggy whispered. "I saw you two wandering off earlier on."

She patted Peggy on the arm.

"We're working things out."

Peggy's eyes brightened speculatively.

"Then you work them out, Duch. They don't come much better than Nate."

Chapter Twenty-Three

LILLIAN PUSHED HER annoyance down as far as it could go and planted a pleasant expression on her face to entertain her husband's guests.

The sclerotic bores always set her teeth on edge, yet she put up with it to give an illusion of domestic harmony. They and their business generally occupied enough of Martin's time to leave her to her own devices, and he gave her enough money to do what she liked with it.

Lillian had to own that, in their own way, she and Martin were a formidable team. They both had their roles and played them to perfection. Furthermore, they both had their affairs and were equally willing to turn a blind eye to keep their aim on a common goal of a prosperous life. She would not put that arrangement in jeopardy.

Still, the continued presence of the bank board chaffed since she had pressing engagement of her own. The stranger, the one who was particularly keen on tracking down Susannah Linwood – beg pardon, *Mrs. Susannah Moorcroft* – awaited her.

While she flattered and charmed her husband's guests, Lillian's true attention was on her own private affairs. She was quite prepared to admit to being intrigued about why such an insipid thing as this Moorcroft woman inspired such devotion from Nathaniel Payne – and such passionate hatred in this Robert Lawnton.

Back in May, she thought to poison Nathaniel's mind against the widow by suggesting there was something more to the woman than she'd led him to believe. That was her mistake. Men were often weak for a woman with mystery, and she had fed into it.

She might have just left it, if not for poking through her husband's magisterial documents and discovering the name Susannah went by was not her legal name. She'd chanced upon a letter from the woman's solicitor in Kent and was pleasantly surprised by his indiscreet revelation that someone else was looking for her, too.

A series of carefully worded advertisements in newspapers around Kent eventually bore fruit.

This Lawnton man claimed Linwood had something from her late husband that belonged to him. He was most keen to have it returned.

Well, he *should* have it, should he not?

And so, if she could not destroy Nate's interest in Susannah, perhaps she would simply have to ruin the woman's reputation.

With a smear on her name, she would lose her license to serve alcohol. The Queen's Head would require a new publican. And, with a word in the right ears and the hand-picked selection of a more "suitable" person for the role, there could be a further fine profit in it for her and Martin to share.

AFTER THEIR GUESTS had departed, Martin Doyle kissed his wife on the cheek. "That was a fine luncheon, my dear, thank you."

Lillian caressed his chin. Martin responded with a fulsome kiss into the palm of her other hand.

"If you will excuse me, I wish to take some air. I will take a walk down to the boathouse."

Martin raised an eyebrow. "Anyone I know?" he asked with only the mildest of interest.

"No dear, no one of importance."

THE INTERMINABLE LUNCHEON meant it wasn't until two o'clock before she could meet her "guest". She did not bother to change from her fine day gown nor remove the pearls that went with it. The meeting should not take long.

Once she pointed Lawnton in the right direction, she could watch events unfold without anyone being the wiser as to her involvement.

The boathouse door was ajar when Lillian entered. On the round wooden table were the remains of a repast. Whoever Robert Lawnton was, he hadn't wasted time making himself at home.

Behind her, the door slammed shut. She swiftly turned to find a large man barring her way. Lillian looked him up and down. He was a big man, indeed, with a not unpleasant face to look at. He was in his late-forties, she guessed, still strong enough to be virile, but the years were beginning to show.

"Lawnton, I presume," she said, with all the imperiousness of her status.

The man twisted a smile and bowed.

"My lady, I fear you have the advantage of me."

She returned the same kind of smile. "How come I find that hard to believe?"

"Does the lady wish to remain *incognito*?"

Lillian shrugged.

"I see no harm in telling you who I am. In this desperate little pocket of the world, my identity wouldn't be difficult to guess. I am Lillian Doyle, wife of the local magistrate, and I happen to be in a position to do you a good service."

"So you said in your letter."

"I know where Susannah Moorcroft is."

The man's expression sharpened and, indeed, hardened.

"She goes by the name of Susannah Linwood and, if you can believe it, she's the publican of The Queen's Head outside the village. She's ingratiated herself quite snugly in St. Sennen society."

"And I assume that's a problem for you."

"A *minor* one I trust you'll rectify for me."

"Why, Madam," he said with exaggerated politeness, "I only wish her to return something of mine that I value."

Lillian laughed.

"A man does not spend two years in prison and not dream about the day he is released and the revenge he intends to exact," she said, quietly satisfied by the briefest flicker across his face of shock at her knowledge of his recently completed imprisonment. "No, I think I know your type, Lawnton, and I don't believe I'm mistaken at the level of mutual antipathy we have for this woman."

SUSANNAH UNLOCKED THE front door to The Queen's Head, struck by the silence. She stepped inside and closed her eyes, recalling what it was like when she first inspected the place more than a year ago.

It hadn't looked like much, but she knew it to be solid. Nothing a little love and attention couldn't fix.

A bit like her, really.

She smiled to herself and closed her eyes to remember.

The windows had been nearly opaque with smoke and grime, floorboards in need of a serious scrub and a coat of varnish, the walls long overdue for a good scraping down and repaint.

When she opened her eyes, she saw what she and Peggy had accomplished. Whitewashed walls, plenty of light through clear windows, solid tables clean until they shone.

She heard Nate enter. He placed two hands on her shoulders and kissed her neck.

"What were you thinking?" he whispered against her ear. She sighed and leaned back into him.

"About how far I've come," she said. She closed her eyes as he kissed her ear.

"You have every right to be proud of this place," he answered as he continued to kiss her neck and further down to her shoulder.

She lifted her arms up and back until her hands reached the back of Nate's head and she savored the luxurious feel of his hair in her fingers.

Nate's hands left her shoulders. The flats of his hands rubbed up and down the sides of her torso from the sides of her breasts down to her hips, and back up and across until his palms cupped her breasts fully.

She surrendered to the sensation, a restless yearning of desire she could no longer ignore.

Surrendered but liberated, free to enjoy Nate's touch, knowing that she was safe, cherished, *desired*.

"Make love to me," she breathed.

"Whatever the lady wishes..." Nate's voice rumbled, sending a line of gooseflesh down her arms and then her legs. She could not hold back the sigh.

She picked up the mischievous note in his voice. She turned in his arms and pressed herself against him. Oh, how she wanted him and, judging what she could feel pressed against her, he was equally ready.

She felt like a virgin bride, newly awakened to sensual pleasures. There was no "before", there was only now. There was only this man.

Once again, she reached up to touch him, his face, his lips, the jet black hair so thick between her fingers. She expected him to kiss her again, but he didn't. It was hard to tell what he was thinking beneath those hooded eyes.

But they never left hers as he scooped her into his arms.

Nate used his foot to swing the door to her private quarters open wide and strode through the parlor and into her bedroom. She thought he might lay her on the bed and, in truth, that was what she wanted – that he would take control while she was carried away on the tide of passion.

Instead, he lowered her gently to her feet beside the bed and looked at her intently.

"Don't close your eyes," he said. "I want you to see *me*. When I touch you, I want you to know it's me who holds you. New memories, Susannah – lasting memories for both of us. There is no space for past memories or regrets between us."

To say anything would force her to conquer the lump in her throat and she would not allow there to be any misunderstandings. She decided words were not needed.

She removed her pelisse and laid it over the bed then reached behind to undo the buttons at the back of her pink gown before pulling it up over her head. Layer by layer, she removed her garments in an unhurried manner, but not with a courtesan's coquetry – rather a deliberate, matter-of-fact undressing until she stood before him naked wearing nothing but stockings in deference to the chill in the air.

As he had asked, she had kept her eyes on him and, although she was the one now naked while he was fully dressed, he seemed more nervous than she. His eyes flickered over her body and any shyness or unease she felt being so exposed was conquered by what she saw in his eyes. There *was* lust there, to be sure, but it was leavened by tenderness.

He took half a step toward her and stopped when she shuddered, but he rightly apprehended the cause of it.

He reached past her to pull back the covers.

"Get into bed, my love," he said. "I'll set a fire."

She did so and drew the covers up to her shoulders. The touch of chilled sheets on her skin heightened her awareness of her body, the weight of the blankets covered her body like a caress. She rolled onto her side and watched him at the grate, raking aside the ashes of the morning's fire and arranging fresh kindling and coal. He had removed his blue coat and the cream shirt he wore stretched tight against his shoulders as he lit a spill of paper and applied it to the kindling.

As though aware she watched, he glanced back toward her and smiled just as the life blew into the makings of the fire. The little flickering flames of the kindling brought light as well as warmth.

Nate set a couple of lamps but, instead of wicking them low, he kept the flame high, filling the room with light.

A rush of heat surged through her veins as she realized why. He intended to make love to her in the light.

He began to slowly undress. Every item of clothing that was removed revealed something more of him, faint scars here and there on his arms, the patch of hair on his chest, the strong muscular legs and buttocks as he removed his breeches and underclothes.

Then he stood to face her.

Oh my!

The evidence of his arousal before her was impressive, and Susannah couldn't help the flush to her cheeks.

He climbed into the bed beside her. She gravitated to his warmth. He kissed her lips slowly with deliberate intent.

"Touch me, beloved," he said. "You trust me with your body, I trust you with mine."

So, this was a man in his prime, powerful and strong. Susannah touched him tentatively at first, watching reactions play across his face, growing more confident as his expression was laid bare. He was making himself vulnerable to her. To know how to pleasure him would also be to know how to harm him.

Her breasts brushed across the hair on his chest and they let out a moan together which mingled in a joint kiss. She was ready. More than ready for him, but he didn't seem inclined to move from his present prone position.

Despite having been married for seven years, she knew now how little experience she had, especially with a man who refused to be hurried, as though her pleasure mattered as much as his own.

Caress met caress. Light touches at first but increasing in urgency as her need for him grew.

"Join with me," she breathed.

"Not yet."

His hand fell from her breast and searched lower to find that place between her legs. He circled her sensitive flesh with his thumb over and over, bringing with it a rising tide of arousal. She was helpless against the surge of it. She threw her head back and cried out in pleasure.

Never had she expected to be overwhelmed by a feeling so powerful.

Nate touched her cheek.

"*Meurgerys... beloved...* open your eyes... look at me."

Susannah did and saw tension in jaw and in his eyes as he held himself back, waiting for her reaction.

"Oh my!"

He chuckled. "A man likes to hear that he's doing something right."

She rolled until they lay face-to-face. He drew her leg over his. She could feel his hardness rubbing against her most sensitive skin. It was a tease, a hint of more pleasure to come.

He entered her slowly, achingly slow until she squeezed him with her inner muscles. He closed his eyes and hissed as though burned. She encouraged him with words as he moved within her, terms of endearment, nonsensical words as her pleasure built once more.

NATE AWOKE FROM a light doze, listening to the comforting crackling of the fire. His still healing ankle ached but, in all, he was a very satisfied man. His fingers played with strands of Susannah's warm brown hair now loose from their confines.

His contentment was soul-deep, as though at last he had found his true home in the arms of this woman who owned his heart. He turned to look at her. Her eyes were closed but she was wearing a very contented smile.

"I want us to be wed soon as possible," he said.

She opened her eyes; they shone a sapphire blue.

"A Christmas wedding? I like the sound of that."

"I'll be leaving for France with Adam next week and I'd rather you weren't here on your own. Come with me to Truro. Stay with Lady Abigail or with Olivia. At least you'll have some company with someone who understands."

She kissed him. "I won't be on my own. St. Sennen is my home. How much safer could I possibly be than surrounded by all our friends here at The Queen's Head? Peggy will be back every day and Tressa will be living here in Peggy's old room. In the meantime, I'm perfectly capable of locking the doors after the last drinker has gone. If it will make you feel better, I'll ask Sam to stay with me. I'm sure he'll be happy to give Clem and Peggy the house to themselves, and he'll get to see Tressa every day. And besides, I'll have Prince with me."

"He isn't the world's best guard dog, you know."

She smiled in acknowledgement of Prince's failings. "When are you leaving for Truro?"

"Next week."

"Peggy will be back by then. I'll come with you and stay for a few days. There are papers I need from my solicitor… my hus… *Jack's* death certificate. Reverend Johnston will need to see it before he'll issue the banns."

The thought came belatedly to Nate. "St. Sennen will learn your married name."

She smiled and touched his cheek.

"It truly doesn't matter anymore. It's only our future that is of consequence."

He kissed her again, lavishing kisses around her ear, and he witnessed the delicious shivers down her limbs.

"I can't seem to get enough of you, beloved."

Chapter Twenty-Four

Charteris House
Truro

S USANNAH LOOKED AROUND the display of brass lanterns, coils of rope, and lengths of chain as seconds ticked away on the wall of clocks. The place seemed deserted.

"Are you sure we're expected?" she asked Nate.

He winked and walked behind the counter. He reached behind a loosely hung map on the wall and a door-sized panel in the wall hinged outward. He held out his hand to her. She drew near and looked up the stairs, then back at him questioningly.

He nodded. She shrugged and preceded him up the stairs.

The funny little shopkeeper with the thick spectacles and another man were hunched over drafting tables, the little man's face a scant three inches from the paper. But it was the older man at the desk that caught her attention. He was dressed expensively but not foppishly. A gold stick pin studded with a cabochon ruby in his white cravat and a broad gold band on his left ring finger were the only obvious displays of wealth.

He rose from his desk on seeing them. Susannah immediately bobbed a curtsy, intimidated by the presence the man exuded.

"Susannah, this is Sir Daniel Ridgeway. Sir Daniel, I have the honor of presenting you with Susannah Linwood... my *fiancée*." There was a particular satisfaction in saying that and not a small amount of pride in watching the peer's face become animated.

"Your fiancée!" The man now bowed to her. "My dear, a pleasure to meet you. Nate has spoken of you often, and my wife, Abigail, was singularly pleased to make your acquaintance a few weeks ago."

Susannah dropped another curtsy. "I'm honored to make your acquaintance, sir. Your wife has been very kind to me."

The sunlines around Sir Daniel's eyes deepened as he smiled. "My wife has a particular interest in creating a rather unique society. I'm glad you elected to join us, Mrs. Linwood."

"Please, call me Susannah."

Sir Daniel acknowledged the invitation with an incline to his head before reaching forward to shake Nate's hand.

"I'm glad you got everything sorted out between you two."

"Yes, you were becoming a right pain about it, too," said the shop-keeper, looking up from his desk with a smirk. "A Payne who's a pain…"

Nate bared his teeth and the little man laughed. "And, Susannah, *this*," said Nate, gesturing to the man, "is Mr. Bassett. He's a forger."

"A recreator of documents and *sourcer* of equipage, if you don't mind, Mr. Payne," Bassett responded. He approached Susannah and took her hand in both of his. "A delight to make your acquaintance Mrs. Linwood. You are far more than this man deserves."

Bassett turned back to Nate with a mischievous twinkle in his eyes. After a moment, he held out his hand to him. "In truth, much happiness to you both."

"Well, being in this room means you are part of The King's Rogues inner circle, so I must swear you to absolute secrecy," said Sir Daniel.

"I'm afraid it's too late, Daniel."

Everyone turned to the new voice in the room. Lady Abigail had appeared at the top of the stairs and paused in the doorway. "Susannah here has already been inducted into *my* league."

The man tilted his head; a smile played about his lips. "Ah, it's a *league*, not a society. Oh well, I know when I am defeated by a superior force."

Lady Abigail raised her eyebrows in triumph. She entered the room bringing with her an entourage, Adam and Olivia Hardacre.

"And did I overhear correctly?" Olivia said to Susannah. "You're engaged?"

Susannah nodded, accepted the fulsome congratulations of the Hardacres as well.

Sir Daniel cleared his throat loudly. "As much as I hate to bring this party to an end," he announced, "this is still a place of business and we have work to do if we're going to make another run into France."

Adam Hardacre's face hardened. "Two weeks is all I need, Daniel."

"Then I shall leave you and take the ladies with me," announced Lady Abigail, putting a hand on Susannah's and Olivia's backs. "We have work of our own to occupy us for the next little while. We expect to see you gentlemen home for supper."

After Lady Abigail shepherded her down to the shop floor, Susannah took one more glance back up at the stairs.

"Don't you worry about what they're doing up there," said Lady Abigail. "I'm going to keep you busy enough that you won't have time to miss them. There are a few things we need to do ourselves."

She led the way across the street to the White Hart Inn where they were ushered upstairs to a private dining salon.

Lady Abigail sat at the head of the table and ordered a light repast and a bottle of sweet sherry, then spoke of little of consequence until after the maid who served them departed.

The only thing which so far distinguished this from a social occasion was the unexpected addition of a blotter and an expensive oak writing case on the dining table.

Susannah struggled to find the same nonchalance as her host, so she looked to Olivia for a cue.

ELIZABETH ELLEN CARTER

Adam's wife seemed to exude serenity, but there was an alertness in her manner, a nervous anticipation that was contagious. Susannah fidgeted with her fingers.

Lady Abigail set her glass down at last and leaned back in her chair.

"Tell me about St. Sennen, Susannah – who can be relied upon, who should be avoided. I try to make it a habit to know all the influential people around Cornwall, but I have to confess I'd never before considered St. Sennen as anything but a rural backwater. Who is magistrate of the area? I have a vague recollection that he's some officious little potentate..."

The unexpected description broke the tension. Susannah laughed.

"I suppose that *does* sum up Martin Doyle. I suspect he is little more than a corrupt petty bureaucrat, but he signs my liquor license and I pay him the quarterly taxes. He has caused me no bother. It's his wife you have to watch out for. Lillian Doyle is a sneaky, dangerous, conniving, unfaithful—"

"Oh, my! I like her already," Lady Abigail interrupted. "What is it about her that suggests she's dangerous? From your description, I assume she's had her claws in Nathaniel sometime in the past. Oh, don't look so surprised, dear. Is there anything you know of that she has over Nathaniel that could compromise us? Or over *you*, for that matter."

Susannah told her what she knew. "She and her husband engaged him as a smuggler. Nate believes Doyle became jealous of Lillian's affair and arranged to have him arrested in France to teach him a lesson."

Olivia looked momentarily shocked by the revelation but recovered quickly. Lady Abigail, on the other hand, took in the information with equanimity.

"There's another thing I need to ask," she said. "Are you aware of any of your late husband's former associates? I've had my agents glean everything on the records, and I've read the coroner's verdict on

Moorcroft's death, but I need to know what is *not* on record."

Susannah blinked rapidly. Lady Abigail had said she knew all about Jack but the bald-faced manner in which she detailed her inquiries shocked her. Her stomach plummeted for a moment as the past disappeared in an instant. Once again, she was the panicked young woman who stood back and watched her husband drown without making the least effort to save him. Did Lady Abigail know even *that*?

She didn't realize she was trembling until she felt the touch of Olivia's hand on hers. Susannah turned to find not censure, but understanding.

"You're safe here with us," she whispered.

"But you won't find pity," Lady Abigail added. "Not from me at any rate."

Susannah noticed Olivia tried to hide a wince at the older woman's harsh words, but nonetheless she nodded.

"There is nothing you've done – or failed to do – that makes a difference to us. There's nothing to be afraid of. We are all sisters-in-arms now."

Susannah picked up her sherry glass to wet her lips. The honey-colored liquid trembled in the glass.

"From time to time, I met several of my husband's associates, but I only knew the name of one man. Robert Lawnton."

Abigail pulled out a piece of paper from the writing box, primed a pen, and wrote down the name.

"He led the search party for Jack and was at the funeral. I expected him to show up at the inquest but he didn't. I spent a year and a half waiting for him to come back, but I never saw him again. I *didn't* want to see him again. So, when the opportunity came to start over with a new life and a new name, I took it."

"And there's been nothing more since?" Olivia asked.

Susannah started to shake her head and then stopped. There was no use denying it. "Six weeks ago, I received a letter from him."

The older woman frowned.

"Rather, my former solicitor received a letter forwarded on by the owners of the old house. He forwarded it on to my current solicitor."

"And what did he say in the letter?"

She sighed. "He wanted to know about some property of Jack's that I had."

"Had?"

"I burned it. It was a ledger. Of stolen goods, I think."

Lady Abigail tutted. "A pity. Never, ever burn something that might come in handy down the road, Susannah. Anything someone wants badly enough to spend years looking for could be useful for – how shall I put it delicately? – oh yes, for *leverage* should the need arise.

"Do you think this Lawnton fellow knows where you are?"

"No, I don't think so. He wouldn't look for me under the name of Linwood. I have no family connection to St. Sennen at all. I can't imagine how he could possibly find out."

The woman looked thoughtful. "I suppose it would be too much to hope he put his address on the letter?" Susannah shook her head. "No matter. Write down everything you can remember about the man. I'll have some of my people run him down and I suspect we can make sure he won't bother you again.

"Now, we'll continue with some immediately pressing matters. I need to ask you again, Susannah, about your willingness for us to make use of The Queen's Head."

"Why is it so important?"

This time Olivia answered. "I don't know if Nate told you the particulars about his and Adam's excursion into France."

Susannah shook her head. They'd been too caught up in Peggy and Clem's wedding and their own reunion to talk *business*.

"They rescued two of our agents who brought back a trove of information," Lady Abigail continued. "We know there is more than one plan to invade England, but we don't know how many of these plots have merit. That's the job of The King's Rogues to find out. What our men brought back suggests a major campaign is being prepared in Ireland."

"A *campaign*? You mean an *invasion*?"

Lady Abigail leaned forward. "We don't know. A suspect ship called the *Stockport* was captured two nights ago off the Scilly Islands departing from Cork. The men onboard started dumping papers overboard so we don't know what's lost, but what was retrieved was a mountain of information in French."

"I'm waiting for them to arrive," said Olivia. "Of course, a lot of it could be in coded language or is so oblique we won't know what might be of use and what is not."

Lady Abigail continued. "Daniel has not had a chance to interrogate the men but he is... we are *all* certain... that with the right incentive, they will furnish us with what we need to know. He's waiting for a report from the captain of the *Stockport*."

Olivia drew the conversation back to Susannah's original question. "From what Adam has said, The Queen's Head is a perfect launching place for a covert trip. It has direct access to the Irish Sea, and it's quiet but not too far from major roads. Sir Daniel spoke about establishing temporary semaphore stations along that stretch of coast as well."

Susannah shook her head. *This was the most remarkable thing she had ever heard in her life!*

She noticed Olivia glancing at Abigail who regarded her with a mild frown. *Oh – they thought she was refusing when she shook her head?*

"Of course...yes," said Susannah, her voice growing in strength. "Whatever I can do I will, it's just that... well, I've never had this type of conversation before. And the idea of having it with other ladies is, well, incredible."

Lady Abigail let out a bright laugh.

"Oh, I can assure you, Susannah, I'm more than capable of discussing the latest *on dits* with the rest of society and agonizing over the newest fashion silhouettes," she said. "And, as it happens, since there is little more we can do in the meantime, I suggest that we go shopping for a trousseau for our bride to be."

Susannah shook her head once again. This time she meant it. "I assure you that's most unnecessary."

"Nonsense!"

"I... I'm not a first-time bride."

Abigail flicked her hand dismissively.

"I shouldn't count the first one at all since the man was such a villain. No, this is a new life for you and Nate. You should start as you mean to go on. I'll introduce you to my dressmaker. You wouldn't think such a talented seamstress would be found this far away from Bath or London, but the number of supremely talented emigres in all corners of the country has been quite the find."

"I have a dress I ordered from a dressmaker in Truro."

"The one on the corner of Lemon and Fairmontle Streets?"

Susannah nodded.

"The very one! You have excellent taste, indeed, and I'm sure Madam Lefanu will be only too delighted for a further commission."

NATE WATCHED ADAM Hardacre erupt like a barrel of gunpowder.

"What do you mean we're not going back to France?" he yelled.

"At ease, Hardacre!" Sir Daniel commanded. "The *Stockport's* capture takes precedence, especially when you take a look at the names of those apprehended."

He picked up a piece of paper from his desk and handed it to Adam. Nate leaned over his shoulder to read it for himself.

When Sir Daniel next spoke, his voice was calm. "I received a coded signal about an hour ago that said one of the men captured may be Harold Bickmore."

Nate watched his friend's reaction, grim and determined as he read over the document.

"I'll leave immediately, sir."

"You'll do no such thing. The weather is set to turn bad, you told me that yourself only this morning. You have a wife to go home to. Don't be in such a hurry that you forget what's important. Those men aren't going anywhere, not until the weather clears."

"We can sail to Old Grimsby in a couple of days' time," Nate assured him. "If we're away at first light and you can get your old chum to talk quickly, we'll be back in time for supper. What do you say?"

Adam nodded, his temper barely under control. He turned on his heel and rapidly descended the stairs. Nate went to follow after him but was stopped.

"Let him go," instructed Sir Daniel. "He'll calm down once he's had a chance to think it through. But watch him when he gets to Old Grimsby. I want to have you as an eyewitness in case Bickmore pulls some stunt."

Chapter Twenty-Five

Old Grimsby
Scilly Islands

NATE FOLLOWED ADAM into the commander's room. Weary from a rough sea crossing, he was happy to be a silent spectator. Yet he forced his focus to the task and observed the man in front of him.

Even though Nate had seen Harold Bickmore twice before, this was the first time he'd had a chance to study the man up close. He had light brown hair and youthful good looks which, no doubt, went over well with the ladies.

On their arrival, Nate detected a malevolent look that quickly disappeared behind a mask of affable indifference. It would be a mistake to underestimate their prisoner.

Previous attempts to draw Adam out on the matter of his one-time friend had proven fruitless. Nate tried to imagine someone as resolute as Adam Hardacre being subordinate to a little prig like Bickmore.

He still couldn't imagine it.

Bickmore sat on a wooden chair, shackled arm and foot, but with an audience to play to, the former lieutenant did not look like a man who risked being hanged for treason. He wore a faint expression of amusement across his face, designed no doubt to irritate his interrogator.

A glance to Adam reassured Nate that his friend wasn't fooled by the charade.

"Ah, I was wondering if they'd bring you over to have a chat with me," said Bickmore in a tone that seemed genuinely friendly.

That was a surprise.

Adam Hardacre adopted the same tone of voice. "Did you think I'd pass up the opportunity, Harold? We didn't get a chance to finish our conversation last time."

Bickmore leaned forward with an earnest expression "How are my two other friends? It was two, wasn't it?"

"Much safer with us than with you, to be sure. Anyway, I'm the one who's supposed to be asking questions."

"Well, now," Harold leaned back in his chair holding up his manacled hands. "I'm your captive audience... ask away. Although I can't guarantee you answers."

"Then let's start with something easy. Are you The Collector?"

Bickmore frowned. Nate concluded the man was genuinely confused by what also sounded to Nate to be an odd question before realization dawned on the man's face.

"Oh – *The Collector*. Wilkinson hated that name, you know. He thought all the code names were ridiculous, but I thought they were rather fun. So, to answer your question, yes, I am The Collector."

"And what precisely were you collecting?"

"Oh, come on, that question is beneath you, Adam. You know *exactly* what I was collecting."

Adam remained silent for a long time, so much so that Bickmore acknowledged Nate for the first time.

"We've met before, haven't we?"

"*Votre Français n'est pas mauvais, mais ce n'est pas la langue des gens.*"
Your French isn't bad, but it's not the language of the people.

"What do you know of the 'language of the people'?" Bickmore responded in his formal, mannered French.

Nate continued in French: "I was there at Fort St. Pierre. I know who you took away."

Bickmore stared at him, more curious than worried.

"Speak English, both of you," Adam demanded.

"We were just renewing old acquaintances, that was all," said Nate.

The interrogation of Bickmore continued. In English.

"What was so important about me that you were planning to take me to France?" Adam demanded.

"Originally, you were supposed to have gone willingly, remember? You signed up to *The Society for Public Reform* on your own. You were going to be our Perkin Warbeck after the war was over and return to England to reclaim your place. Not King of England obviously, but a man the rank and file would follow to overthrow the last of the aristocrats in the highest ranks."

Hardacre barked out a laugh. "I happen to remember my English history. Warbeck died a traitor's death."

Bickmore shrugged, unconcerned.

"You played your part well. I have to admit. I... *we*... all thought you were quite filled with revolutionary zeal."

"And seven men are dead because of it."

Bickmore looked up, lips pursed, appearing to count the number in his head.

"Six," he said at last. "You can't lay the seventh on me. Your sweet governess did in Peter Fitzgerald all on her own from what I hear. Whoever you're working for has done quite the job in covering *that* death up."

Nate made sure he watched both men but he kept an eye on Adam. The only reaction he showed to the mention of Olivia was a clench of his fist which made the crossed anchor tattoo on his hand stand out starkly against his skin.

"Credit where it's due, old man – you genuinely had me fooled," Bickmore continued. "Even that bull-headed oaf Dunbar saw right through you, but I was completely convinced, even when I saw Miss

Olivia outside that strange little chandlery in Truro. It never occurred to me to wonder whose side you were on."

"Why involve her?"

"I put on the show to test you, and to show Wilkinson my judgement was right. I included her because she was getting too curious. If she had started planting doubts in your head, it was going to make our job harder. I knew she was fond of you and you fond of her, so it was going to be a little added insurance to ensure your cooperation."

Nate saw Adam's jaw clench tight. He was fighting his fury.

"Cooperation for *what*?"

Here, Bickmore seemed transformed, energized, animated. He stretched out his arms as wide as his chains would let him. He held their attention like a carnival barker, clearly reveling in having an audience.

"The biggest, most audacious military conquest the world has ever known. By the time we're through, Napoleon will weep like Alexander because there are no more worlds left to conquer."

Hardacre barely stifled an obvious yawn, not above employing a bit of theatre of his own, it would seem.

"And that would be?" he asked, sounding bored with the whole thing.

Bickmore shook his head.

"I can't say. I mean I literally have no more answers to give you. Torture me if you like. I can't tell you what I don't know. What the Emperor has planned is too big for any one man to be trusted with all of the details. I was simply tasked to bring together a group of specialists prepared to betray King and Country and usher in a new Europe, without borders, united under one flag."

"Considering you're in chains facing the noose, has it been worth it, so far?" Nate asked.

"*C'est le guerre*," Bickmore shrugged.

"Tell us what you were doing in Ireland," Adam ordered, changing the subject.

Bickmore shook his head.

"No more questions tonight. Any chance to getting these off me?" He rattled the chains on his arms and legs. "Shouldn't I be treated like an officer in His Majesty's Navy?"

Hardacre shook his head in refusal. "You resigned your commission – something *else* you failed to tell me."

"You never told me you'd turned Agent of the Crown either, so call us even."

"I'll tell your corpse when I *spit* on it on the gibbet." Adam turned to Nate. "Come on, let's get out of here, the stench is becoming intolerable."

"Wait, I have some questions of my own first," said Nate. Adam shrugged. He leaned against the wall and waited.

"The men you were with at Fort St. Pierre. You took away three officers from the *HMS Starbeck*. Where are they?"

"I'm afraid two are detained at the pleasure of the Emperor," said Bickmore. "Hopefully in more convivial surroundings, at least the captain is. One of the lieutenants was killed when a partisan force attacked the detachment that was taking them to Paris. We believe the attempt to liberate them was part of a sabotage campaign you and your little group might know something about."

"Guard!" Adam pounded on the door. "We're finished in here."

He stormed out as soon as the door opened. Nate followed. He gave Bickmore one last look before the guard closed the door and locked it.

"We're not going to get any more out of him," said Adam as soon as Nate caught up with him in the corridor.

"He didn't answer your question about Ireland."

Hardacre didn't slow his pace. "And he's not going to. The best thing we can do is send him to London to put him on trial. If he knows anything, he might use it to plead for his miserable hide, though I doubt it."

Nate shrugged. "Torture may be quicker... *and* more satisfying."

"The man is a fanatic. He'd rather die first."

Nate surged forward and opened the door to the outbuilding, leading the way out into the bitter November night.

"Let's hope Lady Abigail and your Olivia have made more headway with the documents they've retrieved," he said. "Although what we're going to do if they're in code is another thing altogether."

For the first time this evening, Adam returned to his usual even temper. "Olivia's good at ciphers, but Sir Daniel is a truly talented codebreaker. He read mathematics at Cambridge in his younger years, apparently. If anyone can make sense of this then he will be able to."

THE EARLY NOVEMBER market day at St. Sennen was one of the largest of the year. Winter brought uncertain weather and the wisest were stocking up.

Susannah stopped in the middle of a conversation with Peggy and Clem, dropping the bottle of preserves she had in her hand. It landed on the table unbroken and remained sealed, but it toppled and rolled toward a pyramid of jars like a ball toward nine-pins.

She shook her head to clear it and stopped the bottle rolling before it could do damage to the display.

Her friend frowned. "You look pale. Are you all right?"

"I thought I saw someone I recognized, that's all."

"You mean there's someone around these parts you don't know?" Clem teased.

"I suppose you're right." A rueful smile emerged.

"Who was it you thought you saw?" asked Peggy.

Susannah shook her head. "I'm sure it was no one."

Surely it couldn't have been *him*. But it certainly did look like him.

She waited until Clem was in conversation with a couple of men before tapping Peggy on the shoulder and drawing her to the back of their stall.

"What's up, Duch?"

"I thought I saw someone who looked like Robert Lawnton."

The older woman's eyes opened wide, but she didn't say anything for a moment.

"Tressa," she called. "Mind the stall will you, luv? I'm just going to have a chat with Mrs. Linwood."

Peggy steered her away from the crowd to a quiet corner of the green.

"Where did you see him?"

"The other side of the green."

Peggy glanced over there. "Are you sure?"

"No, I'm not sure, that's why I need you to keep your eyes open."

"All right, I will. But what do we do if we see him?"

Susannah fiddled with the ring on her finger, turning it round and round.

It seemed strange to be wearing another one but it was different. It was not the plain, thin gold wedding band from her marriage to Jack, but rather an engagement token from Nate, a ring with nine aquamarines as bright as the summer sky set flat into a gold band.

He presented it to her before he left for the Scilly Islands with Adam. But now her new ring had fallen subject to an old anxious habit.

"I don't know," Susannah confessed. "Make sure you stay close to Clem. Sam will be accompanying Tressa and I home today anyway. If it *is* Lawnton, then we'll deal with him when the time comes."

Peggy's lips thinned. "I'll tell Clem that we'll stay at the inn for a few days."

"You'll do no such thing! I won't have everything upset over a panic about nothing."

"Well it was *you* who said you saw him," Peggy retorted.

"I said I thought I saw someone who *looked* like him. It's been more than two years; how can I be sure of anything?"

"All right, I'll have a good look around. So, what if I don't spot him?"

Susannah shrugged her shoulders "Then it means I'm jumping at shadows, and I'm missing Nate."

"Are you sure?"

Susannah nodded and looked sheepish. "Thank you for looking out for me."

"I'll always be here for you, Duch, you know that."

"WHAT ARE *YOU* still doing here?"

Lawnton opened his eyes and looked at Lillian Doyle balefully.

"You know where Susannah Moorcroft is. Now leave."

The man sat up on the daybed and eyed his "benefactress" with faint amusement.

"Now, how can I leave before I've gotten what she's stolen from me?"

The woman was unconvinced. "You could *ask* her for it. She's supposed to be a very honest person."

Lawnton surged to his feet as quick as his temper. "Honest? Luring her husband to his death in the marsh and watching him drown?"

"*What?*"

Lawnton calmed himself. He was almost amused by the look of shock on the woman's face. The practiced neutral mask which gave the illusion of someone who had only just passed the prime of youth had slipped. In her, he felt a kindred spirit.

"Oh, yes," Lawnton continued, "That one's a cold-hearted bitch if there ever was one, to be sure. She claimed she hadn't seen Jack all evening and only grew concerned in the morning. But I know for a fact she was out there on the marshes that evening and right where her husband died. I fully intend to make her pay. She owes me."

Lillian Doyle wrapped her cloak around herself in an imperious fashion and raised her chin. She nodded toward the door.

"Get out of here."

Lawnton stepped forward in an instant and gripped the woman's arms tightly. He shook her and the shock on her face pleased him.

"*You* don't understand me, woman," he snarled, leaning in. "I need until Sunday when the inn's closed 'til late afternoon."

Lawnton shoved her away from him. To his chagrin, the woman recovered herself far more quickly than he anticipated. The look she gave him now was one of utter contempt.

In that moment, he knew he had underestimated her.

Lillian Doyle brushed down her sleeves and peered down her nose at him.

"You'll have until the end of this coming Sunday. On Monday, I'll be down with all the footmen and your body will wash up at Land's End. *Never* threaten me again."

She slammed the door behind her. The swirl of frigid sea air extinguished the warmth in the boathouse but resentment heated Lawnton from within.

Bitches! All women can rot in hell. Every last useless one of them. They're only good for one thing...

HE WAS CALMER by the time Agnes came down with the food. At least this time, she had brought him something warm to eat, and the ale would go part way to restoring his temper.

He arranged his most charming personality and lavished praise on the dumpy woman until she blushed with it. He drew Agnes close and ran his fingers through her hair tenderly, as a lover might.

"How I'd love to see you dress in satins and pearls. Hair like yours needs to be dressed; shown off. Emeralds would set off the color of your eyes," he crooned.

He brought her into his embrace and whispered in her ear.

"Have you ever gone through your mistress' jewels and tried them on for yourself?"

Lawnton watched the woman's face. She blushed. He knew he'd hit the right note.

"You *have*, haven't you? You naughty minx," he said, lightly pinching her chin. "I won't tell, I promise."

He ran a finger down the side of her neck and across the chest above her ample bosom.

"I'd love to see that," he whispered. "I want to make love to you covered in jewels."

"I... I couldn't take..."

He pressed a finger to her lips, shushing her.

"I would never do anything that would get you in trouble with your mistress, Agnes. But if she's away for the evening, perhaps you can invite me in and..."

He finished the thought with a kiss. The woman gave herself into it and Lawnton knew his ruse had worked.

"The master and mistress are attending a house party on Sunday evening. They'll be away overnight." Agnes offered him what he imagined she thought was a seductive smile. He pretended to be enraptured by it.

"Let me know when and where, my dove, and I will fly to you."

Chapter Twenty-Six

NATE REACHED ACROSS the pew and caressed Susannah's hand as Reverend Johnston read out their names alongside those of another couple for the first reading of the banns. Her gloved fingers curled around his and lightly squeezed.

A murmur of delight went through the congregation. He wondered whether any would be surprised at hearing Susannah's full name – Susannah Louise Moorcroft Linwood. He appreciated the clergyman's tact. By reading out both their full names and adding Susannah's legal name as only part of hers, he had fulfilled his duty and, at the same time, prevented questions of a strange surname being raised.

Through the leather of her glove, his thumb brushed along the smooth tops of the gemstones in the gold ring he had given her.

The ring had caught his eye over the others he scoured through at a market in Truro. He'd reviewed some spectacular jewels. Some had been large stones, others had been elaborate settings of ruby and pearl, yet none of them seemed right to him. And he knew they were pieces Susannah would not wear.

The aquamarines reminded him of the color of her eyes, its simple mounting was practical for the owner of The Queen's Head.

Although he was not the most frequent of churchgoers, he was surprised at how warmly he was welcomed and congratulated on his engagement after the service.

Of the greatest surprise was that Martin and Lillian Doyle *had* attended church. As the preeminent family in the district, they had their own pew, but they rarely made use of it.

Magistrate Doyle had the excuse of frequently being away on business. His wife had no such pretext. To his shame, Nate had been a party to many of her absences from her civil and Christian duty, taking advantage of the household staff being away from the house to conduct their affair on the Lord's day.

Regret settled like a cloud on him and he almost missed the question from one of the congregation.

"When are you and Mrs. Linwood planning to wed?"

Out of the corners of his eyes, he saw Lillian Doyle drawing close, and regret deepened to foreboding.

"Soon, at Christmas," he answered.

He continued receiving the congratulations and made his way with Susannah toward Peggy and Clem. Nate accepted Clem's handshake and warm best wishes gratefully.

Perhaps he was being foolish. The foreboding feeling at seeing Lillian again vanished when he stepped out of the shadow of the church and into the late autumn sunshine. Yet he had a sense that a shadow of a different kind would follow him unless he addressed it face to face.

He kissed Susannah on the cheek.

"You head on back to the inn without me. I have a few people I have to catch up with first." He was as honest as he could possibly be and not reveal his true intent.

Susannah waved him farewell. He watched her walk out of the churchyard with the others until they rounded the corner past one of the houses and the end of the terrace row. Then he turned the other way toward the cemetery that spread around the hill to the east. There was a place out of sight of the village. He knew Lillian would come to him there.

As he went, he paused by the simple headstones that marked the graves of his mother and father. The stones were weathered and worn. It had been too many years since he had stopped here to pay his respects.

He touched one, then the other of the granite monoliths and bowed his head a moment before walking onwards to a bench in the sunlight.

Out of the corners of his eyes, he could see Lillian make her way up the path toward him. He didn't acknowledge her, looking out on the view instead.

The day was clear and he could see down through the valley and its patchwork of fields, rising up to the hills. The movement of large canvas-covered vanes of a windmill caught the sun and drew his eyes. Beyond there, on the hill, was another structure he'd never really taken notice of before, perhaps it was new. It was a semaphore tower. The white-painted arms glowed in the sun but he was too distant to see the particulars of it.

"Well, you *are* serious about the widow, aren't you?"

"I thought I made that clear months ago."

"But *marriage*... I never saw you as the type to fall into the parson's mousetrap."

There was silence between them for a moment. When Lillian spoke, it was almost with sincerity.

"I've tried to warn you about her. There's something not right about that woman. She has secrets, Nate, dangerous secrets."

He bared his teeth, got to his feet and strode no more than a few feet away.

"You need to listen to me," Lillian insisted. "I learned something about her husband. That woman killed—"

"I will not hear of it!"

"My, my, such a show of temper for a conniving little slut."

Nate hauled Lillian up by her shoulders and, for half a second, considered backhanding her. In his mind's eye, he'd already done it and it was *satisfying.*

Instead, he let her go.

Lillian sank back down on the bench.

When he spoke, his voice was harsh with anger barely restrained.

"Susannah has told me everything I need to know about her past and anything she hasn't told me wouldn't change a thing between us. Let it go. I'm your plaything no longer."

His rough handling didn't seem to bother her a whit. She rose to her feet and approached him.

"I don't want this to be a bitter farewell," she said, touching his shoulder. He shrugged her hand away and heard her make a little dismissive snort. "For what it's worth," she continued, "our time together has been pleasurable and profitable, so you cannot blame me for feeling a little nostalgic for what we once had."

He turned to look at her. "Your husband arranged to have me *imprisoned* in France."

A twitch of amusement touched her lips.

"You might find it amusing, Lillian, but other people's lives are not a game. That's something you and Martin could stand to learn, otherwise, one day, it might end very, very badly for you."

He decided not to head back down toward the village, but instead go up to the Trethowan headland and cross over and down along the rough cattle path to The Queen's Head.

He did not look back. He would leave his past with Lillian behind, appropriately in the cemetery, and concentrate on the future – with Susannah and with The King's Rogues, however it might turn out.

As he walked, he looked up at the sky, pale and blue but cold. The coming winter was heralded in the chilly evenings and it wouldn't be too long before the days were short and grey.

There was another reason why he wanted to make sure Lillian knew in no uncertain terms that she and her husband were not welcome in his life anymore. The Queen's Head was to have a full house for Christmas and he didn't want any unwarranted intrusions.

ROBERT LAWNTON LINGERED in the shadows between two buildings and watched those leaving the churchyard.

He spotted a woman in a reddish-brown dress and there she was. Apart from the smile on her face, Susannah Moorcroft was unchanged from the timid little creature she had been when Jack wed her.

She was in animated conversation with another woman he thought he recognized. After a moment, it came to him that maybe the older one was Jack's housekeeper. She was holding hands with some old bloke. Lawnton looked back at Susannah. There was no mistaking *her*. That was definitely Susannah Moorcroft walking around laughing like she didn't have a care in the world.

That was going to change.

He watched the party make their way down the street in his direction, joking and huddled together against the chill. He drew back into the narrow alley as they neared, saw them cross the entrance to the passageway, then slipped back out to spy around the corner after them.

He had no idea why Susannah stopped a moment. Perhaps she could feel the weight of his stare on her. She glanced behind just as he drew back into the alley again.

"What's up?" called the older woman. "Come on, Susannah, it's cold!"

After a moment, he looked out again. She had caught up to them and they continued on their way.

Little did the woman know she had passed by him so closely he might have grabbed her and slit her throat in a single action. But where would the fun be in that?

SPYFALL

Besides, he wanted the ledger and she needed to be alive for that. The book contained the details of their contacts on the Continent who Jack had sold their stolen goods to over the years. With that in hand, and a haul from the Doyle residence, he could slip across the Channel and soon set himself up in Holland or in Naples.

And he didn't intend to swing for killing Jack's widow, either. But he promised himself that when he'd finished with her, she'd wish he had.

To his surprise, she and her friends stopped outside an ironmonger's shop less than a hundred yards further on and went inside.

Lawnton rubbed a hand across his mouth and considered his next move.

Believing himself safe from discovery, he decided to pay a visit to The Queen's Head before heading to his next appointment.

As he walked, he considered the events of recent days. Romancing the lady's maid had to be the single most easy conquest he had ever made. The pitiful creature was starving for a little attention. A word here, a caress there had all but secured him a private invitation to the house.

If need be, he was sure he could count on another week hiding out in the Doyle's boatshed – longer if he romanced the lady of the house herself. Lillian Doyle was a piece of work but not half as hard as she thought she was. The threat to have him killed was all bluff. And he'd warrant she'd never had a man like Bobby Lawnton on that fancy daybed of hers.

Then again, best not stick around too long. If he stayed, the half-glance he and Jack's widow shared across the green the other day might turn into full-blown recognition and that's not what he wanted for now.

No, it was time now to just make the little bitch scared, scared as old Jack must have been as he breathed his last on the boggy marshes.

He stopped a few hundred yards from the inn. Susannah must

have been stupid to buy as isolated a place as The Queen's Head. He adopted the posture of a rambler and walked straight up to the front door. Chalked on a board fastened to the front door was an announcement that the inn would reopen at four o'clock. That was another three hours from now. Plenty of time to look around.

He went around the back of the inn, past the chicken run and the stables. All of this she'd profited from Jack's death. Resentment brewed like a storm.

An old dog bounded up to him more in friendly inquisitiveness than protectiveness and received a pat on its head. Then something attracted its attention in the field and the hound went tearing off, leaving him alone.

He looked through a window into what appeared to be private quarters. He recognized the desk. That belonged to Jack. He went to the next window and peered through. A bedroom. He even knew the bed and its iron balusters.

He wouldn't have time to search though the whole place. But if the woman kept the ledger then it would be in one of those two rooms.

Like the practiced thief he was, he pulled out a slender piece of metal from his coat and slid it between the window frame and the sill, maneuvering it until he could knock the simple latch to its unlocked position.

With another look about on the off-chance he was being observed, he pushed open the window and clambered through.

He leafed through the ledgers on the bookcase by the desk, but none were what he sought. He opened desk drawers and rifled through. The last one was locked. He withdrew from his pocket a smaller iron strap and a hooked length of wire. He worked the lock until it unlatched. Beneath a cloth was a small cashbox. Doubtless the float for the inn's till tonight.

It was tempting to take the money. But he wouldn't if he couldn't find the ledger. Why put the woman on alert and make it difficult for him to come back and search again if he needed to?

He was thorough in his present search, spending far longer than he would normally when doing jobs like this. "Get in and get out quick", that was his motto. "If you stick your neck out, the hangman will find it quick enough".

He started at the sound of the hall clock chiming two.

He would look in the bedroom next.

After a while, he admitted temporary defeat. If she had the book, then she'd hidden it well. He'd even searched around for a safe. Perhaps it was down in the cellar. If so, he didn't have time to look there. The next time he came back, he would have to take more direct action…

As he was about to leave the bedroom, a box on the dressing table caught his eye. He opened the plain wooden casket and found a pair of earrings and a simple gold band.

The wedding band old Jack had put on the useless chit's finger.

He'd told Jack that he was a fool at the time, but the man insisted he knew better. How better to trick the authorities than by having a perfectly respectable wife – the daughter of a vicar even! – living in a perfectly respectable house, acting like a perfectly respectable businessman. That was Jack's argument anyway.

Ungrateful wench. She didn't know when she was well off. Jack had given her the clothes on her back and little jewels for her so she could keep up appearances. What did she do with those pieces?

Anyway, time to put the wind up her. He pulled out of his pocket a small tangle of green ribbon and white lace about three inches in length. He would leave "Mrs. Linwood" a gift. He put it in the box and closed the lid.

Let's see if she remembers.

LAWNTON DID NOT come empty-handed to his assignation that night. He brought a bottle of gin and, in his pocket, a vial of opium. He poured them both a glass of mother's ruin while Agnes sat at the dressing table and opened her mistress' jewelry casket with the key entrusted to her.

He emptied the vial into Agnes' glass behind her back and stirred it in. She accepted the drink he placed on the dressing table. He tried not to smile as she quaffed a large mouthful to cure her nervousness. He leaned down and rained kisses on the back of her neck, loosening her plain hair pins until her locks tumbled down her shoulders. He ran his hands over her shoulders until the wrapper of the nightrail she wore slipped off and down her arms.

"Here," he said. "Allow me."

He twisted her hair and piled it high in a mass of curls and picked up one of a set of ruby and pearl-topped hair pins and set it in, then another and another. Agnes giggled until she hiccoughed and took another swig of gin to stop *that*.

Next, he picked up a pair of earrings, pear-shaped emeralds, and held them up to the lamplight, estimating their value.

He kissed Agnes on top of her head and watched her reflection in the mirror. Her eyes were heavy-lidded from the sleeping draught already. She did not react when he caressed her earlobe and put the earring up to it.

"I don't have holes in my ears like the mistress," she slurred.

"Then let's find something else for you to wear," he said, slipping the earrings unnoticed into his pocket.

"How about this," he said, pulling out a lavish collar of amethysts and diamonds. He settled the jewel around her neck as Agnes' head lolled.

"I... I need to lie down," she whispered.

"Here, drink this," he offered her the glass with the remains of the gin. "You're feeling a little dizzy with excitement, that's all. Finish this and you'll be feeling a lot better."

"I need to lie down…"

"Of course, you do," he soothed. "Let me help you."

He levered her weight up from the dressing table chair but they never made it as far as the bed. Her weight started to slip, so he hauled her into a chair beside the bed.

"I'm not well, Robert."

"Sit there, sweeting, and close your eyes a minute."

The woman did as bid.

He returned to the dressing table and covetously examined the jewelry box. It was tempting to take the lot, but he was far too experienced to allow that.

He selected one or two silver chains to go with the haul in his pocket and a plain gold signet ring. Another piece fell to his hand – a large brooch with an emerald-cut center stone in a grassy green. Perhaps it was an emerald, but likely not; a peridot or tourmaline perhaps.

It was mounted in gold. The gold spread out like vines to terminate in diamonds mounted in the shapes of flowers from which dangled pear-shaped cuts of the same green stone.

Not an exact match for the emerald drop earrings in his pocket, but near enough.

He started at a noise behind him, but it was just the sow snoring, her head lolling back in a most unattractive fashion.

He removed the amethyst collar from her neck and added it to his haul before tidying the jewelry case and locking it, but leaving the ruby and pearl pins in her hair. He surveyed the table to ensure nothing was amiss.

Behind him, Agnes' snoring worsened. He wrinkled his nose in contempt for the woman. He poured another glass of gin and swallowed half of it himself before he touched the glass to the woman's lips. A little insurance to make sure she stayed out until late.

He poured the alcohol slowly down her throat and only stopped when she gagged slightly.

Finally, he closed her hand around the gold jewelry box key.

The way he saw things, when Agnes awoke, she would immediately check the box. Seeing some of the bigger pieces there, she would remove the pieces she wore and return them with nothing more than a pounding hangover and an illusion of an evening of romance to recall. And even when the missing jewels were noticed, she would not give him away – not without admitting her own complicity in an act that would see her immediately dismissed, if not charged.

Robert Lawnton smiled to himself and surveyed the room one more time before he went down the servants' stairs and left by the back door Agnes had left unlocked for him to come in.

He would sleep in the boathouse tonight and, early tomorrow, he would *make* Susannah give him Jack Moorcroft's ledger and be off.

And then he'd be well and truly back in business.

Chapter Twenty-Seven

THROUGH THE WINDOW in the early morning outside, Lawnton caught the figure of a woman hurrying down the path from the main house. Cursing the fact he'd slept later than planned, he fastened the buckle on his satchel and glanced about the boatshed. There was no sign he had ever been here. He looked out of the window once more. The rushing figure was Lillian Doyle.

Steady your nerves, he reminded himself. No one saw you at the house.

The woman crashed into boathouse without preliminaries. Her face was puce with rage.

"Give me back what you've stolen from me and get out of here before I scream the place down and have you arrested for murder!"

Murder?

"What the hell are you talking about, you stupid woman?"

"Agnes is dead! In my bedroom! Wearing my jewels!" She glared at him. "I *know* you had something to do with it."

He allowed himself in a slow intake of breath. *Dead? Fuck...* The stupid sow. It must have been too much opium for her. *Oh, shit.* He decided to brazen it out.

"If you truly believed that, you wouldn't have come here alone," he sneered.

Lillian grew more furious still, but didn't come any closer.

"You fool!" she hissed. "I can't give you up without implicating myself. Now give me back the emerald earrings. I haven't told anyone yet. I'm giving you an hour's head start before I do."

The contempt he now had for the woman before him was visceral.

"Get back to your house, Mrs. Doyle."

Still she would not be deterred.

"Perhaps I should and just show the authorities *this*?" From her pocket she produced the empty opium vial. "You didn't have *this* when you arrived. I know because while you were out one morning, I made a search of your possessions. That means you could only have gotten it from a chemist within fifteen miles of St. Sennen. It won't be too hard to find who sold it to you."

Lawnton found himself with the tremors as though *he* were an opium addict.

"Give that to me!" he demanded, grasping for the vial.

"No!" she responded, snatching it out of reach.

The beast within Robert Lawnton roared.

He surged forward and found his hands around Lillian Doyle's neck. Her half-scream was choked off. His vision turned vermillion red. When it cleared he saw the color again... no, deeper, a puce.

Then he became conscious of his hands and arms supporting the woman's dead weight, her mouth open in a silent scream, her tongue protruding grotesquely.

He shoved her away. The body slumped to the floor and remained there, unmoving. With shaking hands, he picked up his satchel and stumbled out of the boatshed.

Lawnton looked up the cliff toward the house which was out of sight and ran for his life along the cliff path that would take him away from here. But where could he go?

Susannah Moorcroft.

Her name came to him clearly. A guardian angel must have whispered it in his ear.

And yet, the horror of what he had done dogged him, snarled at his heels. He dare not look back. Instead, he kept his eyes fixed on the path before him for dear life until he could see the slate-roofed inn in the distance at the bottom of the hill.

No one would believe it was an accident. He hadn't *meant* to kill the two women. The first death wasn't even his fault. How was he to know that Agnes Sloan would react badly to the opium?

And, as for Lillian Doyle… well, she brought it on herself, didn't she? If she hadn't antagonized him, he wouldn't have lost his temper. But there was no way he'd be believed, not with his form, not with a lifetime of thievery. They'd just say murder was a natural progression. *Oh, God!* If he was caught, he'd swing for sure. *What to do? What to do?*

Jack's widow had a new fancy man with a boat. That was it. Make her give him the ledger and have her lover take him to Holland – *or else*.

Formulating the plan worked like a balm on his shattered nerves. The rushing of blood in his ears ebbed and he could hear sounds clearly once again.

He needed a weapon. *A knife.*

There were plenty of knives in the kitchen of The Queen's Head.

Damn looking casual like a rambler.

He began to run.

"Fetch the jar of flour, Tressa, and I'll show you how to make some of those fancy French pastries," said Peggy. "Them Frenchies make them look like a big deal but there are a few tricks you can learn to make it easy."

Susannah smiled and looked up as the younger girl turned to Peggy with a dubious expression.

Normally she would have done the accounting ledgers in her parlor, but the fire had already been set here and since the doors weren't open until one o'clock, there was no one to look out for in the bar.

Woof, woof, woof!

Susannah shared a concerned glance with Peggy whose fingers were covered in rubbed-together flour. The woman frowned back.

"That's not like Prince to—" said Peggy.

Crash!

The sound of a smashing window was unmistakable.

"I'll see to that," said Susannah.

"I'll come with you, Mrs. Linwood," Tressa volunteered.

"Take the Billy club by the door," Peggy added.

Susannah's hand was already around the smooth wooden club. She took it and passed through into the bar. In the dining room, three diamond-shaped panes were smashed. A fist-sized rock sat surrounded by the glistening shards of glass.

She unlatched the front door and raced out. There was no one about, but Prince bounded up to her, continuing to bark most insistently.

"What is it, boy? Who broke my window?"

The pointer bounced about her feet and continued to bark but, over the noise, she heard something else, a scrabble of footsteps.

She held the club more firmly in her grip, wishing not for the first time that Nate had not gone out to St. Sennen early this morning with Adam Hardacre.

Susannah moved around the west side of the building where the windows to her bedroom lay.

The chickens seemed agitated, they congregated in the farthest corner of the hen house. Had their vandal been around here? Or had Prince's barking set them off? She glanced across the field to see if she could spot anyone running away. There was nothing.

She came to the door to the mud room and the double trap doors that led down to the cellar. The side door was locked and the cellar's doors were closed. She moved around to the kitchen side of the inn.

Still, here, was nothing unusual.

"I saw no one, no one at all," she called, opening the kitchen door inward.

There was silence, nothing but the crackling of the kitchen fire in the grate.

"Peggy?"

The kitchen was empty, she heard only silence.

Susannah set the club back by the door and bolted it shut for good measure.

"Peggy? Tressa?"

She pushed open the swinging door to the bar only to come face to face with Peggy, her eyes wide, face pale. Catching the gleam of the knife was second, recognizing the man holding it was third.

"Hello, Susannah, my darling. Did you miss me?"

"Lawnton," she said, her voice much more calm than it ought to be under the circumstances. "Please let Peggy go."

"You've got something I want, Susannah."

She swallowed. *Dear God, he really had returned for the ledger – the one she had happily burned a few weeks ago.*

"Where's Tressa?"

"The girl?" said Lawnton. "She seems to have bumped her head."

Susannah eased herself past the kitchen door and into the bar. Tressa lay prone on the floor and moaned faintly.

"Let Peggy go," she said "We need to help Tressa."

"You have the ledger?"

"You have my word you won't see it unless you let Peggy go."

Lawnton barked out a laugh. "I'm a desperate man, Susannah. You don't know just how desperate I am. They'll be after me soon. But I won't let them take me. I'll not go back to Causton Prison. I won't swing, I promise you that."

Lawnton nudged Tressa with his foot, brushing her skirts out of the way. He revealed the ring set flush in the floor.

"Where does this go?"

"The taproom," Susannah answered. "The cellar."

"Not out to your boatshed?"

Susannah shook her head.

"About your ledger, I..."

She swallowed tight as Lawnton's grip tightened on the kitchen knife. Peggy let out a small whimper and squeezed her eyes shut.

"If you tell me you don't have it, Susannah, then I have nothing to lose. You see, I've killed a woman... no, I've killed two. If I kill another three, am I any less damned?"

Leverage. The words of Lady Abigail came back to her. *Anything someone wants badly enough to spend years looking for could be useful...*

Susannah summoned up every ounce of self-possession she had while, inwardly, she prayed frantically.

"I have it," she lied. "But I don't have it here. I was too afraid to keep it at the inn, so I kept it safe. No one but me knows where it is."

Susannah kept her eyes on Peggy's terror-filled face, pleading silently that she would not contradict her.

"Where?" Lawnton demanded.

"The smugglers' cave."

"The one on the beach on the other headland?"

She nodded. Lawnton watched her like a hawk and pressed the knife even closer to Peggy's throat.

"You're not lying to me are you?" The man was becoming more and more agitated. "Like the way you lied about Jack's death? Because you *did* lie to the coroner, didn't you, slut?"

Peggy hissed with pain and a thin line of blood bloomed at her neck from where he pressed the sharp blade.

"Tell me the truth!"

"Lawnton, stop!"

"Answer me, bitch!"

Peggy cried out in pain.

"I did! I lied! I lied! I was there! Now let her go!" Susannah screamed, unable to stop the sobs rising from her throat. "You want the truth? You want to know what happened the night Jack died? You want the ledger? Then let her go. Let her go now."

She fought her sobs as she stared at Lawnton. Both panted with emotion and terror.

Beware lest thy sins find thee out.

If Lawnton did not believe her, then they were all dead.

Suddenly, the hand holding the knife was thrust in her direction.

"Open the hatch!"

Susannah did so, terrified. Did he mean to put them all down there? If he did, what then? A horrible image flashed across her mind of Lawnton setting the inn alight with them in it.

The man shoved Peggy forward toward the open hatch.

"Get down there."

Susannah and Peggy shared a frightened glance, but Peggy did as she was bid, starting toward the opening.

Lawnton directed his attention to Tressa. The girl had regained consciousness and struggled to a sitting position. She was deathly pale and holding a hand to the back of her head.

"You, too, girlie."

Tressa crawled to Peggy who took the young maid into her arms and helped her down the ladder into the cellar.

No sooner had Peggy's head disappeared below floor level did Lawnton kick the heavy hatch shut. The slam was so loud Susannah literally jumped. The knife pointing in her direction was shaking.

"What have you done, Robert?" she asked softly.

"Shut up! You'd better not be lying to me, Susannah. I'd rather damn my soul and take you with me."

She gulped.

"I'm not lying to you, Robert."

She nodded her head toward his shaking hand.

ELIZABETH ELLEN CARTER

"You're in shock. You need a drink… brandy."

It was strange – the more agitated Lawnton became, the calmer Susannah felt, especially now Peggy and Tressa were out of immediate danger. Lawnton glared at her as if he could intimidate her with the force of his expression. Once upon a time, he could. She refused to be cowed now. She was not the same woman she was three years ago.

All she needed to do was to get Lawnton away from here. When the inn didn't open as usual, someone would come looking for her.

"Put the bottle on the counter," he ordered.

Susannah took the decanter from the shelf behind her and placed it on the bar. She could smell the fruity fermentation as he opened it and took a swig directly from it, tossing the glass stopper aside. His hands still shook. They seemed red somehow but she was sure they were not covered in blood.

Breathe in and out. The longer he lingered here, the better for both she and Peggy.

"Where's your lover then? The one with the boat?"

"At the harbor in St. Sennen, preparing to head out this afternoon," she said making sure she kept her voice as calm as possible.

She watched him consider her answer, clearly making plans.

"If he wants you alive, he's going to have to do what I say then, isn't he?"

It was only now Susannah felt the pinpricks of fear rising up her arms.

"The smugglers' cave will do well enough, won't it?" He snatched her arm and squeezed tight. She let out a cry of pain.

Thumping started from the floor below where she heard Peggy's muffled protests.

Lawnton stomped on the floor twice.

"Shut up, woman!" he yelled. "Shut up before I deal with you!"

LAWNTON KEPT A relentless pace up Arthyn Hill. He gripped her wrist tight, dragging her over the headland and down the path that led to the beach.

She had no coat. She shuddered and gulped in the salt air, the cold tang of it hurting her lungs almost as much as her feet ached from the forced march. At last, they stood just a few yards from the cave.

"Where is it in there?"

Where's what?

She stared at him for a moment, not comprehending his words. Then she remembered a split second before his open hand smacked hard across the side of her face, causing her to stagger back.

"Come on, you stupid woman. The *ledger*. You promised me the bloody ledger."

She took another step back. The sand was packed firm underfoot. The high watermark seemed much higher than usual. *Easier to run on....*

A gull wheeled past just over Lawnton's head and she took advantage of his momentary distraction to turn on her heels and flee.

Her abductor caught up with her quickly, throwing himself against her back. Strong arms reached around above her waist and squeezed the air from her lungs. She had the presence of mind to close her eyes and her mouth as she landed face first on the gritty sand. Lawnton's body crashed on top of her.

She tried to scream but the sound of it was lost against the noise of the wheeling seagulls and the pounding of the surf.

Lawnton tumbled her onto her back and straddled her.

Slap!

"Where *is* it?"

"You'll never find it," she gasped. "I hid it too well."

"You don't bloody have it, do you?" Realization dawned on his features so clearly it was as if she could read his mind. *It was all for nothing...* "That's it, you bitch," he panted, gaining his feet and dragging her up with him, hauling her closer and closer to the roiling grey sea. "This is where *you'll* know fear. I'll watch you drown like you watched Jack drown. A fitting end for you, you bitch."

As the waves rolled in, he pushed her head underwater. She closed her mouth and her lungs screamed in protest but, by some miracle, a wave knocked Lawnton off his feet. He lost his balance, and his grip on her neck.

She stood in knee deep water, gasping for breath. Lawnton prepared to lunge at her again.

Something rose within her. Now it was she who offered him a savage snarl.

"Kill me and you *will* swing," she said. "If you really did kill someone else, then your only hope is getting Nate to take you to Ireland or France or Holland – wherever it is you want to go. But if you kill me, you'll dance on the end of a rope!"

Lawnton growled. Instead of an open-faced slap, it was a fist. And that was the last thing Susannah saw.

Chapter Twenty-Eight

NATE KEPT A watchful eye on the sky above. He knew better than to be fooled by the glimpses of blue between the clouds.

Somewhere out in the ocean beyond, there was a monstrous storm revealing itself in the high tides and the change of air pressure that always presaged nature's capricious mood.

He readied the *Sprite* to go out for one last look along the Irish coast, looking for anything that resembled the maps the spies from France had recovered. If the weather worsened as he expected, this would be the final voyage for the year – that suited him just fine.

The weather could do what it liked then. He would be married in a few weeks, and he and Susannah would savor their first Christmas together.

He smiled at the thought as he coiled a spare line and glanced over the dock then back up at the sky. Fat grey clouds were beginning to thicken there.

Adam needed to be back here soon if they were going to catch the tide.

Nate continued to tidy the boat, making sure everything was se- cure just in case they needed to batten down the hatches. He picked up his box of tools and headed below deck.

No sooner was he in the cabin than he heard a set of footsteps above.

"'Bout time you showed up," he shouted with a touch of good-natured exasperation. "Loose the lines and weigh the anchor, we're not going to have better weather than this."

There was no response. Nate went back out onto the deck and found everything exactly as he'd left it.

He could have sworn he'd heard Adam come aboard. But there he really was, making his way along the pier at a clip. The man made the small jump from the jetty to the boat and immediately started loosening the lines. Nate shrugged and turned his attention to raising the anchor. He felt the draw of the current pull the boat away from its moorings.

"I've just heard back from *Aunt Runella*," said Adam. "We have a more specific area to search this time – Dungarvan to Wexford."

Nate gave his friend a look. "Just sixty miles of coastline, then?"

The man shrugged and started pulling on the line to raise the sail. "It's a hell of a lot better than the two hundred we were looking at just a month ago."

There were few people Nate trusted to run his boat, but Adam had quickly become one of them. They fell into a comfortable working routine to safely take the *Sprite* out into the increasingly choppy estuary.

Nate watched the surge of the water pushing its way through the mouth of the river but the boat sliced its way through the waves, its bow rising and falling in dramatic fashion.

He braced himself at the wheel. If the swell out at sea was as bad, they were in for a rough time, indeed. *Just as long as it wasn't as rough when they were fleeing the Frenchies.*

Once they had left the estuary, the rise and fall didn't seem as bad. Weak shafts of light pushed their way through the clouds which would help improve their visibility.

He'd rather be closer to Ireland and drop anchor overnight to give them a full morning to survey the coastline for God-knows-what. And with the wind before them, they could be back at St. Sennen before the storm bore down on them.

"Do you know where the hell we're going?" Nate yelled.

Adam wove his way across the heaving deck with a compass in one hand and a folded map in the other. He approached the helm.

"Keep her northwest."

Nate glanced down at the compass, then looked up at the pale white sun, its face obscured by clouds, and fought with the wheel to correct his course.

"You may as well get below and get some rest for a few hours," called Nate. "There's no point in the two of us being exhausted."

Hardacre waved a hand in acknowledgement.

"I'll relieve you for the first watch," he answered.

Nate nodded in return.

First watch.

Nate chuckled to himself. On a boat like the *Sprite* he was cabin boy, seaman, bosun, and captain all at once. There were no niceties like setting a watch. It was "all hands on deck, all the time" when he was single-handedly sailing her.

He listened to his boat. Every sound she made told him what was needed next. When he was imprisoned in France, he would dream of being on her deck and sailing her once again. He would bring to mind how the boards felt under his feet, he could feel the carved spindles of the vessel's wheel in his hand, the fight and pull on the lines to keep the sails in trim.

Alone in the dark confines of the oubliette, he would close his eyes and feel the sun on his face and see the bright blue sky of a perfect English summer's day. He could ignore the cold and the stench of the pit for a little while when he reached down for pleasant memories to help sustain him.

He had vowed then that he would be on the water once again with the wind and the briny air of the sea filling his lungs. Never again would he allow himself to be trapped on land for any length of time.

Ah, but that was before he met Susannah. Still waters ran deep with his beloved. He was pretty certain he could know her for a lifetime and still not plumb her depths.

When the weather improved, he would take her sailing again. He had a feeling she would take to it. And there was a secluded cove only a few hours from St. Sennen, where a stream became a waterfall and plunged directly into the sea.

He smiled at the idea of making love to her in the open air, the summer sun touching her skin as he caressed her. It was a rather nice fantasy and he happily indulged it until the chill November wind and fast ebbing daylight could no longer be ignored.

He lashed the wheel into position and set about setting a lamp or two on deck.

There was no sign of Hardacre to take his watch.

He stomped heavily over the cabin in a none-too-subtle hint.

That man could sleep like the dead. Perhaps he should go down and wake him. Instead, he merely opened the door and yelled down to him.

"Hey! Hardacre! Wakey, wakey, old man!"

Satisfied he could hear a man moving about, Nate returned to the helm.

Unsteady feet climbed the steps up to the deck.

"Did you drink a bottle of rum before nap time?"

The figure emerged onto the gloomy deck and lurched awkwardly as the *Sprite* rolled.

"You're drunk!" Nate laughed.

It wasn't until the figure got closer that he saw the blade of the knife glint in the lamplight. It took another moment or two after that to realize the man, tall and broad, was not Adam Hardacre.

Nate recognized him as the stranger he'd confronted in the streets of St. Sennen on the night before Clem's wedding. *The footsteps he'd thought were Adam...*

"What are you doing on my boat?"

"You're going to take me to Holland."

"Oh no, we're not. We're halfway to bloody Ireland!"

"Then turn her about!"

The knife shook in the man's hand. Nate looked at it with contempt before casting a watchful eye on the sail before him.

"We're all dead if you use that on me, because I'm the one sailing the boat."

"Then I'll just have to do it myself."

The man surged forward and tackled Nate around the waist, pulling him to the deck. They grappled, the boat beneath them heaving in the increasing swell.

Nate managed prise the knife from the man's hands. It skittered somewhere in the blackness, useless to him but at least now useless to the stowaway. Nate launched himself, slamming his full body weight on the man, knocking the wind out of him, and pinning him to the deck. He pressed a forearm across the man's chest.

"Now, who the hell are you, and where the hell is Hardacre?"

"You don't need to be worrying about him," the man puffed. "You should be concerned for Susannah."

Nate fought a violent urge to seek answers with his fists. "Explain yourself."

"The little whore's tucked away safe for now. Get me to where I want to go, and I'll tell you where she is."

Nate lifted the man by his shirt and slammed the back of his head on the deck.

"Where's Susannah?"

Nate wasn't sure if the violent shaking he was giving the man was not actually tremors in his own body.

"Get me to Rotterdam," the man gasped. "The longer you delay, the less time you'll have to find her."

"Tell me now and I won't throw you overboard."

"If you turn us back, I'll jump myself and save you the trouble. I am *not* going back to England. I'd sooner drown than face prison and the hangman's noose."

Something within him recognized the true desperation in the man's words. Nate's own smothering fear of being trapped in dark, confined spaces underground emerged to the fore and found its kin in the man beneath him.

"It'd take us four days to get to Holland under fair skies. I don't care what kind of madman *you* are, but in two days *I will not* be out at sea with this storm bearing down on us. I'll take you to Ireland and no further. That's my first and final offer."

The tension leaving the man's body seemed to be his acceptance. Nate released his grip and rose to his feet. He needed to be at the wheel and work out where the hell they were.

"Do we have an agreement?"

The man nodded.

"Then since you're going to be crew for the next few hours, you may as well tell me your name."

"Lawnton," he replied, coming gingerly to his feet. "That's all you need to know."

WHEN SUSANNAH AWOKE, her head pounded and she feared that she was frozen stiff from the cold and her wet, salt-crusted clothes. She managed to move her arms a little but found them bound; so, too, her legs. As awareness returned, she felt a gag and a covering over her eyes.

She rolled up into a sitting position. When she twisted her wrists around in the cloth binding them, she felt it slip. She tugged her wrists apart and found the knot that bound them together tightened while actually making the binding round her wrists a little more slack. It took some minutes working until one wrist was free.

She immediately tore off her blindfold. Its removal made no difference. It was pitch dark. As she tugged away the gag across her mouth, she realized she was deep inside the smugglers' cave.

Lawnton had used her own petticoat to bind her even though she could not see it. She could only feel the missing underskirt as she began to fumble at the knotted cloth that secured her ankles. This was more difficult. She stretched her fingers, hoping to work some warmth into them, and tried again. The longer it took the more she feared the tide of panic rising in her.

She breathed in deep, hoping the headache would ease. The air smelled musty and yet dank. While the ground she was on seemed dry, it was difficult to tell with her dress still wet.

Without light to give her an indication of the day, she didn't know whether she worked five minutes or fifteen to untie the knot that kept her ankles bound. Once free, she gathered her arms around her knees and shivered.

She thought of Nate and his dread of confined spaces. Did he know moments of terror like this?

It was tempting to fall into the looming panic. She felt hysteria touch the edge of her consciousness. Oh, the temptation to sob uncontrollably was there, and she toyed with it, giving it the reins for a moment before pulling it back under her control. She should be grateful she was still alive.

Flashes of memory flickered vividly – Peggy's terrified face, Tressa's prone body, Lawnton's demonic countenance, the beach. Her eyes still stung from their exposure to salt water and her throat ached in pain from the seawater she unwittingly swallowed.

Concentrate!

So Lawnton had taken her into the caves beneath Arthyn Hill. How far did they extend? No one seemed to know. Not even Clem who said he'd never ventured beyond the smuggler's grotto. Some of the regulars at The Queen's Head hinted at a labyrinth dating back to the time of King Arthur, but she had dismissed them as tall tales.

You can't just sit here. Think!

"Hello!" she called out.

Strange, she expected to hear an echo, but she didn't.

She wasn't quite sure what that meant. But surely if Lawnton had brought here, then there had to be a way to get back out. She concentrated on what she could hear. A steady rush of water she guessed, but the sound was distorted in the twists and turns of the caverns.

There!

A distinct touch of moving air on her cheeks. A way out. She started to rise but only got as far as a crouch before she bumped her head. She fell again with a frustrated cry.

It was to be hands and knees then. But where had that breeze come from? Now it was still, apart from the haunting moans of wind going elsewhere through the caves. She willed the touch of air to return and it did. To her left.

This time, she crawled cautiously. Grit from sand and shells along with the hard, unyielding surface of the rock grazed her hands and knees.

Every few feet forward, she would stop and listen, and wait for the moving air to guide her.

She called out again, not so much in the hope of rescue, but rather to get a better understanding of her surroundings. If there was an echo, it would indicate a chamber; if there was not, she was somewhere else. A passage perhaps. Who could tell in the total darkness?

And the breeze lied to her.

Abruptly, she banged her head against a dead end. She screamed in frustration, pounding her fists against the rock.

Whispering voices in her mind alleged her fate was no less than she deserved for her wickedness for letting Jack drown. Her choice had hurt innocent people like Peggy and young Tressa and, as for her – she would die here alone with Nate never knowing her fate.

She wept until she felt weak and boneless, staring into the blackness.

No. I am stronger *than this.*

If she stopped and gave in to her exhaustion and despair, she would sleep. The dark would claim her first and then the cold.

Despite the pounding of her head, she must not give in.

If she did not give up, there was hope, she told herself, even though every part of her ached. She would only count to thirty before moving on.

Did she hear a sound?

"Hello!"

The caves remained mute.

Chapter Twenty-Nine

THE *SPRITE* PLOUGHED on through the waves. Nate used the tumultuous seas to hide the fact he was making incremental changes to his heading.

Every so often, he would glance down at the hatch to below decks. It had been more than half an hour, at a guess, since the unwelcome stowaway revealed himself and there was still no sign of Adam Hardacre.

That was not good.

So far, Lawnton hadn't noticed the change in direction. Nate gambled that the man wasn't a seafarer. He certainly wasn't much of a sailor. He was subdued and never ventured too far away from the sides. Between squalls, Nate would hear the sound of retching.

Sometime later, out of the corners of his eyes, he saw a shadowy figure emerge at last from the hatch.

Adam hunkered down beside it and didn't move for several minutes, apparently getting the lay of the land. Finally, he cautiously made his way across to the helm, making very certain to stay out of Lawnton's eyeline.

He stopped by the mast and crouched down. Nate adjusted his position to provide additional cover.

"Nice to see you awake," Nate muttered under the wind. "I was trying to work out what I was going to tell Olivia if your nap was a permanent one."

Adam rubbed the back of his head and winced.

"Who's our passenger?" he asked.

"The name's Lawnton. He wants us to take him to Holland."

Adam snorted. "Why haven't you tossed him overboard already?"

"Because he says he has Susannah."

Nate heard his friend hiss the curses he himself had uttered a half-hour before.

"Where is she?"

"I don't know, he refuses to say. He also says he's afraid of the hangman's noose and I've seen enough frightened men to believe he's telling the truth about that."

Lawnton stood up unsteadily and glanced Nate's way. "Well?" he demanded. "We don't seem to be getting any bloody closer to Ireland."

"You're supposed to be keeping a lookout for the lights on the coast," Nate returned. "Do *you* see any?"

The man harrumphed and made his way to the other side of the *Sprite*. Hardacre moved around the mast to avoid detection. Nate understood why without being told. As long as Lawnton believed Adam was incapacitated, he would be less on his guard.

"Got a plan?" Nate inquired down to Adam.

"Not really," he said. "Try and get him to tell you where Susannah is. We'll work it out from there. What's our heading?"

"Southeast. The wind is running with us, we should see the Cornish coast within the next two hours."

THE ANONYMOUS COACH rolled to a stop outside The Queen's Head.

Sir Daniel Ridgeway didn't wait for the footman. He had opened the door and dropped the steps before the coachman had even applied the brake.

He knew something was amiss the moment he saw the inn from the top of the crossroads.

The last of the sunlight changed from yellow to orange and what he'd thought were lights in the windows were instead an illusion, fading as the sun descended.

There ought to be smoke from the kitchen and dining room fires drifting skyward. The place had a deserted air. He tried to resist a superstitious shudder of being too little, too late once again.

He held a hand out to help his wife down first, then Olivia Hardacre.

"No welcome for us, eh?" Lady Abigail remarked.

She looked back to Olivia who was now making her way down the steps. Her brows were furrowed as she made her way directly to the door.

"Adam responded to the coded message this afternoon, so he knows our plans," said Sir Daniel.

"There's no note on the door," said Olivia. "But I can see a light in one of the rooms so there is someone here."

"Go secure the horses," Sir Daniel told his coachman. "We'll be staying anyway."

The door to The Queen's Head opened. A short, grim-faced man looked out and Sir Daniel stepped forward.

"Who are you?" the man asked, uncertainly.

"Sir Daniel Ridgeway and party."

The man looked him up and down and relaxed.

"You're the friends Adam Hardacre has spoken of. I'm Clem Pascoe."

"You're Nate's friend," Olivia said.

"Aye, that I am. You'd best come in. There's been bad news and worse."

The three new arrivals followed Clem inside.

"Me and my son got here not long ago, found my Peg and the

lassie locked in the cellar. They've been there for half a day. I sent Sam to the village to get help."

"And Mrs. Linwood?" Daniel asked.

Clem silently led them into the private parlor. A few lamps were lit and a warm fire burned in the hearth, but this was not a happy place.

Two women sat on the settee, each with blankets around their shoulders.

"Where's the kitchen?" asked Olivia. "We'll start with tea and warming up some food to eat."

That seemed to rouse the younger one who, a moment before, had looked ready to burst into tears. "I'll show you the kitchen," she said, getting up.

Lady Abigail took the younger girl's place on the settee.

Daniel looked at the older woman. Even from this distance, he could see a faint pink line across her throat.

"Peggy?" Clem said gently as though he were trying not to spook a frightened mare. "Tell Sir Daniel what you just told me... about Susannah."

Peggy looked up at him, her bottom lip jutting out. "He burst through the door like he was Satan himself and hit poor Tressa on the head with a wine bottle. His name's Robert Lawnton. He was confederate of Susannah's late husband. Ooh, he's a bad one. I... I told Duch that, he's a bad one."

Peggy accepted a glass of brandy from Clem and took a large swallow.

"And he's taken Susannah?" Lady Abigail asked gently.

Peggy took in a deep breath and nodded. Daniel's heart sank. The weather was beginning to turn and the inky skies had stolen whatever light there was in the day. He knew from Nate's plan that the incoming tide over the next few days would bring a storm surge.

He was beginning to regret sending Adam and Nate out in it.

"Where?" he asked. "Did Lawnton say *where* he was taking Susannah?"

"She was *so* brave," whispered Peggy. "That man held a knife to me. I thought I was going to die. Susannah persuaded him to let me go. She said she'd take him to the smugglers' cave."

"Why would she do that?"

"He was desperate like, because he'd killed someone, so he said," said Peggy, and then without pausing for breath: "He wanted Nate to take him to Holland and he wanted the ledger that Jack Moorcroft had, except we didn't have it anymore, we burned it, but we couldn't tell Lawnton that because he would have slit my throat quick as a wink, so Susannah told him a tale to get him away from here…"

"Peggy," Lady Abigail said gently, "you said this man claimed to have killed someone? Killed who?"

Daniel heard the sound of pounding feet and a youthful voice calling, "Da! Da!" He turned to the door as a young man burst through it.

"Da!" he exclaimed, addressing Clem. "There's news all over the village. Mrs. Doyle from the big house – she's been strangled! And her maid, she's been done in, too!"

This must be Sam, thought Daniel. The young man noticed him and Abigail belatedly, and cast a puzzled glance at his father.

"It's all right, Son, these are friends," Clem assured him. "Did you get help to find Mrs. Linwood?"

"Aye, a dozen men are on their way to the beach now, but they're worried about the tide with that storm sitting out at sea."

"Then we don't have time to waste," said Daniel. "My men and I will join you."

LAWNTON WAS BECOMING increasingly agitated as the seas grew rougher. "What are you doing, man? Do something, for God's sake!"

he called out.

An hour ago, the lightning only flickered through the voluminous clouds on the horizon. Now, jagged bolts were visible, accompanied by booming thunder, carried on the wind that was now approaching gale force.

Nate braced himself at the helm. It wasn't going to be long before he would have to consider dropping anchor and riding out the storm, or lashing himself to the wheel.

"You'll be on dry land in an hour," Nate shouted back, the lie uttered with confidence. "I've kept my end of the bargain, Lawnton, now tell me where Susannah is."

Lawnton croaked out a laugh.

"She's in Hell... where she belongs."

Nate squeezed the *Sprite's* wheel so tight his knuckles cracked.

Patience...

"If she's dead, you bastard, then I've no reason keep you alive, *do* I?" Nate ground out through clenched teeth.

Lawnton waved a dismissive hand. "She'll be all right for a few hours at least, if she doesn't do anything stupid like try and find her own way out of the caves."

As far as Nate was concerned, there was only one place that could be – the smugglers' caves under Arthyn Hill.

"She'd better be *all right* otherwise I'll track you down, kill you and take great pleasure doing it."

"You *do* have it bad for her, don't you? You'd better watch your step, mate, you might find yourself dead, too – oh, not by my hand, but hers. That prissy little miss killed Jack. If she dies, I'll have done you a good turn, mate."

Nate quelled the urge to kill the man where he stood.

Lawnton turned starboard and stumbled over to the side of the boat. "The lights!" he cried, pointing.

Nate had noticed them already *and* knew exactly where they were.

On the Trethowan headland, the Doyles' mansion was lit up like a beacon. Bright yellow shone from every window as though every lamp in the place had been lit.

He used Lawnton's distraction to lash the ship's wheel. In the shadows, he saw Hardacre ready himself to catch their stowaway unawares.

They were coming in fast on the shore. Below the cliffs, the Doyles' boathouse was lit up, too. A jagged run of lightning illuminated the scene. The sea appeared only yards away from the boathouse. If the storm surge continued, it might very well wash the structure away.

Belatedly, Lawnton recognized their location.

"You double-crossing bastard! You've brought me back to England! I'll not set foot on shore for the hangman. I'd rather die here and take you with me."

The *Sprite* pitched in the increasingly heavy seas as the water beneath them became shallower. The deck fell away from under Nate's feet as Lawnton launched himself. The two men collided. Nate's head hit the now rising deck, stunning him. He felt Lawnton get in two heavy punches before his vision cleared.

Hardacre, now would be a good time for you to show up...

The boat pitched once more, giving Nate the advantage. He shoved Lawnton off him and got to his feet. His attacker staggered wildly as a gust of wind hit broadside, pushing them toward the rocks.

"Hardacre! Take the wheel. Get us away from the rocks!"

Nate felt Lawnton's arms encircle his chest from behind. Nate stepped forward, then threw his head back. There was the satisfying crunch of a nose being broken.

He rounded on Lawnton and got in a solid punch which sent the man sprawling among the jumble of line on the deck but it was not enough to knock him out. Lawnton rose.

"Jib-ho!"

Nate ducked automatically at Adam's bellow.

Lawnton did not.

The boom swung in a wide arc across the deck. Lawnton saw it at the last moment and got his head down under the jib but a tangle of trailing line gathered under his chin and dragged him backwards across the deck and overboard. There was a scream then a much louder sound of thunder overtook it.

In the flash of lightning that followed a second later, Nate saw Lawnton hanging in the ropes, clawing wildly at his neck as they tightened, his feet kicking in the waves.

Nate turned away and ran to help Adam. Together, the two men struggled to bring the mainsheet under control. While Adam contended with the lines, Nate resumed control of his boat and prayed they had done enough to stop them foundering on the rocks. He waited for the sound of the hull scraping, but there was none.

He spared a glance along the length of the boom just as lightning flashed again. A limp figure hung beneath it.

Nate readied himself to duck on the reverse swing back but the boom stopped just before it crossed the gunwales and would not move. He nodded for Adam to investigate though he suspected he knew the cause.

On the Arthyn headland above the caves, he saw a line of torches making their way across and down to the sand.

"Jib-ho!"

This time, the boom swung as it ought and the *Sprite* picked up speed.

Adam made his way back to the helm, puffing with exertion. "Lawnton's dead. I cut the line and let him drop."

Nate simply nodded. "Then let's not hang about."

Any exhaustion he might have felt vanished. His only concern was Susannah.

He knew the caves flooded a couple of feet in during a regular high tide. During major storms, they were completely inundated. And he'd have to go in...

Memories of his imprisonment in France returned with shocking clarity. The horror of being trapped underground with no light in a confined space – his heart beat in triple time. But his fear *for* Susannah was greater than his own.

He spotted a light and turned the *Sprite* to the shore.

"Hold on! I'm going to beach her!"

He drove the *Sprite* at full sail up onto the beach. The keel dug hard into the sand. Adam threw out the anchor while he furled the sails. Nate knew the risks – if they didn't get Susannah out before the tide reached its zenith, he'd lose her and the *Sprite* would be dashed against the cliffs. He would lose everything he loved and everything he'd ever worked for.

He jumped off the boat. Water was already lapping around his calves above the usual high tide mark.

Over the wind and the first few drops of rain he heard a high-pitched whistle. A man swung a lantern to attract his attention. Nate could make out a glow from inside the cave entrance. He ran with Hardacre at his shoulder.

"Thank God you're here," Clem called.

"Where is she?"

"Dunno, man! We've only just arrived."

"Help us get the dinghy from the *Sprite*," Nate ordered. "Then get everyone else out of here."

Chapter Thirty

SUSANNAH'S LIMBS PROTESTED as she crawled blindly away from the dead-end passage. She counted her progress in the motion of her hands and knees. Ten counts of ten, she promised herself. Ten counts of ten and she would stop for another rest.

By the time she had counted to sixty, the moving air was more than a whisper – it was a distinct breeze with the tang of sea salt on it.

In the blackness, she squeezed her eyes closed tight until she saw red spots dance before her, just to remind herself what was open and what was closed.

She ached mightily. Everything ached in the bitter cold. The wind from outside wailed mournfully through the cavern. She breathed in deep, hoping the smell of salt air wasn't an illusion. It wasn't. She sucked in another lungful, beginning to revive from her lethargy.

"Hello! Is anyone there?"

Her call was drowned out by the sound of surging water but it gave her hope.

If she could hear the wind and the sound of water, she must be close to the entrance!

She sat and reached up, feeling for the roof. She could not touch it. She crouched and reached up and around her and felt nothing but air.

Suddenly, that was more frightening than the narrow apertures she had wormed her way through. If she walked, a deep drop could kill her. Worse still, the thought of being trapped underground with broken limbs and her last moments being of pain and terror.

"Help me! Oh God... someone, please help me!"

Breathe in, breathe out, breathe in, breathe out...

She battled her fears one by one, starting with the one that whispered in her ear – *you deserve to die here alone. Alone, unloved, unmourned...*

A lie!

Nate loved her. He would not leave her. He would do everything in his power to find her. And there was Peggy, her dearest friend, who tried to protect her from the worst of Jack's temper, who held her together in the aftermath of his death. Peggy would try to find her. And wonderful Clem who she loved as a brother.

She owed it to them to not give up on herself.

In that, she found the strength to go on.

With both hands on her head to protect it, Susannah rose to her feet without once making contact with a ceiling. She raised one tentative hand. Her fingertips scraped across rock.

Oh, blessed relief to be able to stand! She stretched her cramped muscles and reached out. She was cold, sore with a few cuts and bruises but otherwise uninjured. That was another thing to be thankful for.

She planted her feet and stretched out to the right to feel for a wall. There was nothing. She did the same thing on the left and, at the far extension of her fingers, she felt rock. She shuffled over and nearly hugged the wall.

Being on two feet was not much faster than crawling but it was kinder on her knees. She used the wall on her left to guide her way and reached forward blindly with her right while shuffling along to feel whether the next step was on solid rock or a void. All she knew was she was heading up a slight incline with a breeze on her face.

She listened. There was something beyond the wind and the water. Perhaps the sound of voices.

Hope growing, she continued slowly forward to where the sound appeared to be coming from. She blinked and squeezed her eyes tight before opening them.

Was there light? Or was that, too, an illusion? She continued to follow the breeze. The tang of salt air was stronger here. So, too, the swirl of damp air. The strange sounds continued.

A flash of lightning briefly illuminated the cave before it turned back once more. Close enough now for light to reach inside! Thunder rumbled and bounced around the walls.

"Hello!"

Hello!

That didn't sound like her echo.

"Hello! Who's there!"

"Susannah!"

The sound of her name was so faint, she wasn't sure whether she'd heard it or it was nothing more than her imagination.

She shuffled along again then stumbled on loose stones and fell.

She screamed.

"Susannah!"

Nate ran, leaving it to Adam to haul the little rowboat through the knee-deep water.

"Nate!"

He ignored Adam's call. He held the lantern high and glanced in the chamber where he had stowed the goods he had brought back from France.

Susannah was not there.

Nate called her name with increasing urgency.

Several seconds passed before he heard an answering call and headed for the deeper parts of the cave that he had only once explored as a boy.

Back then, he had not been afraid, but back then he had not experienced the claustrophobic horror of the oubliette. Nonetheless, he rushed on, knowing that hidden around an ancient tumble of rocks was another chamber.

"Susannah!"

FORTUNATELY, SHE HAD fallen no further than on her bottom.

"Susannah!"

Now the echoing voice was real.

"Stay where you are! We'll find you. Stay where you are!"

"Help!" she cried.

"Sing to us, Susannah."

Sing?

Her mind went blank.

"Sing us a song, my darling, and we'll come to you."

She took a deep breath and sang the first thing that came to her mind.

Early one morning,
Just as the sun was rising,
I heard a young maid sing,
In the valley below.

Oh, don't deceive me,
Oh, never leave me,
How could you use
A poor maiden so?

Susannah heard faint scuffling noises so she continued on, louder this time.

Remember the vows,
That you made to your Mary,
Remember the bow'r,
Where you vowed to be true.

Oh, don't deceive me,
Oh, never leave me,
How could you use
A poor maiden so?

Tears welled. If she wasn't mistaken, she thought she heard other voices joining in the chorus.

Oh, Gay is the garland,
And fresh are the roses,
I've culled from the garden,
To place upon thy brow.

Oh, don't deceive me,
Oh, never leave me,
How could you use
A poor maiden so?

Thus sang the poor maiden,
Her sorrows bewailing,
Thus sang the poor maid,
In the valley below.

The sounds became closer still and the echoes of other voices were now unmistakable.

Tears flowed, beginning to rob her of her voice and when she came to the chorus for the last time, voices stronger than hers completed the lyrics.

Oh, don't deceive me,
Oh, never leave me,
How could you use
A poor maiden so?

Yellow flashes of light were now visible on the roof of the cave.

"I see you, Susannah!"

It was Nate! Although she couldn't see him, she moved toward the sound of his voice.

"Don't move! For God's sake, stop!"

Susannah saw the edge in the lamplight a split second before she would have stepped off into the swirling water below. It looked like the thickest stout ale, black with a yellowish-white froth, but deadly and menacing.

She glanced back along the way she had come. *Dear God!* For the last twenty yards, she had been on a narrowing ledge, feeling the rock wall on her left and completely unaware that to her right was a drop into the water below.

NATE LOOKED ACROSS to the ledge where Susannah stood. The joy of finding her safe was tempered by the fact that she was not yet out of danger. Even from here, he could see her shuddering violently in her cold, wet clothing. She moved sluggishly and looked utterly exhausted. Even if she could swim, she would likely not have the energy to keep herself afloat, and only God knew what lay beneath the surface of the water here. And it was rising faster than he first feared.

"Get in the boat. We haven't got long," Adam warned. Nate hauled himself aboard to join Adam, who had taken the oars.

"Stay where you are, Susannah!" Nate called. "We're coming to you!"

He turned to Adam. "I can see the end of the cave wall. The rocks over there... get us to them and I'll climb up to the ledge from there and lower her down."

"Make it quick," said Adam, hauling on the oars. "You've seen how fast the water has come up since we've been here. If it keeps going at this rate, we'll be trapped."

Nate slowly rose to his feet, finding his balance in the rocking boat, then stepped out onto a rock protruding just a couple of inches above the water. He reached up to the ledge along which Susannah had walked and pulled himself up, feet scrabbling at the rock face for purchase.

It was an achingly slow process to shuffle along the ledge to her. A glance back at the boat showed him the water level had risen once again. The rocks he had climbed up from were now submerged.

Dear God, how had Susannah managed this in the cold and the dark?

A week, a month, a year seemed to pass before he was close enough to reach her huddled on the end of the ledge.

Tears sprung in her eyes as he reached her and took her in her arms. She was ice cold and shuddering with a combination of chill and shock. He held her close as much to impart warmth as it was to show his relief. He kissed her damp hair and blue lips.

"I knew you would come for me," she whispered.

Nate closed his eyes and allowed himself a moment to regather himself.

"Hey, you two," Adam called from below where he was now maneuvering the rowboat. "There's not a moment to waste!"

Nate patted Susannah's back to get her attention. She answered him with a nod.

On his instructions, she sat on the brink of the ledge so her legs dangled over the edge.

"Ready?" he asked, squeezing in behind her and slipping his hands under her arms.

She nodded and slid off the edge. Nate bore her weight, lowering himself until he lay prone on the ledge, eyes screwed shut with the effort.

"I've got her!"

He looked down to see Adam standing in the rocking boat with his arms around Susannah's hips. He let go and saw the boat rock uncertainly as Adam took her weight and brought her down onto the center thwart. Nate waited until he had moved her safely astern and considered his own descent. There was no way he could drop down into the boat without upending the thing.

"Push away!" Nate urged Adam. "I'll have to drop in the water."

Adam used the oars to draw the boat away in the increasing churn of water. Nate lowered himself over the edge, his hands now so cold he could barely feel his fingers.

He dropped into the frigid waters below and was buffeted against the wall of the cave by the whirling current. He pushed himself up to the surface with a gasp to find an oar blade within an arm's length.

He grasped it and, with a couple of powerful kicks, managed to reach the side of the dinghy. The cold from his immersion went bone deep and he didn't protest at receiving help to haul him in over the side.

He joined Susannah huddled on the stern thwart. Adam took his place on the center thwart and rowed hard, a grim set to his jaw. The water would now be eight feet deep, Nate estimated. The roof of the cave was so close, Adam had to slump down to clear it.

"Keep going," Nate urged, determined not to let his teeth chatter any more than necessary. "The cave entrance is three yards away."

"How much room do we have?" said Adam.

"Three feet. Better duck!"

Adam nearly doubled himself over while Nate pushed Susannah down into the bottom boards of the dinghy. He only just managed to join her himself as the forward gunwales clashed against the rock above.

"This is a tight fit," Adam muttered, squirming uncomfortably down onto the bottom boards up front.

"How much room have you got?" asked Nate. "Is it enough to get your feet up?"

"Just."

"Then we're going to have to 'walk' her out. Ready?"

Nate raised his legs until they touched the roof of the cave.

Adam grunted his reply which Nate accepted as an affirmative.

One foot in front of the other, the two men pushed the little boat down against the rising of the tide and forward against the incoming flow into the cave.

"I can see sky!" Adam called from his position.

Susannah muttered a prayer of thanks through chattering teeth. Nate grinned.

The relief was short lived. A surge pressed the boat against the cave entrance, its timbers groaned ominously. There was a bright cracking sound.

"We've just lost the oars," said Adam.

"Push down!" Nate yelled to Adam. "Squeeze her out!"

Susannah's voice was soft but grim. "Nate, the boat is leaking."

He knew that already – his back was now in water.

"One more push! Come on! One more, you bastard!" Nate swore to no one in particular, legs straining against the rock above.

Then the water dropped momentarily with an outgoing surge. It was just enough to pull them out and into the open sea. Nate struggled to sit up and what his saw made his heart swell with pride and relief. There, riding her anchor close by was the *Sprite*.

Over the sound of the wind and waves, Nate heard an "Ahoy there!". Men on the deck threw out lines. By some miracle, one landed close enough to grab and tie around the forward thwart so they could be pulled alongside the *Sprite*.

Susannah was hauled up first by Sir Daniel and Sam, next was Adam. By the time Nate was aboard, the dinghy – rowlocks smashed off, gunwales splintered, planking sprung from the battering in the cave mouth – was filling with water fast. He cut the line and let the little boat go. It swept back to the now submerged cave mouth, crashed once against the rock, and sank.

Waiting for him on the deck of the *Sprite* was Susannah, shivering in the cold night air. Nate hugged her tightly despite being freezing and wet himself, and kissed her over and over until he'd run out of breath.

"There are blankets below," he told her. "Get changed and get warm. We'll be back at The Queen's Head before you know it, my love."

He watched as Susannah allowed Sam to shepherd her below decks.

"Hey ho!" Clem called. Nate found him at the wheel. "Come and take over, Captain. I'm gettin' a bit seasick tryin' to hold her here!"

Nate clapped his old friend on the shoulder with thanks. Cold and as tired as he was, Nate knew of no better remedy than being the master of his destiny.

Chapter Thirty-One

Christmas Eve 1805

THE HOWLING GALES and driving storm on the night of Susannah's rescue had lasted three full days before abating to miserable bouts of rain for the next week or two. But now, sunlight leaked through the curtains and, although it was early, the day was already promising to be crisp and clear.

Susannah lightly dozed, safe in Nate's arms.

It was supposed to be bad luck for the groom to see the bride before the wedding on the big day.

She idly wondered what kind of additional penalty there was for seeing the bride naked.

She decided she didn't much care for the tradition. No bad luck could touch them here beneath the warm blankets of her—*their*—bed.

They had endured enough misfortune and now it was over.

After the rescue, they had learned the circumstances of Lillian Doyle's death. As detestable as the woman was, she did not deserve to die like that. And poor Agnes. Her fate was even more ignoble, if that was possible. It hadn't taken long for details to spread in St. Sennen about the salacious circumstances of *her* demise. It was said the girl detested pity in life but couldn't avoid it in death.

Nate had told her about Robert Lawnton stowing away aboard the *Sprite*. He said little about how the man met his death, save that he was swept overboard. His body had not been found and, by now, it would likely be unrecognizable even it did wash up somewhere along the coast.

She suspected Nate had withheld some of the telling in order to spare her. She would not press him. In time, she might ask. But now was not that time.

The Queen's Head stirred with sounds from the kitchen of breakfast being prepared for their guests and friends – Sir Daniel and Lady Abigail, Adam and Olivia Hardacre.

Susannah didn't feel the need to rise. The kitchen was in good hands with Peggy and Tressa, now both fully recovered from their ordeal.

Susannah had only just begun to feel fully recovered herself. The chills she'd experienced for several days had been dispensed with thanks to a dram or two of whiskey and Peggy's special broth. But the aftereffects of Lawnton's ill-treatment of her on the beach and the deep exhaustion from her ordeal in the cave had lingered on a while longer.

Spending days upon end in bed with Nate had been the only medicine she truly needed. After all, when one was chilled, sharing body heat with another was accepted medical wisdom, was it not?

Susannah considered that so much of her life had been about duty and responsibility. Now, she was learning that pleasure should not be overlooked. It was simply enough to enjoy a moment for what it was.

She had waited for so much in her life that now she didn't want to wait any longer. Tonight, she would be Mrs. Nathaniel Payne, recognized by church and state. But here, just the two of them under God, they were already man and wife.

She turned in Nate's arms to find him awake and watching her.

She wanted his touch. Wanted *him*. How exhilarating it was to put herself in his hands completely. The wantonness of her thoughts continued to surprise her. She smiled and impulsively leaned forward and kissed him on the lips.

His answering touch emboldened her. She offered him a coquettish smile.

Nate hauled her up to his side, his fingers spread wide across her back, while his lips found their way to her cheek and her neck.

"I love you," he whispered.

She touched his cheek, bristles rough against her hand.

Susannah felt the weight of his expression. She knew what he was thinking. The desire on his face answered a call deep within her. She wanted him, couldn't get enough of him, and she wanted him now.

"I love you, too," she said running a hand down his back to his buttocks where she pressed her hand to bring him closer. She felt him stir.

Nate grinned. "Are you trying to seduce me?"

"Am I succeeding?"

She watched as he openly pondered the answer to the question. How wonderful it was to savor lovemaking with light touches, a slow tease. Her fingers brushed over his body, learning him; knowing him.

He leaned forward and she opened herself for the kiss. It was soft and languid. Susannah lay back on the sheets and gifted him a smile. He followed until he lay alongside her, propping himself on one elbow.

She watched him trace a line along her collar bone, down her arm to her hands where his work-roughened finger drew circles in her palm before returning to her collar bone. Now, he traced a finger across the top of her breast, down to her torso and waist and further, touching her hip and the top of her thigh.

He repeated his action on the other side. Susannah sighed.

"Relax," he said. "Let me pleasure you for a while."

Rather than relaxing, it made her aware of her own body. The gentlest of caresses brought with it a cascade of gooseflesh in its wake. Her body remembered the pleasure Nate had brought to her the night before and wanted more of it.

He palmed her breasts, then gave them lavish caresses with his mouth and tongue, the cold morning air striking them, causing even more gooseflesh to arise. Her nipples hardened and didn't go unnoticed. He teased them with his fingers and then again with his tongue while his hand ran down the outside of her thigh.

She raised her knee. The blankets fell and his hand caressed her inner thigh above the knee, first one and then the other, his fingers stroking bare flesh unhurriedly. She ran her bare feet along the cotton sheets and squeezed her toes. She let out a sigh that was half-longing, half-contentment.

His grey eyes were mesmerizing in their intensity. The depths of his desire and his love were written large on his face. It was overwhelming. She closed her eyes.

"Please, don't hide from me, look at me...you are the most beautiful woman I have ever laid eyes on."

When she opened them, she blinked back tears. Nate touched her elbow gently. Susannah took a moment to compose herself.

"I want you," she breathed. "Show me again what it's like to be made love to."

He lifted her hand to his lips and kissed it once, softly, before laying more raw open-mouthed kisses on her palm, up her arm, across her breasts. She held him there, the dark strands of his hair sliding through her fingers.

Then he slid lower, his hands holding her hips still as he brought his mouth to that place between her legs. She cried out although it had been only the barest touch. Then his tongue darted out, driving her to madness with the sensation of it on her, bringing waves upon waves of pleasure until she was breathless with it.

Nate pulled back, then turned them both until he lay on the bed with her on top of him.

She touched him as he had her – with reverence and care – and watched as his body reacted to her kisses and caresses. The hitch in his breathing and low moan of pleasure emboldened her as her fingers circled the hardness of his flesh.

Oh, she was ready for him now. Never had she been so aroused. She straddled his waist and rubbed herself against his erection, shocked by the pleasure of that small contact of flesh.

"Susannah..." She silenced him with a kiss and lowered herself onto him slowly, gasping as her body grew accustomed to his.

He gasped as though branded. Now they were joined. The feeling was exquisite – the cool air on her back and the heat between her legs. She began to rock, searching for the pleasure anew. Nate held her hips, encouraging her, guiding her, but allowing her to take the lead.

His face, caught up in his own pleasure, aroused her more. She touched that sensitive part of herself in time to the rhythm she set until the last moment when she closed her eyes, crying out as her vision filled with a thousand stars. Nate's grip on her hips tightened as he thrust up into her, his own release close. She forced her eyes open to watch his face seek then find the pleasure that she herself knew.

His eyes flew open. He gasped and thrust his hips harder, bringing her another jolt of pleasure.

Then he cried out his own release.

He rolled them both over until she was beneath him and covered her with kisses.

"I love you," he said.

Susannah repeated the vow she'd made, the one she would repeat in a few hours' time before their friends at the church in St. Sennen.

"Nate Payne... I love you."

Epilogue

1 January, 1806
Charteris House
Truro

B ASSETT WASN'T SURE what had awakened him from his slumber. He opened his eyes, then lay there to listen.

There the sound was again. No mistaking it this time. There was someone in the back alley behind the shop, trying to break in.

He reached out and found his spectacles, then threw back the bed covers and sat up on the side of the bed to slip on his boots. Standing, he picked up his brocade dressing gown to go over his bed shirt.

Lighting a candle, he left his quarters and crossed the mapping room to look down through the window near Sir Daniel's desk.

He wasn't sure, but there may have been a figure running away down the alley.

He ventured down the stairs and unlatched the hidden door behind the shop counter. His wall of clocks marked away the seconds with a comforting *tick-tock*.

He checked the front door as a precaution ahead of checking the back. Whoever it was hadn't managed to get into the shop at least. In truth, he'd be surprised if they had, as both front and back doors were reinforced. After all, in their line of business it paid to be careful.

Bassett's sensitive nose detected something. It was familiar, a bit like pine.

He opened the door to the storeroom to make his way through to the back door. Wisps of smoke were visible here. A glow caught his eye. A reflection of his candle in the transom window? As he neared the back wall and the door out into the alley, he could feel the heat as well as see the glow beneath the door. A pane above suddenly shattered with the heat, showering him with glass.

Bassett ran up the narrow back stairs up into the living quarters.

"Joe! Joe, get up!"

He burst through the apprentice's bedroom door and shook the lad awake. "There's a fire outside the back door. Take the two strongboxes outside by the front and get some help."

The lad leapt to his feet and began running to the map room.

"Shoes, boy! Get your shoes on first!"

"Yes, Mr. Bassett!"

Bassett scuttled back downstairs into the storeroom. Flames licked around the sides of the door. He picked up a bucket filled with sand and tossed it in a futile attempt to quench the fire.

By the time he had disposed of a second bucket, Joe had descended the front stairs and opened the front door. The rush of cold air drew the flame further in at the back. Tongues of flame lapped along the ceiling. The entire thick timber door was engulfed.

Bassett backed away from the heat. Everything that was irreplaceable to The King's Rogues was now in Joe's hands. The fire burned hot and brighter than he expected. This was *not* caused by a careless dropping of embers or a discarded cigar.

In the shop, the air shimmered with the heat of a blaze well established in the back of the building. It would be in here very soon.

Bassett looked mournfully at his beautiful, beautiful clocks – such precision, such craftsmanship! He wasn't a man often given to emotion but hearing the discordant sound of clockwork springs distorting in the oppressive heat nearly made him weep.

He withdrew to the outside and joined the bucket brigade which concentrated on trying to save the two shops either side of the chandlery. For Charteris House itself, it was too little, too late. Flames burst through an upper window and waved like pennants.

Although dressed in nothing more than his robe, bed shirt and boots, Bassett didn't feel the cold. He was numb.

"Mr. Bassett, is there *nothing* we can do?"

His apprentice Joe, face soot-stained, looked at him with wide, mournful eyes.

"Get one of our horses from the stables and race as fast as you can to Sir Daniel. Tell him the fire was no accident."

"What? How do you know?"

"Someone set it by the back door, poured turpentine all over it before lighting it – and stayed long enough to watch it go up." He glanced about the gathered crowd. "And he may still be here."

Joe's jaw dropped.

"I suspect *that*," he continued, handing over a folded piece of paper, "because someone slipped this into my dressing gown pocket when I was wielding the buckets."

Before Joe could ask any more, the sound of bells chimed discordantly from the distressed clocks inside.

Bassett spun round to look at the shopfront, suddenly remembering. "My God! The key!"

He took off at a run back toward the burning building without a second thought.

"Mr. Bassett!" the youth called out.

"Follow orders, Joe!" Bassett yelled back. "Go to Sir Daniel!"

JOE LOOKED DOWN at the note he had been given. It was addressed to Adam Hardacre in a flourishing hand. It read:

This is not over,

Harold Bickmore

The apprentice rushed to the stables several streets away, rousing the ostler from his bed. No sooner had he mounted than the ground shook and a fireball of yellow and orange appeared above the roofs of the buildings between the stables and Charteris House.

The horse reared and tried to bolt. Joe used all his skill to control the startled beast and send it in the right direction, weeping all the way to Bishop's Wood for his friend and master.

The End

Adam Hardacre will return in book three of The King's Rogues:
Spy Another Day.

About the Author

Elizabeth Ellen Carter is an award-winning historical romance writer who pens richly detailed historical romantic adventures. A former newspaper journalist, Carter ran an award-winning PR agency for 12 years. The author lives in Australia with her husband and two cats.

Made in the USA
Coppell, TX
25 July 2024

35180884R00177